Hitting the Heavens

Hitting the Heavens

An Adrian Boyle Catalan Mystery

Barbara Rennie

Copyright © 2020 Barbara Rennie

The moral right of the author has been asserted.

Apart from any fair dealing for the purposes of research or private study, or criticism or review, as permitted under the Copyright, Designs and Patents Act 1988, this publication may only be reproduced, stored or transmitted, in any form or by any means, with the prior permission in writing of the publishers, or in the case of reprographic reproduction in accordance with the terms of licences issued by the Copyright Licensing Agency. Enquiries concerning reproduction outside those terms should be sent to the publishers.

This is a work of fiction. Names, characters, businesses, places, events and incidents are either the products of the author's imagination or used in a fictitious manner. Any resemblance to actual persons, living or dead, or actual events is purely coincidental.

Matador
9 Priory Business Park,
Wistow Road, Kibworth Beauchamp,
Leicestershire. LE8 0RX
Tel: 0116 279 2299
Email: books@troubador.co.uk
Web: www.troubador.co.uk/matador
Twitter: @matadorbooks

ISBN 978 1838594 237

British Library Cataloguing in Publication Data.
A catalogue record for this book is available from the British Library.

Printed on FSC accredited paper
Printed and bound in Great Britain by 4edge Limited
Typeset in 11pt Minion Pro by Troubador Publishing Ltd, Leicester, UK

Matador is an imprint of Troubador Publishing Ltd

for Kenneth Tuson

1

A CHILLING CRY ROUSED PRIVATE Investigator Adrian Boyle, interrupting a dream of Ana. The cry came from somewhere down in the woods. He thought it was one of the wild boars, *jabali*. Hunters were swarming the mountainside of Pedralta. Shots from their high-powered rifles had been pounding out all morning.

He glanced at his mobile. Noon. Lying on top of the duvet, still dressed in clothes from the night before, he listened. All was quiet now. He rolled to the side and looked at the empty place beside him. Her pillow was untouched. It was unhealthy to dream of the dead. Who had told him that? He closed his eyes and tried to get back to sleep but that cry interfered. He had heard it before. It wasn't the squeal of a *jabalí* in the throes of death at all. It was human.

Slowly, he made his way to the French windows and onto the terrace, his headache hammering with every step. The coastal town of Sant Martí lay far below. Leaning against the wrought iron railing, he stared down into the woods. A gust of cool air blew at the back of his head then swept with a whoosh over the umbrella pines sloping halfway down the mountain. Poking out from the trees were several houses like his, white stucco with Catalan stone and terracotta-tiled roofs, making up the tiny urbanisation of Roca Alba. The woodland alongside Roca Alba was jammed with hunters' trailers and SUVs.

He heard a car speeding through the woods below. The sound of grinding gears made him wince as it crunched along the gravel track, obscured by the trees. Moving across the terrace, he managed to catch a glimpse of a small silver car but he was unable to identify its make.

He phoned his friend at the *comisaría*.

A woman answered. 'Deputy Inspector Pujol.'

'Rosa, it's Adrian,' he said, surprised at the hoarseness of his voice.

'*Guapo*, good-looking. You don't sound too good.'

'Touch of flu,' he lied. 'That's all. Listen. I've just

heard a cry, a scream down in Roca Alba. The hunters are here today. Perhaps someone was hurt.'

'Nothing's been called in so far.'

'It happened only five minutes ago. And then a car shot out of there and onto the road. Something's not right.'

'I'll send someone up there to check it out.'

'I can meet them down there,' he said, immediately regretting the offer.

'No, no. Take care of yourself. Go to bed. Anyway, you don't want to spread it. I don't want my officers coming down with the flu.'

Adrian drank a mugful of water, downed two ibuprofen, bent towards the bedroom mirror to examine his bloodshot blue eyes and vowed to take better care of himself. But then he eyed the smidgen of whisky left in the bottle on the bedside table, which had been half full the night before. For the purposes of hair of the dog only, he finished it. He took off his shirt and jeans then climbed into bed, drawing up a pale waffle blanket that he remembered buying on a day trip to Oxfordshire with his wife Ana.

It was late afternoon when the sound of an ambulance siren woke Boyle. The hunters had returned to their vehicles below and flashing blue lights moved through the development. He dressed quickly and hurried down the stone steps beside his house, armed with a walking stick to protect him from the hunting dogs. Lining the dirt track to his house was a steep, rocky bank that dropped to the properties below. Rather than walk the long way round, he took the short cut. In amongst the shrubs of wild rosemary and sage, he found the narrow footpath and began to descend the bank some twenty metres down into the woods to the edge of the urbanisation. He reached the bottom, under a thick canopy of umbrella pines. There was a pungent smell of damp and decay.

The hunting dogs began to howl, sending a chill down Boyle's spine. Often in the afternoons, the hunters would be joined by friends and family. They would roast the boar on an open fire, sing traditional Catalan songs and dance the Sardana, but there was no sign of that today.

Boyle came to a clearing where Can Bosc stood. Like most houses built on Pedralta, it had two storeys, with views over the valley and the Mediterranean. On the side wall of the building, huge letters were sprayed in vivid red paint, in Catalan. '¡*No Cazes!* ¡*No Mates!*' 'Don't hunt! Don't kill!' Boyle steered clear of several dead boars neatly lined up just beneath the scrawl.

At the front of the house, lights were blazing in an open garage and two men in worn rubber aprons were butchering one of the boars on a long table. They worked quickly. There was blood everywhere. Boyle stood at the edge of the property, transfixed. The pangs of hunger that had plagued him turned to nausea as he watched the men work. Above the garage, on a terrace that stretched the length of the house, a dirt-covered hound whimpered as he stared down at the prime cuts of boar laid out. One man carefully wrapped them in bin liners while another hosed the blood from the drive.

Boyle recognised his neighbour sawing away on a leg. He was tall for a Catalan with long, steel-grey hair tied back into a ponytail. Widower Faustino Duran, the owner of Can Bosc, was the only other person besides Boyle who lived on this mountain all year round. At first, when Boyle and his wife had moved up here, they had hoped to build a neighbourly friendship with Faustino, once inviting him over for a speciality of Ana's, *setas con caracoles*, but he never turned up. Even after Ana died last year, Faustino made no attempt to offer his condolences when they passed in the road. Boyle's father-in-law, Narcis, had told him that Faustino hated foreigners but that didn't make total sense; Ana was from Sant Martí. He could at least have been civil to her.

When Faustino caught sight of Boyle, he frowned. 'Can I help you?' he shouted in Catalan, as if Boyle was a complete stranger.

'What's going on?' Boyle asked in Catalan.

'It is none of your business,' Faustino replied, waving him away with a bloodied saw.

Boyle flexed his fingers, fighting off the urge to thump Faustino, and moved on.

In the distance, near the exit to the main road, there were about a dozen hunters gathered round their vandalised cars, bundling their dogs into trailers, preparing to leave. Boyle moved closer to get a better look. Two police officers were in amongst the hunters, taking statements. A member of the forensic team was dusting the cars for fingerprints.

An attractive woman in a red hunting jacket was standing at the back of a silver Land Rover Discovery, which Boyle had seen many times in the area. The woman was Señora Clavaguera, wife of Eduardo, the property magnate and art collector who owned most of this mountain. Slender, with her dark hair braided to the side, she was focused on her Lynx straight-pull bolt action rifle, dismantling it and wiping each piece with a cloth before placing it in a case in the back of her SUV. At her feet, a dock-tailed brown and white spaniel gulped water from a bowl. Standing close to her was her tall brother-in-law, Salvador Clavaguera, the mayor of Sant Martí. *Useless mayor at that,* thought Boyle. *The road up to this mountain was an abomination.* Salvador had his rifle still slung over his shoulder. Boyle smiled to himself. He wouldn't trust Salvador with a water pistol, never mind a high-powered rifle.

Carefully stepping around huge potholes on the road, Boyle made his way down the dirt track, following the route the flashing lights had taken. He passed several white houses, all with red anti-hunt slogans slashed across them. The houses were already closed up for the winter, with green metal shutters securely fastened over doors and windows. He peered into their gardens, carpeted with pine needles, the pools covered with blue tarpaulin.

A *Mossos d'Esquadra* four-by-four drove up the track, heading for the main road. The vehicle stopped when it reached him and the driver's window slid down, revealing Deputy Inspector Rosa Pujol, the girlfriend of Boyle's sister-in-law, Montse. The *Mossos* uniform was smart as police uniforms go. The well-cut pale blue shirt and navy trousers suited Rosa and Boyle knew she was proud of the three gold stripes on her epaulets.

'Adrian. How's the flu? Are you feeling better?'

'Much better, thanks,' said Boyle, bringing a hand to his face and rubbing his three-day beard. 'What happened?'

'One of the hunt protesters died. Fell off the roof at Casa Cielo. Montse and I knew him through his mother; Cisco was her only child. Oh God,' she said, placing her elbows on the wheel of her car and resting her head. 'How am I going to tell her?'

All the experience in the world never made it easy to tell someone that their loved one had died. 'What happened?' asked Boyle.

'After vandalising the cars and houses up here, it

looks like Cisco decided to paint at Casa Cielo. Have you seen it?'

'Only once. That was enough,' he said.

'It's an acquired taste.'

Casa Cielo was the last house on the development, on the shoulder of the mountain, with a sheer drop to scrubland and forest below. Owned by art collector Eduardo Clavaguera, husband of Tina, it had been unoccupied for years. The story was that Clavaguera had felt sorry for the local graffiti vandals when they were caught by the police and offered them the walls of Casa Cielo to paint however they liked.

'So, he went to the house, and when he climbed out onto the roof to paint the tower, he must have slipped and fell,' said Rosa. 'It is a drop of at least forty metres. What a stupid, stupid boy.' She looked at Boyle. 'The doctor said he died between eleven and one today.'

Boyle looked over at the hunters. 'Were any of them around when it happened?'

'No witnesses. The hunters were all on the other side of the mountain and heard nothing.' She looked at him, interested. 'When did you hear the scream?'

'At about twelve – and then soon after, I saw a silver car speeding up this track towards the main road. It was a small car.'

'What make?'

'No idea. The trees blocked my view.'

Rosa nodded. 'Small silver car. That should be easy. There are only about a million cars that fit that description in Catalonia.'

'Well, that's your job, Señorita. I'm sure you're up to it.'

'To be honest with you, Adrian, I feel there's something not quite right about this.'

He put his hands on the door of her car and leaned in. 'What do you mean?'

'I had no idea that Cisco was an anti-hunt protester. He wasn't political like many graffiti artists. He just wanted to do his art.'

After agreeing to meet up for a meal with Montse sometime, they said their goodbyes and Rosa drove off.

Boyle continued down the dirt track, stepping across gullies that ran down either side of the road, caused the year before by heavy rains. After about twenty yards, at the end of a long drive, he could see Casa Cielo perched on the edge of the cliff. It was an L-shaped house with a round Catalan *torre*, tower, and the walls of the house were covered in paint. Boyle was unable to make out the subjects in the fading light but he knew it was worse than when he had seen it two years before. Now it appeared to be one dark, tangled mess. *Like something out of Grimms' Fairy Tales,* he thought.

He followed the track below the house, which

wound to the left, hugging the cliff face of the development. An ambulance was parked on the path. Two paramedics carried the dead boy to the vehicle, the body wrapped in a foil blanket aflame with the last rays of the setting sun. Boyle didn't envy Rosa having to tell the boy's mother. That was one job he was glad to be rid of when he left the police.

2

Boyle drove down into Sant Martí. Easily finding a parking space for his ancient Rover at the seafront made him want to punch the air with elation. The tourists were gone. He shrugged on his pale jacket, took his laptop case and turned the key in the car door to lock it. Noticing there were fewer leisure boats in the marina further lightened his mood. The holiday season was finally over. Surrounded by hills of pine and cork, Sant Martí was one of the oldest towns on the Costa Brava and a favourite with tourists. The population more than doubled during the summer and although Boyle knew how much local business relied on that trade, he, like most of the inhabitants, celebrated at the sight of the bright red lights as the end-of-season traffic crawled out of the valley.

He turned down a narrow street that gave out onto the main square. On the east side of the plaza was the ochre-coloured, newly renovated Gothic town council building. Boyle cut across the square between the kiosks of the open-air market towards Calle Joan Vall, where he worked. There were five case reports to deliver to his sister-in-law lawyer, Montse Ferran, and the promise of more work. For the past five years he had done investigations for Montse, mostly trailing errant husbands, searching for missing persons and doing general work for expatriates abroad. His office, situated in a three-storey terracotta building off the main square – one of the many properties owned by his father-in-law, Narcis Ferran – was conveniently located just down the corridor from Montse.

'On November the fifth, Rosa and I are getting married,' said his sister-in-law. Boyle stared at her, so surprised that he was unable to utter a word. They were standing in her large, smoke-filled office, lined with shelves, jam-packed with case files. There were not enough hours in the day for Montse, who handled both civil and criminal cases. Boyle placed his file of case reports on her desk and joined her at the open window overlooking the food market in the main square.

He had never seen her so happy. Petite and full-figured, she had short brown tousled hair and a splash of bright red lipstick on her lips. Holding her cigarette flamboyantly high, her eyebrows were raised almost jokingly. She often had that look and for a moment it threw him. Perhaps she was just joking.

'A civil partnership?' he asked.

'No *cariño*, 'marriage'. In Spain we are allowed to marry,' she said. 'We want you to be there.' She reached out, taking his hand.

'Yes, of course. I'd love to come. Congratulations,' he said as he kissed her on the cheek. But he was unsure how he really felt. The women had met two years before when Rosa had given a talk at a refuge centre Montse had set up for abused women. At the time, Rosa's marriage to another cop, Inspector Marc Saldoni, was ending. Within days, they were living together as mates. Montse's parents had no idea about their daughter's real relationship with Rosa and from what he could gather, neither did anyone in Sant Martí, which was a close-minded, old-fashioned town.

'Have you told your parents?'

Montse looked at him as if he were mad. 'I don't want them to know. Ever. And you mustn't tell anyone.'

'Of course not. But why are you doing it?'

'For legal reasons, mainly. Rosa and I have bought a house together. What if one of us should die? I want protection for us like any married couple,' she explained. 'We have waited this long because we didn't want to marry so soon after Ana… out of respect for Ana,' she said, glancing down. She looked up at him. 'And for you, Adrian,' she said, swinging his hand, tensing her mouth, fighting back a tear.

'Thank you,' said Boyle, unable to imagine how he would commemorate the anniversary of his wife's death. He wanted it to pass without his noticing, without his having to feel anything.

There was a quick rap on the door and Deputy Inspector Rosa Pujol came in carrying a briefcase, her thick wavy hair tied back. When she leaned over to kiss Montse her navy jacket inched up, revealing her nine-millimetre Walther p99 pistol holstered to her hip.

Rosa turned to Boyle and smiled. 'You've heard the news?'

'Yes. Congratulations,' he said, hugging her.

'The wedding party is only six. Carmen, her children and you,' said Montse.

'Where are you having it?'

'In the town hall in Sitges. Where do you think? The church?' Montse said with mock horror. Montse and Rosa laughed. 'Even if they would have us, I don't think we'd want them. Anyway, it's an excuse for a real *knees-up*,' said Montse, effortlessly slipping the cockney phrase that Boyle had taught her into her Spanish.

Rosa and Montse exchanged a look. 'I have something to discuss with you if you have time,' Rosa said to Boyle.

He suggested they go to his office.

Down the corridor from Montse's office, Boyle raised the Venetian blinds and opened the windows while Rosa, unable to hide her innate nosiness, began scanning the large square space. There was a plain desk with a swivel chair, a worn sofa, two equally worn chairs for clients and a grey filing cabinet. Maps of the local towns, villages and urbanisations covered the walls.

Rosa frowned. 'You need to brighten this place up a bit.'

'I don't do decoration,' he said.

She picked up a small silver bowl from his desk. 'I haven't seen this before,' she said, peering at it and reading the engraving slowly in her primitive English. 'Detective Superintendent Adrian Boyle. From your friends at the London Metropolitan Police.' Looking up at him, she said, 'Superintendent. *Gwow!*'

He loved her Spanish twist on 'wow'. Words beginning with 'w' were demanding on the Spanish tongue. Spanish dictionaries gave them less than a page and most of those were words like 'windsurfista', 'whiskeria' and 'waterpolista'. Boyle's lips curved into a smile. He never corrected her. He dragged a chair over for her to sit on.

'You know my ex-husband has just been made Chief Inspector.'

'My sincere condolences. At least he's not your boss,' he said, sitting back against his desk, facing her. The divorce of Marc Saldoni and Rosa Pujol had not been an amicable one and the station where they both worked had taken his side in the matter. Boyle used to be friends with Marc but he had taken Rosa's side because of Montse.

'He is moving up through the ranks while I am stuck to the glass ceiling.'

'Don't hurry too much. My inspector days were some of my best. It can be surprisingly dull at the top.'

On that note, she glanced at her watch and sat forward. 'You remember the boy who fell at Roca Alba last week?'

Boyle nodded.

'Well, the investigating judge, Gabriel Llfranc, has ruled it an accident, so we've had to drop the case. But Cisco's mother thinks he was murdered and she'd like to hire you to look into it.'

'What do you think?' asked Boyle.

'Something's off. At first, we thought that Cisco

was one of the anti-hunt protesters who vandalised Roca Alba last week. But his mother insists that he had no interest in that movement. Though he *had* vandalised places in the past with his graffiti, it was never anti-hunt. There's a case report in here dealing with an incident of graffiti damage in Sant Martí and another in Santa Nuria two years ago,' she said, opening her briefcase and taking out a manila file. 'But his mother says that since then, he only painted at legal sites. Also, another thing – his scooter, a red Honda Elite, his smart phone and his sketchbook, which he had with him that day, are missing. The judge thinks that the hunt protesters must have taken them.'

'Any signal from his phone?'

'Nothing, it's dead.' Rosa got up and began to pace. 'The judge didn't give us enough time to look into it properly. He closed the case too soon, more interested in his precious government targets than the truth. They weren't going to do an autopsy at first but his mother insisted, which is her right.'

Boyle nodded. 'Anything come up in that?'

'Just that Cisco had no drink or drugs in his body. But we found a packet of cocaine in the brush near him. His mother says that Cisco didn't touch drugs, that someone must have planted the cocaine.'

'He could have been waiting to take the cocaine later. Parents rarely know what their children are up to.'

Rosa paused and looked at Boyle. 'It doesn't sound like you are interested.'

'I didn't say that,' he said, but that's what he felt. If it did turn out to be a murder investigation, it would be the first time in over five years that he had handled one. He wasn't sure if he was up to it.

Rosa sat next to him on the desk. She was so close that any closer, she would have been sitting on his lap. The Spanish women he knew were all very touchy-feely. Boyle was just beginning to get used to it, just beginning to understand that it wasn't a come-on.

'Look, a boy is dead,' she began softly. 'There is some doubt as to whether it was an accident or not. All I know is that I would have given it more time, spread the net a bit wider, interviewed more people. But I can't do that now because the case is closed. Will you help me out?'

'Of course I will,' he said. Rosa was like family. He wasn't going to say no.

She smiled and handed him the folder. 'Case notes and autopsy report. I will help you all I can to obtain records, anything you need. And it goes without saying that no one must know I'm involved. I'd lose my job.'

'Of course, don't worry.'

Rosa got up to leave, pausing at the door. 'You can speak to Juanita Perez today. She's coming in to see Montse briefly this morning. Say an hour from now?'

Boyle nodded, feeling as though he had done something right.

After Rosa left, he took the case notes out of the police file and slipped them into a green pocket folder. He had just enough time to review the notes before Montse turned up with Cisco's mother. Juanita Perez was petite with raven hair scraped back from her moon-shaped face into a ponytail; definitely not Catalan – South American, Boyle reckoned, about forty-five. Grief consumed her. He had seen that empty expression many times during his twenty years in the police force. When greeting Boyle, she held out her hand and he took it, squeezing it gently to reassure her. At that moment he knew he would do all he could to find out what had happened to Cisco, anything to lift her gloom.

Montse said goodbye and he opened the door wide so Senora Perez could enter.

Senora Perez paused, saying. 'Señor Boyle, do you mind if we go somewhere where I can smoke?'

They sat at a table outside Café Bon Día in the market square. She smoked a cigarette and sipped a *café con leche*. He drank fresh orange juice. They spent a few moments watching people at kiosks around the square buying fruit and vegetables picked that morning from farms along the Costa Brava. From a small van, two men unloaded anchovies that had been caught offshore during the night and carried them into the municipal covered market. At one kiosk, Boyle saw two wide-eyed rabbits squeezed into a cage, ready for the pot. Had he been alone, he would have teared up. Funny that the potential demise of a rabbit brought out more emotion than hearing about the death of Cisco Perez. What was wrong with him? Did he feel that Cisco was partly responsible for his own death?

Boyle faced Juanita Perez. 'In your own time, tell me what happened.'

She stubbed out her cigarette and winced. 'At nine o'clock in the morning, Cisco went to paint at Casa Cielo. And then the next thing I know, Inspector Pujol rings to tell me that he…' She lowered her head and took a shaky breath.

In the middle of his chest, Boyle felt the familiar, hollow pain he had every time he thought of Ana and how he would never see her again. 'I'm sorry, Señora. But it was a dangerous thing to do, no?'

Juanita shook her head. 'Not for my Cisco. He was like a mountain goat, climbing since he was small. And balancing high up, he painted the most beautiful pictures.' She began to cry. The tears flowed. She reached into her bag for a tissue and mopped her face.

'I am so sorry, Señora.' He put his hand over hers. She gave her eyes one final dab with the tissue, took a deep breath and looked at him.

'Apart from the fact that you think cocaine was planted, why else do you think your son was murdered?'

'Those houses on Roca Alba with all that anti-hunt rubbish painted on them, Cisco would never paint anything as ugly as that. He was an artist. And another thing. Not only was his sketchbook taken, but someone broke into our flat this week and stole *all* his sketchbooks.'

'Was anything else taken from your flat?'

'No.'

Boyle thought for a moment, then asked, 'Why would anyone steal Cisco's sketchbooks?'

Juanita looked at him as if he had taken leave of his senses. 'To sell them!'

'Is there a market for them?' asked Boyle, thinking how out of touch he had become.

'Of course. Cisco was famous – well, famous in his world. He sold drawings on the internet. For real money,' said Juanita. She was suddenly distracted, squinting at something. Like a car going from zero to one hundred in an instant, her placid face became enraged. She stood up and pointed. 'Murderer! Murderer!' she shouted.

Boyle jumped up and held her by the shoulders. 'Señora! Calm down.' He glanced around and recognised the man she was accusing – property developer Quimet Navarro, dressed in a cashmere cardigan and carrying a man bag, no doubt stuffed with cash. He was walking towards the entrance to the café. People in the square were beginning to stare at Juanita. Quimet smirked at Juanita then turned to Boyle and shrugged, lifting both his hands in innocence as if to say "what's going on?"

Boyle could feel Juanita quiver with rage and knew they had to leave quickly. He let go of her just long enough to take a five euro note out of his pocket and throw it on the table, which was a mistake. She flew off towards Quimet, her hands out in front of her, aiming for his eyes. Boyle hurried after her.

Quimet had stepped away from the door, ready for Juanita, and catching her by the wrists, he held her back from him. 'Silly bitch,' he said. 'What is your problem?'

She screamed, 'You killed my son!' and lifted her knee towards his crotch, just missing. Now everyone in the square was staring at them. Quimet bared his horse-sized teeth, pulled Juanita to him and shook her with excessive force. She was whimpering as Boyle moved behind Quimet, grabbed his elbows, jerked them behind his back and yanked them high. Quimet shrieked with pain and released Juanita. Boyle marched Quimet to the door of the café and shoved him inside. Juanita was quiet as Boyle put his arm through hers and led her away.

At one point, Boyle turned and saw Quimet standing at the open door to the café. He held a finger up to his temple and announced to him, 'She's fucking loco!'

3

Boyle led Juanita Perez to a bench on the esplanade at the seafront where they sat down. She burst into tears. *She probably needs grief counselling more than she needs a private detective,* Boyle thought. He put his arm around her and waited for her to cry it out. A cold mist was coming in from the sea. He watched the ghostly image of a yacht sailing, pitching up and down. After a few minutes, she pulled away, took out a tissue and blew her nose.

'Thank you, Señor Boyle.'

'Señora, there is a place where you can go for counselling.' It was a service that had been suggested to him after his wife's death, which, despite the agony of the past year, he had yet to attend.

She crinkled her nose. 'Oh no, I don't need that!'

'Señora, I know you are going through a terrible time, but I can't help you if you behave like this. Do you understand?'

She lowered her head. 'Yes, I do. I'm sorry. I won't do it again.'

Boyle studied her. 'Why do you think Quimet Navarro was involved in your son's death?'

She opened her bag, drew out a cheap brand of cigarette, lit up and took a drag. 'He was there that day, hunting.' She then hesitated and gave him a wary glance, as if unsure whether to go on. 'Two years ago, Cisco got into trouble with the police. My husband had had a stroke. He ended up in a wheelchair and lost most of his memory. Cisco took it very hard. He was angry. He went and sprayed graffiti all over Sant Martí and Santa Nuria with his best friend Miguel. They did it for two weeks without getting caught. Of course, Cisco's graffiti was beautiful,' she said with pride. 'But Miguel has no talent. He made a real mess.'

There is no beauty in graffiti, thought Boyle behind a mask of sympathy. *It is vandalism, pure and simple.* If Juanita Perez had not been in such a fragile state of mind, he would have told her so.

'One night, they sprayed the new flats of Quimet Navarro's. You know, the ones along the bypass?'

Boyle nodded. Quimet Navarro was known to be an ambitious property developer and his latest build of eighty flats, constructed on one of the old farms of the Clavaguera estate at the bottom of Boyle's mountain, was a real eyesore. The locals disliked it. Boyle remembered seeing the complex covered from top to bottom with graffiti and laughing out loud. Even though he detested graffiti, he had to admit that he loathed this garish complex even more. He had wondered why Eduardo Clavaguera had sold the land to Quimet in the first place. It was common knowledge that before the Spanish Civil War, the vast acreage of the Clavaguera estate had been the domain of the Navarro family but somehow the Navarros, had ended up on the losing side of the conflict and lost their land to the Clavagueras. Even though the Clavagueras and Navarros hunted together, everyone assumed that the age-old hatred still existed between them, although Boyle had never seen any sign of it.

'And the boys also painted two of the new buildings in Santa Nuria. They're owned by that Swedish man, Gunnar Lundgren. Miguel was high on cocaine and drink and making a lot of noise. The police were called. It took thirty thousand euros to paint everything again. Thankfully, Miguel's father is rich and he paid for it. I don't have any money.'

'You think the developers murdered your son?' Boyle asked in disbelief.

She nodded. 'I think they hired someone to kill him.'

'But they didn't hurt Cisco's friend Miguel. Why not?'

'Probably because Miguel is the son of Eduardo Clavaguera. You know who I mean?'

'Yes.'

'Eduardo is an art collector. He saw Cisco's work and loved it so much that he decided to help him. He let him paint at Casa Cielo and then set up a studio there for him to paint canvasses.'

Boyle tried to imagine how a sophisticated art dealer could be interested in a boy who defaced everything with graffiti.

'Cisco was supposed to have an exhibition of his paintings in Eduardo's gallery in Barcelona next month,' she said. 'His first. He was working hard towards that.' There were tears in her eyes. She wiped them away.

'Do you have your son's address book?'

'No. He had everything on his smart phone and that's missing. He took it everywhere with him and it's gone, along with his scooter.' She lifted her hands up in exasperation. 'And I'll tell you this: whoever took all those things killed my son.' She threw her cigarette on the ground and crushed it under her boot.

Juanita gave Boyle a cheque for two thousand euros. At his charge of fifty euros an hour, that was forty hours work. Having pleaded poverty a moment ago, he was surprised that she had that kind of money and questioned her about it. She explained that it was from her son's account. 'Cisco is paying for this,' she said.

Boyle was unsure if he could help. The missing smart phone, scooter and sketchbook indicated that someone might have been present when he fell. Was it just a robbery gone wrong? Whoever took the sketchbook could possibly have stolen Cisco's other sketchbooks from his parents' house at a later date. And what did all this have to do with the hunt protesters? He felt a tingle of excitement move up his spine. It didn't sound like a straightforward accident, no way, and it was exactly the sort of conundrum he thrived on.

After banking the cheque, Boyle went to his local bar, El Cisne, and had anchovies on tomato bread and an espresso. Back at his office he made a few calls. Cisco's best friend, Miguel Clavaguera, answered on the first ring. Boyle detected disappointment in Miguel's voice when he introduced himself and explained why he was ringing.

'I can't help you,' Miguel said. 'I didn't see him for ten days or so before he died. Anyway, I've already told the police everything.'

'Could you spare…'

'No, I'm sorry. I have nothing to say,' Miguel said. And the phone went dead.

Not the greatest conversationalist, thought Boyle. He then punched in the number for Cisco's other best friend, Luis Sureda, hoping he would have better luck with him. His mother answered and said he was at work. When Boyle asked where he was employed, his mother ignored the question, told Boyle she would pass on the message to ring him and then hung up. He rang two more numbers straight away. The office of property developer Gunnar Lundgren said he was in Sweden until the following week and would ring back when he returned. When Boyle spoke to Eduardo Clavaguera, he was able to make an appointment to see him the next day at his house in Santa Nuria. Boyle asked if he would be able to speak to Eduardo's wife Tina as well but learned that she would not be there. Boyle thought he should interview Quimet Navarro, but wondered if he would be approachable so soon after Juanita's outburst at the café.

Boyle took the police file from the top of the filing cabinet. He opened a file marked Cisco Perez and took out the autopsy report. He glanced at the photographs from the scene. They showed Cisco on his back, his head twisted unnaturally. The *forense medico* estimated that Cisco died around midday, between 11am and 1pm. The stated cause of death was the fall from the roof of Casa Cielo. He had slipped off the roof and over the cliff, tumbling over stony ground, and landed on his back forty-five metres below, breaking his neck and dying instantly. *Well, at least he didn't suffer long,* thought Boyle. The scrapes, bruises and breaks were all consistent with a fall from that height over rocky terrain.

The report mentioned that green, pale pink, blue and brown paint was found on his clothes and hands and under his fingernails. Although there was dirt and gravel found under his fingernails, there was nothing there to indicate that he had fought with anyone before he fell. However, Boyle thought it was interesting that there was no mention of red paint, which was what the hunt protesters had used, on his hands. If Cisco had been spraying with them, there definitely would have been some residue of red paint on his hands.

There was no drugs or alcohol found in his body. Boyle made a note to ask if there were fingerprints found on the packet of cocaine that Rosa said was discovered near Cisco's body.

There was no red paint found near the mural Cisco was working on, just spray cans of blue, green, brown and flesh-coloured paint.

Boyle read the hunters' statements. There were eight hunters on the other side of the mountain when Cisco fell. They included Tina Clavaguera, her brother-in-law Mayor Salvador Clavaguera, Faustino Duran and Quimet Navarro. None of them had heard anything. The spaniel belonging to Tina found the body at 4.30pm after they had finished hunting.

In his final statement, Judge Gabriel Llfranc concluded that Cisco's death was a tragic accident. He surmised that Cisco had first committed acts of vandalism to the houses and cars, alone or with others, then gone down to Casa Cielo to paint and there, on the roof, he had lost his balance and fallen. Boyle shoved the report back into the file. What a slapdash job. Even he could see that, most likely, Cisco had had nothing to do with the hunt protesters. And if he had, where was his scooter, his smart phone and his sketchbook? And what about the sketchbooks taken from his house? There was no indication yet that Cisco had been murdered but Boyle sensed that it wasn't a simple death by accident.

BOYLE PUSHED OPEN THE GLASS DOOR TO THE El Dorado restaurant and found a seat at the sleek wood and steel bar. The waiters in black were setting tables for dinner and preparing their stations. It was a newly modernised restaurant set in a nineteenth-century building on a corner in the main Rambla d'Antoni. With two walls of French doors that opened onto the street, it looked like something you'd see in Barcelona, not a sleepy town like Sant Martí that had sixty thousand people in the summer but only twenty thousand 'real' inhabitants the rest of the year.

Boyle's other sister-in-law, Carmen, glided up

to him and put her hands protectively around his shoulders and rubbed them as if he might be cold. She had the same classic Catalan looks as her dead sister Ana. Slender with fair hair, her nose was straight and she had large, warm brown eyes; 'Salvador Dalí eyes', Boyle called them. He remembered those same eyes that had first attracted him to his wife Ana in London over twenty years earlier. She was a newly qualified nurse at St Thomas's, working the night shift in A&E. He was a constable on the Metropolitan Police force, luckily with the same unsociable hours, and had come to interview the injured victim of a mugging. After the patient had had his arm put in a cast and was tucked up for the night, Boyle hung around. It was unusually quiet in casualty. Ana brought him tasteless coffee from a machine and a packet of custard creams, and in the hushed, dimmed corridors of the hospital they talked.

'We have *calamarsets* tonight,' Carmen said as she took a bottle of beer from the cooler and poured it for him. Boyle took a seat and smiled. This was his favourite time of day, time with his other sister-in-law.

Carmen ran the restaurant for her semi-retired parents, the Ferrans. They were socialists and moneyed, their property portfolio including four grand buildings on the seafront. The socialism and wealth never sat right with Boyle, although his wife had told him he was naïve to think that that combination was a problem, especially in Spain where the history was complicated. The Ferrans never showed off their wealth though. There was little jewellery, no furs or fancy cars, unlike so many other people on the Costa Brava who made an art of displaying their money.

Carmen placed a dish of olives and sliced chorizo in front of Boyle and then leaned across the bar, her flowery perfume enveloping him. 'Montse and Rosa getting married. Can you believe it?' she whispered.

He looked down at the appetizers. 'They are serious about each other, there's no doubt about that,' he said, taking an olive and popping it into his mouth.

'I have nothing against Rosa.' She put her hand over his. 'In fact, I like her. But she is as straight as this bar.'

'They've lived together for two years. Rosa isn't going anywhere,' he said.

'You can't possibly see this as a good thing?' She took her hand away and stood back as if she were punishing him. 'I've nothing against women being together. Montse's had girlfriends in the past – but they hadn't been married to men before. I am still worried that Rosa will meet some man and run off.'

'Marriage is a strong commitment,' he said.

'Don't be ridiculous. Marriage doesn't keep people together. It means nothing today,' she said. Boyle bit his tongue, knowing she was referring to her husband Pau who had left her two years before for another woman. Her eyes began to water. Drops appeared and ran down her cheeks. 'That bitch is pregnant again,' she said, taking a napkin and holding it to her face to catch the tears.

'I'm sorry, Carmen.'

'Never mind. I really am over Pau. It's just I worry about how it will affect my children.' She looked Boyle in the face and reached across the bar.

'Hold my hand,' she said. 'Please.'

He cupped his hands around hers, a stab of guilt coming from out of nowhere. Her fingers were bony and cold from the beer. He could feel her relax, then she smiled at him, her eyes half closed like a cat.

They saw the waiters milling around the kitchen door. She let go of his hand and said, 'Thanks, *cariño*.'

He watched Carmen move towards the ultra-modern kitchen, where the waiters gathered around her for their nightly chat. Boyle observed her from behind. With her shoulder-length hair and the way she held herself, slightly favouring one leg, she could easily pass for Ana. He felt an ache of longing in the pit of his stomach.

After, she asked Boyle what he was working on and he told her about the death of Cisco Perez. She was horrified and said that graffiti was all the rage at her son Antonio's school and that Cisco was their hero. Boyle asked if he could chat to Antonio about it.

'It would be good if you could talk some sense into

him,' she said. 'Warn him how dangerous it can be.'

Boyle had dinner at a table near the bar, where the family always ate. Opposite him was Carmen's new white laptop, intermittently beeping whenever a new message came through. He had to fight the urge to turn the screen around and sneak a look. He had had dinner here at least three times a week since Ana had died. It was at the funeral that Carmen had told him that he always had a place to go, that he would never have to be alone in the evening, adding that having him there would also make it easier for her. Carmen would sit with him in between seating her customers, playing head waiter and taking orders. The loss of Ana had been tough on both of them and they quietly mourned her together.

In their early forties and childless, Boyle and Ana had left their jobs in London, moving down to Spain to work and be near Ana's family. Three years later, Ana died of an inoperable brain tumour. She was a surgical nurse with a specialty in neurosurgery and Boyle was convinced that she knew what she had months before she was diagnosed, that she knew it was terminal, so kept it from them. He was her main carer for a year, probably the hardest thing he ever had to do, and he had felt a terrible combination of sorrow and relief when she died.

Boyle had long finished his post-prandial *café solo* when Antonio arrived. He was thirteen years old and had a long fringe swept across his forehead, practically covering his eyes.

'Mama said you wanted to talk about Cisco Perez?' he said, sitting opposite Boyle and placing his red laptop on the table.

'You knew him personally?'

'No. But he was a well-known writer.'

'Writer?'

'Graffiti artists call their work "writing".'

'What do you think of his work?'

'I used to like it but then Cisco became big-headed.'

'How so?'

Antonio looked behind him and clocked his mother laughing with customers across the room. He turned back to Boyle. 'At first, Casa Cielo was there for all writers to use,' he said in a lowered voice. 'I went up there a few times with some of my friends. The house was always left open then. It was fun. There was plenty of wall space. One day, four of us went up there. I had sprayed over one of Cisco's tags with white paint and was working on something. All of a sudden, this old guy grabbed my arm and shook the spray can out of my hand, yelling at me to stop. He was crazy, asking who did I think I was, spraying over brilliant work with my rubbish? Couldn't I see how much better Cisco's work was than mine? Blah, blah, blah. He was a real weirdo. We left and never went back.'

'This weirdo – do you know who he was?'

'Señor Clavaguera.'

'Miguel's father?'

'Yes. Then I heard that the place was locked up and that only Cisco was allowed to work there.'

'Why did you paint over Cisco's work?'

'The walls were totally covered. You had to keep painting over one another's work. Anyway, you take photographs of your pieces. Sure, when you paint something good, it hurts to see it covered over by something that's not as good as yours. But it's not important.'

'It's not?'

Antonio shook his head. Stubborn as a mule.

'Even when someone replaces your masterpiece with something that's not quite as good?' asked Boyle.

'It's not about who's the best artist, it's about everybody expressing themselves with their own tag – you know, your individual graffiti name. Everyone's tag is important,' he said with an intensity that worried Boyle. 'Now, the best writers are the ones who are fearless. Going to places that are difficult to reach, where you have to be brave. High on a crane, let's say, or hanging from a bridge. Or, like Cisco, from the roof of Casa Cielo. It's called "hitting the heavens". That's what made Cisco great.'

Boyle cringed inwardly at the thought of his nephew hanging from a bridge. 'Doing graffiti on bridges and cranes is against the law. Are you aware of that?' Boyle said.

'Yes, Uncle,' Antonio said, mindlessly scanning the room to see who was in the restaurant. He then opened his laptop.

Boyle closed the computer and pushed it to the other side of the table. 'I'm talking to you now, Antonio.'

'Yes, Uncle,' he said with a little smirk reserved for those dinosaurs who could never understand the younger generation.

'My concern is for your welfare.'

'Yes,' he said, beginning to sulk.

'I mean it,' said Boyle, worried that he was losing the little boy he had once had so much influence over. 'I want you to stop painting in illegal places.'

'You really don't understand,' said Antonio. 'Sometimes we just paint abandoned buildings that no one cares about, that are going to be torn down anyway. Or underneath old bridges, where no one can see it. That's all. Besides, the police still don't know who I am.'

'They will if you keep it up,' said Boyle.

'Yeah, but they could never prove anything because they don't know my tag. They don't know *who* I am. Your tag is your secret signature,' he said with pride.

5

The Clavaguera estate was set in fifty acres of hilly woodland in the *pueblo* of Santa Nuria, just over the hill – as the crow flies – from Boyle's house in Pedralta. The dogs in the estate were already barking as Boyle drove up to the main gate, immediately setting him on edge. He slammed his fingers on the automatic button to close his window as the massive grey metal gate slid open with a hum and a dozen dogs surged forward, encircling his car, leaping up and down, barking hysterically. Most of them looked like hunting dogs, with a couple of Jack Russells jumping the highest and yapping the loudest.

Boyle flinched when an Alsatian appeared from out of nowhere, shoved its nose against the car window, bared its teeth and growled. He moved forward slowly on the gravel drive, careful not to run over any of them. As the pack followed the car up the drive, he wondered how he was going to get from the car to the house without being mauled to death.

Off to the right, Boyle noticed two gardeners covering a row of olive trees with protective green netting in preparation for winter. In the distance, standing near an orchard of apple trees, were two other gardeners, not working but watching him. It wasn't till Boyle saw the large semi-automatic weapons strapped to their sides that he realised they were security guards. *Why does Eduardo Clavaguera need heavy security? Sure, he is a multi-millionaire but he isn't exactly an oligarch.*

The drive opened up to a broad forecourt in front of an enormous Catalan country house that had the clean honey-coloured stone characteristic of a recent renovation. Everyone in the valley had been talking about the vast amounts of money Eduardo Clavaguera had spent on the house. Boyle parked close to a garage with four cars parked outside. The dogs stood near the driver's door and stared at him, clocking his every move. There was no one about. While he waited for salvation, he scanned the cars, recognising Tina Clavaguera's Land Rover, now painted a silvery blue.

The last time he had seen that car, it had been covered in anti-hunt graffiti. There were a further three small cars – a navy blue Mercedes SLK, a silver Peugeot 207 and an old silver Clio.

A young maid in a blue and white uniform appeared and whistled for the dogs and they ran off with her. Unaware that his hands were clamped on the steering wheel, Boyle released them and flexed his fingers. A plump older maid met him and took him across the courtyard towards the house. He followed her through double oak doors to a reception area, where she told him to wait. It was cool inside and smelled of lavender polish. Faded thin tapestries covered the stone walls above dark, imposing antique furniture.

A tall, distinguished-looking man entered the room. He was an eccentric dresser, wearing a silk leopard print shirt with casual trousers. He had a goatee, and straight salt-and-pepper hair that was combed back, revealing a high, smooth forehead. He extended his hand to Boyle.

'Good morning, Señor Boyle.'

'Thank you for seeing me,' said Boyle, shaking hands with him. Clavaguera had an air of entitlement. Boyle, having come from the poorest of the poor, was always attracted to and envied this quality in a person. Ana had possessed it. In police work, this was a weakness that he had struggled with but eventually conquered. Witnesses were always under suspicion until proven otherwise, no matter from which drawer they emerged.

'Come in,' said Clavaguera, leading him into a cavernous two-storey drawing room with a skylight. It was an art gallery more than a drawing room, the immense white walls covered with oversized modern paintings. Seating ran up the centre of the room in sections, comprising sofas, chairs and coffee tables.

Out of politeness, Boyle drew near one of the paintings and peered at it. Executed in dull colours, it was a dense tangle of lines and drips.

'It's a Jackson Pollock. What do you think?' asked Clavaguera.

'I'm not a fan,' said Boyle. 'But I'm not surprised you like it. It's not unlike the graffiti I hear you like so much.'

'But this painting is slightly different from graffiti,' said Clavaguera. 'It's worth forty million euros.'

Boyle was amazed. 'Is that why you have security men outside?'

There was some quiet laughter from Eduardo. 'Just two, but both Pedro and Manel are ex-army and former police snipers. The paintings in this room are worth around eighty million, and that is a conservative estimate,' he said, turning to face the room, hands raised like a priest. 'And this isn't everything. Most of my paintings are on loan to museums all over the world.'

Boyle wasn't a collector of anything; it was too much work. Possessions needed to be insured, cleaned, repaired and worried about – although he wouldn't say no to a new car. His Rover was on its last legs.

Eduardo gestured for Boyle to sit. They sat opposite each other on deep, worn leather sofas. Eduardo leaned forward and asked. 'You said on the telephone that you wanted to question me about Cisco. What is it you want to know?'

'I was hired by Juanita Perez to look into his death. She thinks he was murdered,' answered Boyle, observing Clavaguera's reaction carefully.

'I can't imagine who would do such a thing. Everyone loved Cisco,' said Clavaguera with what Boyle thought was genuine sincerity. 'He was extremely close to my whole family, like a son.' Clavaguera's eyes were glistening. He glanced down at his hands intertwined on his lap and when he had composed himself, faced Boyle again. 'He was a brilliant painter but like many graffiti artists, he was reckless. He didn't have to climb on the roof at Casa Cielo and paint the tower. But unfortunately, he was addicted to the dangerous aspect of the art. He was an adrenaline junkie.'

'I'm sorry, but I must ask you this question: where were you the day Cisco died?'

'I was here all day. The workers on my estate can attest to that.'

I bet they can, if they want to keep their jobs, thought Boyle. But he held back judgement; Clavaguera appeared to be truly upset about Cisco's death.

'Why did you let them do graffiti at Casa Cielo in the first place?'

Eduardo gave an embarrassed smile. 'It was a shock to me and my wife when Cisco and Miguel were arrested for vandalism all those months ago. But once I saw how brilliant Cisco's work was, I knew I had to help. I think that graffiti is a brilliant medium in its proper place – at chosen sites. I studied painting in Barcelona when I was young. When kids go to art school now, they're offered media or film studies. I wanted to encourage Catalan painters. And the idea of making my old house in Roca Alba an art object appealed to me.' Eduardo paused and sighed audibly. 'I thought it would be safer there. I never thought for a minute that Cisco would climb out on the roof to paint the tower.'

'Does your son still paint there?' asked Boyle, remembering what his nephew had told him.

'My son worked there in the beginning but it soon became apparent that he was never going to be the artist Cisco was – a bit like me with my failed painting career – so he stopped. He works for me now in my gallery in Barcelona.'

A young, serious-looking maid entered and set down a tray with two espressos, a pot of steamed milk and a plate of sweet, round *bunyols*. The sight of the pastries made Boyle's mouth water. He had woken too late for a proper breakfast.

'Would you like milk?' asked Clavaguera.

'Yes please,' said Boyle. As Clavaguera poured the milk into the espresso, Boyle noticed his shiny, manicured nails. "Never done an honest day's work" came to mind and he pushed the unhelpful thought aside.

'Can you think of someone who might have wanted to harm Cisco?'

'No,' said Clavaguera.

'What about the developers, Gunnar Lundgren or Quimet Navarro?'

Eduardo smiled and shook his head. 'What a ridiculous idea.'

'His smart phone and scooter are missing.'

'So I hear. I put that down to robbers. These eastern European gangs are becoming a real menace.'

'But they wouldn't be interested in a sketchbook, and that was missing. Apparently Cisco took it everywhere with him,' said Boyle, as he lowered a rock of brown sugar into his coffee and stirred.

Eduardo took a sip of his espresso, saying nothing.

'And later, the rest of his sketchbooks were stolen from his room in his parents' flat,' added Boyle.

Eduardo looked up with an expression of surprise and confusion. 'I never heard that.'

Eduardo's surprise seems authentic, thought Boyle. 'Do you have any idea who might do that?'

'No. I don't.' Eduardo motioned to the *bunyols*. 'Why don't you try one?'

Boyle picked up a pastry, which was still warm, and bit into it. Sweet custard oozed out. It was so good that he momentarily forgot what point they were discussing. 'Delicious.'

'My wife made them,' said Clavaguera with pride.

Boyle was impressed that a Spanish wife with a house full of servants would do her own baking. He finished, then wiped his mouth with the small linen napkin provided. 'Give her my compliments.'

Eduardo smiled. 'I will.'

It wasn't until they were on their way to another gallery off the main one to see a painting of Cisco's that Boyle remembered his next line of questioning. 'Cisco was found with a packet of cocaine near his body. Do you know anything about his cocaine use?'

Eduardo paused. 'I thought he'd given up drugs. I am ashamed to say that my son Miguel took cocaine as well. But both he and Cisco had stopped. Now it appears that Cisco hadn't,' he said, his smooth brow wrinkling.

Is Eduardo worried about his own son's sobriety? Boyle wondered.

'The autopsy showed he had no cocaine in his blood,' said Boyle.

Eduardo nodded. 'I can understand Cisco not wanting to take drugs while he did his art. He was disciplined, always one for delayed gratification. He took his work very seriously.'

Eduardo took Boyle up to a life-sized mural covering one wall. It was colourful and realistic in style, four people standing together: the Clavagueras – Eduardo, his wife Tina and their two grown children, a boy and a girl. They were surrounded by their dogs, with their house and the hills behind them. Boyle stared at the mural in amazement.

'Isn't it incredible?' asked Eduardo.

'Extraordinary,' said Boyle.

'And he did most of it with spray cans,' said Eduardo, backing up and motioning for Boyle to do the same. 'It has an ultra-real quality that is marvellous.'

'A bit like a cartoon in some ways.'

'Exactly. It is a style uniquely Cisco's.'

In the lower right-hand corner of the painting, something caught Boyle's eye. There was a tag in a black rectangle where the artist's signature would normally be. It was a word, or two perhaps – he couldn't tell. Calligraphy drawn with fine lines of red, pink, green and black, too intricate to read. Boyle moved closer, trying to make sense of it. He did manage to pick up the letter Z filling the rectangle, but the rest was indecipherable.

'What does it say?' he asked Eduardo.

'It's Cisco's graffiti tag, *El Cazador*.'

The Hunter, thought Boyle. *A strange tag for an anti-hunt protester.*

Before leaving, Boyle asked if he could have a look at Casa Cielo. He needed to examine the place close up, to see where Cisco fell. Eduardo didn't hesitate. He gave Boyle a key to the house and added that he had enjoyed meeting him, even though it was under "such sad circumstances". In the car, Boyle checked his smart phone, a device he was now able to navigate with ease after much help from his nephew Antonio. There was a text message from Rosa.

We've found Cisco's scooter, it said. *Ring me.*

6

Boyle put a call through to Rosa immediately. She told him that the scooter had been in an accident, and that a fourteen-year-old boy had been riding it. 'His name is Manel Torres and he lives on Can Pedro – a farm at the bottom of Pedralta. You know it?'

'Yes,' said Boyle. It was one of the several farms owned by the Clavaguera estate.

'The boy's in surgery at the moment. They're fixing a broken leg. We should be able to question him later.'

'What about the parents?'

'They know nothing about the scooter. *Nada*,' she

said, and then, after promising to keep him informed, she rang off.

As Boyle drove back into Sant Martí he noticed the stratus clouds drifting across the sky from the Pyrenees, which was a frequent early afternoon occurrence in the Vall d'Aro.

There were only three customers inside Café El Cisne when Boyle entered, which was slow for lunchtime. Carlos, the owner, fit as a matador with a moustache from the seventies, took his order. Boyle had met Carlos twenty years before, on one of his many holidays to Catalonia with Ana. It was just after Carlos had moved here from Andalucía, and over the years Boyle had seen him work in a number of different cafés as a waiter; El Cisne was the first café Carlos had owned. Over that time, he had begun to know Carlos well. Carlos knew everyone's business and loved to tell Boyle about it. Boyle thought that he had missed his calling. He would have made a great cop.

Carlos served Boyle calamari Andalusian style – deep fried with a light batter – and wiped down the counter as he chatted.

'I heard you had a problem yesterday at Café Bon Día with one of your clients and Quimet Navarro.'

Boyle told him about the case. There was always the chance Carlos could help; he had in the past. While Boyle ate his calamari, they moved on to other topics. Carlos complained about how bad the summer had been for all the hotels and restaurants in the area and how many of them were preparing to close down for the whole winter rather than just the usual month of January.

'Will you shut for three months?' asked Boyle.

'I'm not sure yet. But everyone is suffering. Except for our friend Señor Navarro,' Carlos said, lowering his voice. 'He and his best friend the mayor, Salvador Clavaguera.' Boyle put down his knife and fork and listened. 'Salvador Clavaguera swears to his constituents that he left the property business when he became mayor. But it doesn't look like that to me,' said Carlos. 'Sure, he closed down his *inmobiliarias,* estate agencies – well, four out of five anyway. His wife took over the last *inmobiliaria* under her name, Deirdre. It's her business now,' said Carlos with a shrug. 'So they say.'

Boyle had met Salvador's wife Deirdre once with Ana, when they had first begun looking at properties in Sant Martí. He remembered her because she was English, from Preston, and stood out among the Catalans with her bright red hair. 'Where is it?'

'Over in Calle Joan Marigal,' said Carlos.

After lunch, Boyle walked over to the other side of town, past the Belle Époque casino, where the retired men sat outside playing cards, smoking and drinking brandy. He saw the sign, "Fincas Deirdre", from a distance and although it was not yet two o'clock, he could see that the exclusive-looking *inmobiliaria* had already shut for the afternoon. He crossed the street and checked the door for opening times. There were none. A large board in the window advertised Quimet Navarro Properties. *So Quimet and Salvador are helping each other out through Salvador's wife,* Boyle thought. There was a photograph of the grand development with six peach-coloured three-storey blocks, containing eighteen flats each. This was the set of buildings that had been vandalised by Cisco Perez and Miguel Clavaguera a year and a half ago. The flats were built on land that used to belong to Eduardo, Salvador's older brother. Over the past few years, Eduardo had sold it off to Quimet Navarro to develop. Boyle knew from his sister-in-law Montse that the first thing Salvador Clavaguera did when he became mayor was re-zone the land from agricultural to residential. People found it strange that the old adversaries were doing business together. The Clavagueras had been given the vast estate of the Navarro family after the Civil War, and some said that it left them destitute. Were the Clavagueras now trying to make some amends by selling it back?

Boyle wanted to have a look at Casa Cielo. As soon as he got to his car, his mobile rang. It was Narcis, his father-in-law. 'Adrian, I must see you.'

At first, Boyle thought something must be wrong

with his mother-in-law. 'Is Esther alright?' he asked.

'She isn't ill, if that's what you mean. But we *both* need to see you as soon as possible, please.'

The palatial modernist building on the seafront was called Casa Ferran. It had been built by the ancestors of Narcis Ferran after they returned from Chile, where they had made a fortune mining for gold and copper. The house was so large it was often mistaken for a hotel.

Boyle ignored the modern buzzer and rapped the enormous, hand-shaped brass knocker on the door. Narcis answered and they shook hands in the cool tiled foyer. He was tall with thick white hair that Boyle knew was too long for his wife's taste. 'Thank you for coming, Adrian,' he said in a subdued manner, waving him into the drawing room.

Dark, heavy furniture packed the spacious room, with framed antique maps of South America and murky paintings by Catalan masters covering the walls. Precious porcelain and silver were displayed in glass cabinets, all passed down from the family of Narcis Ferran I Vall, a family that could be traced back to the fifteenth century. Boyle remembered being overwhelmed and intimidated the first time he had entered this room. He had inherited one suede fringed shoulder bag from his hippy mother after she had died from a heroin overdose. In it was a wallet containing one pound and seventy-five pence, a national insurance card and a bus ticket dated the day she died, 11 October 1976; a torn envelope had a shopping list marked in pencil – milk, tea, bread and cigarette papers for roll-ups. She smoked both marijuana and tobacco.

He used to think it sad and was ashamed that his mother's worldly goods had amounted to so little, but now he realised that it had given him a tremendous sense of freedom. He would have been weighed down by the responsibility of an illustrious family legacy and the demands that property and money made on people – the duty to pass on chattels and success to the next generation. If he and Ana had had children, they would have been part of that. A sudden twinge of regret surprised him.

The room opened up into a dining area with French doors overlooking a garden surrounded by a high wall. He remembered happy family lunches here with Ana, her parents, Montse, and Carmen and her children, in the days when her husband Pau was still around.

His mother-in-law Esther was standing as Boyle entered, perfectly turned out as usual, with her neat, short bouffant hair and nails that were manicured once a week. She was wearing a simple navy blue dress, her pretty face was pale etched with sorrow, still mourning for her daughter. The bright lipstick she had worn for years had been replaced by a muted tone. She held out her hands for Boyle. 'Hello Adrian.'

He took her hands, which were icy, and covered them with his own to warm them, and they kissed each other on the cheek. 'Are you well?' he asked, and then regretted it immediately.

She pursed her lips as if to say, "How can I be well with Ana gone?" He squeezed her hands in understanding.

Boyle sat in a chair facing them. On the massive teak coffee table between them was a silver tray with a blue and white porcelain coffee pot and matching cups and saucers – Meissen, Ana had told him. Next to the tray was a red envelope addressed to *Sres. Ferran I Valls*.

Esther poured the coffees. 'How is everything up on Pedralta, at the house?' she said, handing Boyle a cup.

'The hunters are busy three days a week, making a lot of noise.' Boyle stopped suddenly. He hadn't wanted to mention death of any kind, yet what did he do as soon as he was through the door? Bring up hunting. What an idiot.

'Oh yes. It's that time of year again. It comes around so quickly,' said Esther, her lips beginning to tremble.

Narcis watched her with a combination of empathy and irritation, then picked up the red envelope and handed it to Boyle. 'We received it this morning. Open it.'

Boyle could feel their stares as he withdrew a card. On the front was a photo of a bottle of champagne and written across the top, "¡*Felicidades!*" "Congratulations!" Inside the card were the typewritten wishes of the sender: "We were delighted to hear about the upcoming marriage of your daughter Montse to the lovely Detective Inspector Rosa Pujol." Of course, there was no signature. Boyle looked up at Narcis and Esther sitting motionless on the sofa, as if they had stopped breathing.

'Is it true?' Narcis asked.

Boyle glanced at Esther. Her large eyes opened wide, begging him to say it was not. 'Yes, I'm afraid it is,' he said.

Esther bowed her head for a moment and when she finally looked up at Boyle, her eyes were glistening. 'Montse comes to Mass with me every Sunday and takes communion. How can it be true?'

'Rosa?! Rosa is a lesbian?' Narcis said with an expression of incredulity, but not offering the same surprise about his own daughter. 'But she was married,' he added, his focus still on Rosa. It was a joke between Boyle and Carmen that Narcis fancied Rosa, that his attraction to her was something he found difficult to hide.

'That doesn't mean anything today,' Esther threw at her husband, with a look of disgust. She closed her eyes and sighed.

'May I keep the card so I can test it for fingerprints?' asked Boyle.

'No. We'll keep it. We don't want everyone knowing,' said Esther, straightening up and grabbing the card out of his hand. Her eyes were dry and her face hard. 'Montse doesn't care about anyone but herself. She has always been selfish.' She glared at Boyle. 'Who is going to this *wedding*?'

Boyle flinched and she saw it.

'Not you, surely?' she said with disbelief.

'I am. And so are Carmen, Antonio and Isabella,' said Boyle, putting down his coffee cup and wondering how Montse and Rosa were going to react to this. *Not well,* he thought. 'Are you going to talk to Montse about this?'

'No,' she said, shaking her head. 'And I don't want you telling them either.'

Narcis touched his wife's hand. 'We have to talk to them at some point, *cariño*.'

'Why? They've kept us in the dark about all of this. Why should we say anything to them?'

'Perhaps there is something we can do to stop the wedding.'

Not a chance, thought Boyle.

When Esther showed Boyle to the door, she slipped in the last few words on the matter, as she always managed to do. 'We won't accept this marriage, you know. Ever.'

Boyle speculated who had sent the card and why. So far there was no blackmail mentioned. Often these things were about money. Did Rosa's ex-husband have something to do with it? Had he found out about the upcoming wedding? After all, Rosa had left him. Was sending this card a way for Chief Inspector Marc Saldoni to get back at his ex-wife?

7

AT THE BASE OF PEDRALTA, ON HIS WAY UP to see Casa Cielo, Boyle passed several smallholdings owned by Eduardo Clavaguera, who rented them out to farmers. There was a police SUV parked along the track leading to the farm belonging to the family of Manel Torres. Boyle hoped that when the boy woke up, he could shed some light on what had happened to Cisco. He could see the recent damage from the wild boars. Neat rows of courgettes and barley were intermittently broken where the wild boars had run amok, the earth turned over in that haphazard animal way. Winding its way up the mountain, the road went high into the woods of umbrella pine, cork trees and holm oak. Bumping along where the tree roots had buckled the tarmac, Boyle wondered what damage this daily thrashing was doing to the shock absorbers of his fifteen-year-old Rover, not for the first time. Near the top of the mountain, he turned down a track leading into the small enclave of Roca Alba.

He passed Can Bosc, followed by other homes in the development, some still defaced with anti-hunt slogans: *¡No Cazes! ¡No Mates! Cazadores Asesinos.* Why would Cisco, who the judge had named a suspect in this vandalism case, use The Hunter as his personal tag? It didn't make sense. And perhaps Cisco's mother was right that her son would never have painted this rubbish. It wasn't his style. In which case, then who had done it? And did they have anything to do with his death? Boyle first went to the track below Casa Cielo where Cisco was found. He pinpointed the boulder on which Cisco had fallen, saw the brown traces of blood that had stained the rock. He spent an hour searching through the brush for Cisco's missing smart phone, but found nothing.

Standing in front of Casa Cielo, there was no way of telling what colour it had originally been because, except for the windows, it was completely covered in graffiti. In the clear light of day, he could see shapes overlapping in a multitude of bright yellows, purples, reds, oranges and greens, combined with black and white lines, forming writing so dense it was impossible to read. As he moved closer, Cisco's tag, *El Cazador*, seemed to pop out of the maze here and there. Recognising it, he felt a sense of satisfaction.

The house was L-shaped, mostly on one level, but the right side dropped down to include a garage beneath it and in the middle of the building there was a Catalan tower, a *torre*.

With the key that Eduardo had given him, he unlocked the door and entered the house. Sunlight filtered through the clean windows. It surprised Boyle how well tended the property was, resembling an art gallery rather than a home. There was no furniture but graffiti portraits and designs covered every wall. In the second reception room, Boyle came across a mural with figures. It was the sort of painting he liked, realistic and simple, not unlike the family portrait at Eduardo Clavaguera's house. The painting was set in a busy town square with a fruit and vegetable market in the background. In the foreground were the figures of a mother holding a baby and a father standing alongside them. The mother was clearly Juanita Perez; therefore, the baby must be Cisco and the man, her husband. The parents were gazing at their son. Juanita was smiling at Cisco, who was grinning back at her. It would have been a happy portrait but for the father, who had a haunted look. Why would Cisco choose to depict his father this way?

Boyle's mobile rang. It was Rosa, from the hospital.

'I spoke with Manel Torres,' she said.

'Is he alright?'

'Six weeks in a cast. He'll be fine. He says he found the scooter in the brush near their farm. He has no idea who left it there.'

'Do you believe him?'

'Yes. He has an honest little face. They're doing forensics at the site now and searching his house. Perhaps Cisco's phone is there. Also, we've found several different fingerprints on the scooter. Mostly friends, I imagine. But I'll send them over to Girona and they can search the database, see if they match up with any of the anti-hunt people.'

'Can you do me a favour?' asked Boyle.

'Of course.'

'Eduardo Clavaguera sold Quimet Navarro acres of land to build his complex. Can you find any documents of sale or tax... anything? It was once farmland but made *zona residencial,* so rumour has it, by Mayor Clavaguera. Can you look into that?'

'I've heard that rumour. I should be able to find something,' she said, her voice suddenly dropping to a whisper.

Teasing her, he said, 'You're not getting into trouble, are you?'

'My ex-husband just walked by. Ignoring me, of course, but he has ears like satellite dishes.'

'You're not saying anything a cop wouldn't say in a police station.'

'I don't want him knowing any of my business.'

Boyle thought about the card that was sent to Narcis and Esther and reckoned Rosa would go spare if Marc Saldoni happened to be behind it. 'Alright now?'

'He's gone. But before I go, I want to tell you about the spray cans the protesters left behind. Six of them. They must have worn gloves because there were no fingerprints on the cans, but each was stamped with a handy serial number. So, we know where they purchased the paint. And now we're trawling through hours of CCTV to see if we can spot any known vandals. It will take some time but hopefully we will come up with a match, *ojal*á.'

'What brand is the paint?'

'Pintura Estrella.'

They said they would meet up some time during the week and said their goodbyes. Boyle put the mobile back in his pocket and focused on the graffiti. He wandered from room to room, drawn in by the paintings, beginning to get a sense of who Cisco was and thinking that he would have liked the boy, because what was clear from every scene and face that he had painted was his compassion for people.

In the foyer, he climbed a spiral wrought iron staircase that led into the tower and a spacious round room. French doors gave way to a wide terrace sunk into the roof, which spread out in a gentle downward slope. On the left, the terrace overlooked a deep gorge of shrub and brush. Boyle reached out and touched the roof tiles. They were damp. The roof was covered with dew and patches of fine moss, this section of the house facing the north side of the valley. There were skid marks in the moss where Boyle presumed Cisco had slid – or was pushed – and fallen forty metres below.

Cisco's last painting was on the wall of the tower, but Boyle was unable to see it without climbing out onto the roof. Not fond of heights, he saw there was a possible viewing place down in the garden.

The garden terrace was built out to the edge of the cliff with an iron guardrail. A rocky shale wall dropped away from the house into thick brush and umbrella trees, and he could just make out the dirt track far below where Cisco had landed. He stared up at the tower, at Cisco's last painting. It was a larger-than-life mural of a woman reading a book. This was the first time Boyle had seen her image in the house. She was young, not exactly pretty but handsome, relaxing in a wicker chair. The forest loomed behind her. She appeared to have just glanced up from her book, an expression of curiosity on her face. And in exquisite detail, flying towards her, was a bullet just before impact. *What is that all about?* thought Boyle. *Who is she?* He studied the paperback that she held in her hand, her fingers splayed across the front cover, partially obscuring the title. But he had seen the word enough to recognize it. The title was *El Cazador*.

The forested area of the painting was unfinished. Cisco must have been working on it when he died. That would explain the cans of blue, green and brown spray paint that the police had found on the roof terrace. Boyle remembered that no red paint had been found on the terrace. Or on Cisco, for that matter. Another reason, he felt, why Cisco had nothing to do with the protestors. Anyway, why would Cisco, after vandalising all those houses and cars, then come and work on a mural at Casa Cielo? Wouldn't he have left quickly with the others? And it was telling that there was no anti-hunting graffiti at Casa Cielo. He took out his smart phone and photographed the image from several angles, focusing on the woman's face and the bullet.

The smell of cigarette smoke wafted on the breeze. There was someone else about. There had been no sound of an approaching car or anyone walking down the drive. Whoever it was must have already been here when he arrived. He followed the scent back into the house and approached a door just off the kitchen. Carefully, he opened it. Stairs descended into the garage and, going by the strength of the tobacco smell, Boyle knew there was someone down there. He listened for a moment and, hearing nothing, crept down the stairs, straight into a three-car garage that had been turned into an artist's studio. Wooden racks stood against the closest wall, where a couple of huge blank canvasses were filed, and alongside them were racks containing spray painting cans stacked in rainbow order. He sidled closer to examine the cans. None of them were the *Pintura Estrella* brand that the protesters had used.

The girl was so out of it, she had no idea Boyle was there. She was sitting on the side of a bed with her head in her hands and a cigarette dangerously close to burning her fingers.

'*Señorita,*' Boyle eventually said.

The girl jumped up, lost her balance, dropping her cigarette on the floor, and had to put her hand on the wall to catch herself. Boyle crushed the cigarette under his foot. She was thin, wearing low-slung jeans that revealed sharp hip bones and a high-riding tee-shirt that looked like it had shrunk in the wash. Her long, greasy hair was split down the middle. He recognised her, having seen her face in the family portrait that Cisco had painted for Eduardo Clavaguera. It was his daughter, Laura. She stared at him, glassy-eyed, definitely high on something.

She looked at him like he was the help. 'What are you doing here?' she asked.

'I could ask the same about you, Señorita.'

'Eduardo owns this house,' she said, slurring her words. 'He lets me visit when I want.'

What Spanish girl calls her father by his first name?
'Your father gave me the key.'

Her face twisted in disapproval. She was preparing to say something nasty, by the look of her, then, as if forgetting what she wanted to say, she gazed out of the window overlooking the forest.

'Are you alright?' Boyle said, approaching her.

'I'm okay,' she said, not looking at him.

'What have you taken?'

She regarded him and shook with silent laughter.

Boyle took his mobile from his pocket and began to search for a number.

'What are you doing?' she asked, struggling to become alert.

'Ringing your father.'

She lunged to take the phone from his hand but he caught her and, grabbing her wrists with one hand, he sat her down on the bed.

'Don't ring Eduardo. Please!'

Boyle paused. 'You can't stay here alone. Not in the state you're in.'

'Let me ring someone else.'

Boyle studied her pleading face, wondering who the "someone else" might be. Was it her mother, Tina? Curious as to who it might be, he agreed.

Ponderously, she searched for a name on her

smart phone and pressed it. 'Can you pick me up now?' she said to the person at the other end, using the voice of a child ready to burst into tears.

'What have you taken?' Boyle asked after she got off the phone.

'Valium.'

'How much?'

'I don't know, but not enough to die, unfortunately.'

Boyle took her by the elbow and helped her to her feet. 'Why would you say such a thing?'

'Mind your own fucking business,' she snapped, saying it without looking at him.

On the way back to his car, he asked her a few questions. She seemed more amenable. Perhaps she was embarrassed about her outburst. *She should be,* thought Boyle. It was at times like this that Boyle was glad he had no children. How would he cope with a daughter like Laura Clavaguera?

'Did you know Cisco Perez?' Boyle asked after a while.

She tripped on an uneven flagstone in the drive, nearly falling over. Boyle caught her under the arms and helped to steady her.

'He was my boyfriend.'

So, Cisco was Eduardo Clavaguera's favourite artist and his daughter's boyfriend. More connections. More reasons for foul play, by the looks of it. He wondered what Eduardo and his wife thought of their daughter. They must know she had a drug problem. Did they kill Cisco over it?

'I was sorry to hear about Cisco,' he said.

'You seem to be the only one who is.'

'What do you mean?'

'Nothing. I mean nothing,' she said, slowing down, barely able to get one foot in front of the other. Boyle propped her up by the arm and steered her along the drive towards his car. He drank a bit – he wasn't a saint – but he loathed drugs and what they did to people. Upon reaching his car, he helped Laura over to a bench and sat her down. He stood near her. Her eyes were closed and she was smiling.

'I'm investigating Cisco's accident for his mother.'

Laura opened her eyes and sniggered. 'Let me guess. She thinks he was murdered.'

'And what? You don't?'

Laura gave Boyle a blank expression.

Boyle took a calling card out of his wallet. 'What do you think, Laura?' The girl shrugged. He handed her the card. 'If you need to, contact me.'

She took the card and rolled her eyes. 'You can go now,' she said, dismissing him.

'That's alright, Señorita. I'll stay with you until your lift arrives.'

'No, thank you. ¡*Vete!* Go!'

'I want to see that you're safe. Is your mother picking you up?'

'Keep away from me. Don't you get it?'

'Okay, I'll go, but if I see you drugged to the eyeballs again, I will contact your parents,' Boyle said, moving to his car and climbing in. He glanced at her before turning the key. She was staring ahead, in la-la land. *Her boyfriend has just died,* Boyle told himself. *Try to show a bit of compassion.* But he didn't feel it. Never mind the parents, for all he knew *she* could be responsible for Cisco's death. People are often murdered by someone close to them, so the nearest and dearest are usually the first ones put under the microscope. He started the car. At that moment, Laura looked over at Boyle. Her arrogant manner was gone and in its place was an expression of such deep sorrow and vulnerability, it brought a lump to his throat.

He pressed a button and his window slid open. 'Are you sure you're alright to wait alone?'

'Yes, I'm fine. They won't be long,' she said, her voice now choked with tears.

He smiled at her sympathetically and drove off.

Halfway down the mountain, he pulled into a dirt layby and switched off the engine. He had a clear view of the road that rose up from Sant Martí. There was no traffic. There rarely was, because a dead end waited at the top of the mountain. Boyle wanted to make sure that someone was collecting Laura. If they didn't come for her within ten minutes then he would go back and take her to her father. Not long after, he saw a Mercedes sedan speeding uphill, practically flying over the warped tarmac. As the car passed, he recognised the driver. It was Laura's uncle, Salvador Clavaguera, the mayor of Sant Martí.

8

'Señora, is it possible I might see you at your house?' Boyle asked Juanita Perez on the phone. He felt he needed to see where Cisco had lived.

'My house?' she said with uneasiness. 'Why?'

'To have a look at Cisco's room. There might be something that will help with the investigation. To see where his sketchbooks were taken, perhaps?'

'But the *policía local* have investigated that already.'

Why was she backtracking? 'Don't you want me to come to your house, Señora?'

'Yes, of course. It's just that… No, you are welcome to come.'

'Is this afternoon alright?'

'Now is better, Señor.'

Juanita Perez lived on the ground floor in a rundown block of flats away from the coast, in Llagostera. It was at the end of the road with an entry phone for access, but the front door was broken. When Juanita answered the door to her flat, she smiled at him; a smile of expectation. She expected him to find her son's killer but the problem was, he didn't know if one existed and would need hard evidence of murder for it to stand up in court.

'The door to your building is broken,' he said as he entered the flat, which stank of stale cigarettes. They paused in the cramped foyer.

'Yes, they haven't fixed it yet,' she said without interest. 'I think you need to talk to that man, Faustino Duran. He's the one who lives near Casa Cielo,' she said with a low voice.

'Why him?'

'Ask him why he was always saying nasty things to my son. He was never nice to any of the kids.'

No surprises there. Faustino was charm-free. 'Did he ever threaten Cisco?'

'I don't know,' she said as she opened the door to the kitchen and put her finger to her mouth for Boyle to be quiet. 'My husband's here,' she whispered as she waved him in and closed the door.

Felipe Perez was in a wheelchair, slumped over a

pine table, fast asleep. The door to the electric oven was open and heat blasted into the room. Felipe looked wizened, his rounded back revealing each vertebra under his oversized sweatshirt that must have fitted him in the past. He couldn't have been more than sixty but looked eighty and had the bloodless pallor of a dying man. Juanita smiled as she put her hands on her husband's shoulders and kissed the top of his bald head. He was in a deep sleep, his hands wrapped around a huge magnifying glass for reading the newspapers, several of which were stacked up against the wall.

She turned down the oven. 'He's always cold,' she whispered, trying to make everything sound as normal as possible, like people do when living with the dying. 'Would you like a coffee?'

'No thank you, Señora.'

Juanita and Boyle left the kitchen and approached another door. Boyle paused in the foyer. 'How do you manage?' he asked.

'He sleeps most of the time. I'm able to help him out of his wheelchair, into bed, to the toilet. Dolores, from the social services, helps me twelve hours a week. She gives him a bath, cuts his nails or watches him when I go out.' Juanita tucked her hair behind her ear. 'He can't speak properly now but I understand most of what he says. He wants to be at home. He hates hospitals and nursing homes. Anyway, he's been worse.'

From where Boyle stood, "worse" meant "dead", but Felipe Perez was still alive. He had seen it before – people gripping onto the remnants of life while death moved in and made itself comfortable. Often it was because they didn't want to leave a loved one behind. Was Felipe hanging on for Juanita?

'Cisco's room is in here,' she said, her face tensing as she pushed the door open. She indicated with her hand for Boyle to enter before her.

It was a small room with white walls, a neatly made single bed and one window, which overlooked the block of flats next door. There were a dozen books piled on a shelf along with Manga comics – the kind he had seen his nephew reading, a few oversized art books and several clear plastic boxes containing pencils and markers.

On a desk sat a large computer, surprisingly old-fashioned for a young, hip man. 'Señora, is it possible to take a look at this?'

'It doesn't work. He was going to buy a new laptop. Cisco used his smart phone for everything and that's gone,' she said, sitting on the bed.

'What about the sketchbooks? Were they here?' asked Boyle, pointing to an empty shelf.

'Yes, but I don't care who stole the sketchbooks. I just want you to find Cisco's killer.'

'But they may be related.'

'I don't think so.'

Boyle felt this was a strange thing for her to say. 'I was up at Casa Cielo this morning,' he said.

Juanita's face lit up. 'Isn't Cisco's work wonderful?'

'He was a very talented boy, Señora.' Then he paused and said, 'I met his girlfriend there.'

'Who? Laura?' she said, wrinkling her brow.

'Yes.'

Her look turned sour. 'Cisco did go out with her for a while, but it was never serious.'

'There were drawings of her all over Casa Cielo,' said Boyle.

Juanita shook her head, as if the suggestion was an insult. 'She was never his girlfriend. But she was always hanging around my son. Very, very possessive.'

'There was a studio at the house. From what I gather, he had lived there part of the time.'

'No,' she snapped. 'He spent little time there. Mostly he wanted to be at home with me and Felipe. Anyway, he loved his mama's cooking,' she said, biting her lip.

He sat down beside her and took her hand.

'I know this must be difficult for you.'

'Yes,' she said, wiping away tears with a swipe of her hand. 'But you must help me.'

'I'll do everything I can,' said Boyle.

He saw a wardrobe opposite. It looked like it came from Ikea, like most of the furniture in the room. 'Do you mind if I have a look?'

She nodded her head.

Hanging inside were jeans, sweatshirts and an anorak. In the chest of drawers were tee-shirts, pants and socks, all neatly folded, no doubt by his mother. She must have done everything for him. Boyle had seen this kind of motherly devotion over the years while working for the Metropolitan Police, usually while investigating the victims of crimes. He was always amazed by the care most mothers gave their children. Ana had told him that was normal. Boyle had been the product of institutions. He had been in care from when he was a baby until he was sixteen, then joined the army and then, at twenty-one, the Met. Although in his early years his mother had visited him once a week, she never took care of him from day to day. The thought of all that motherly attention brought about a feeling of claustrophobia, but at the same time, he was deeply envious of anyone who had had it. It was an uncomfortable mix.

In another cupboard, he found rock climbing equipment; ropes, crampons, and even a hard hat. Cisco clearly didn't think he needed them on the roof at Casa Cielo. Next to the hard hat was a bulky concertina file for bills and receipts, for his Santander bank account. 'May I take this?' Boyle asked. Juanita lifted her head in agreement.

Then Boyle remembered something. 'You told me that Cisco didn't take drugs. Eduardo Clavaguera told me that, two years ago, Cisco had been a cocaine user.'

She tensed. 'Yes, alright. He did use it back then. But only for a little time. He hadn't taken it for two years before…' She stopped talking and stared out the window.

'I'm sorry, Señora, but I must ask you these questions if I am going to be able to help you. Isn't it possible that he began using cocaine again and that packet found near him was his?'

'No. That cocaine was planted to make him look bad. What I tell you is correct. I knew my son better than anyone.'

Boyle followed Juanita into the living room, where Cisco's paintings covered the walls. She went straight for a packet of cigarettes near a sewing machine and lit up. There was a worn three-piece suite covered with neat piles of clothes. There was a filled clothes rack and an ironing board in the corner. It was more of a workroom than a living room, Boyle guessed. On a round table he noticed a shrine with a statue of the Virgin Mary, blue votive candles and glass rosary beads. Juanita cleared a space for him on the sofa. 'I pray to *la Virgen* every day. She gives me strength,' she said, gesturing for him to sit. 'I'm doing a novena to help us find Cisco's killer.'

'Good,' said Boyle. Being a lapsed Catholic, he thought the novena would help Juanita more than the investigation.

She took a seat at her sewing machine, which was next to an open window looking out onto the main road. 'This is what I do,' she said, indicating the room. She seemed stronger and more confident behind the machine. Boyle smiled at her. 'I am lucky with my work because I can stay at home with Felipe,' she said, placing her cigarette in an ashtray. She took a skirt and began to unpick the hem.

'Do you have family here?'

'No. My family are in Colombia. I never met my husband's family. They are from Catalonia but moved down to Cadiz years ago. Felipe never got on with them.'

'Would it be possible to speak to your husband?'

She paused. 'I can answer any questions you have.'

'It's just that he might have noticed something... How was he when he found out about Cisco's death?'

Juanita put down her work and came and sat next to Boyle. 'He still doesn't know,' she said. And then, as if realising how awful that must sound, she blurted out, 'It would kill him if he found out.'

'He isn't aware his son has died?'

She closed her eyes.

There was a first time for everything. This was the first time in Boyle's work that he had dealt with a person who had kept the death of a child from their spouse. 'How did you explain his sudden disappearance?'

'Felipe gets confused about me, and I'm his wife.

It's the stroke. Half the time he remembers me but the other half, he thinks I'm an old girlfriend or someone else from the past. He used to forget that Cisco was his child. He didn't recognise him. Cisco found this very disturbing. Felipe can remember some things from the past better than he can things that happened a few minutes ago. And he doesn't always know where he is. He was in hospital for three months after he had the stroke and he often thinks that he is back there, locked up, and he begs me to get him out. "Please help me escape!" he cries. So, when he remembers who I am and that he has a son, he'll ask, "Where's Cisco?" and I say, "You've just seen him. He was here a minute ago. He's off to Barcelona to look for work. Don't you remember?" And he believes it. "*Si, claro,*" he says.'

Boyle remembered the newspapers on the table where Felipe was sleeping. 'What about the newspapers and television?'

'I haven't bought the paper since it happened. He's reading old papers and doesn't know it. And he thinks the television is broken.'

'What about the funeral?'

'Felipe wasn't there, of course. None of his family knows. But all of Cisco's friends came. The church was full. Padre Gomez said a Requiem Mass for him.' Juanita put her hand to her mouth and began to cry. 'I can't bear to tell my husband about Cisco. It would kill him. I can't lose Felipe. He's all I have left.'

9

'The road up to my house gets worse every day,' said Boyle, sitting down in one of two expensive leather armchairs opposite the mayor's massive teak desk in the palatial office in the *ayuntamiento,* town hall.

The mayor, Salvador Clavaguera, nodded his head, puffed up like a cockerel, infused with his own self-importance. The resemblance to his older brother Eduardo was striking; he was a flabbier version with the same smooth, high forehead, but there was a dullness in his eyes showing he lacked the intelligence of his brother. Salvador was at the end of a four-year term.

The office of Mayor of Sant Martí was normally held alongside full-time employment. This was a practice many locals did not agree with. It risked corruption, particularly for those involved with the buying and selling of property. Salvador had been a property developer, working first with his father Fernando and brother Eduardo in their successful family business, and then later, after leaving the firm, running a string of his own *inmobiliarias,* estate agencies. But when he became mayor, he announced that he had retired.

'We will resurface it eventually, Señor Boyle.'

'When? Can you give me a date?'

Salvador gave a small laugh, the kind you give to an idiot who could never understand. 'How can we possibly justify spending all that money to maintain a road just for you and Faustino Duran?'

'It's hardly just for the two of us. Hundreds of tourists visit Pedralta every year, not to mention the trails around the mountain used by hikers from all over the world,' said Boyle. Beyond the track to Boyle's house was the famous boulder of Pedralta, the largest rocking stone on the Iberian Peninsula.

'I sympathise with you. I really do. The Cami a Pedralta is an abominable road, but with the economy the way it is now... I'm afraid I can't help you at this time,' he said, rising to see Boyle out.

Boyle stayed seated. He had known what the outcome of this conversation would be; the mayor always offered up the same excuses. 'How well did you know Cisco Perez?' Boyle asked, changing the subject.

'Who?' asked Salvador. The mayor's face dropped and Boyle knew he was lying. Salvador knew who Cisco was, of course he did.

'Cisco Perez. The graffiti artist. He died up at Casa Cielo last week.'

'Oh yes, now I remember. I didn't recall his name. It was very tragic,' he said, feigning sympathy. 'Well, I never really met him.'

'Never?'

'No, why would I?'

'He was your nephew Miguel's best friend, for starters, and your niece's boyfriend.'

'I rarely see my niece and nephew. You know how young people are now. Haven't got enough time for their parents, never mind their aunts and uncles,' he said, moving around his desk to show Boyle the door.

Boyle took his time getting up. 'You picked up your niece only yesterday from Roca Alba.'

'Are you spying on me now, Señor Boyle?' said Salvador, holding his hand up to usher Boyle out.

'I happened to be at Casa Cielo and spoke to her.'

Salvador looked surprised. Perhaps Laura hadn't told her uncle that she had seen Boyle. 'So?'

Boyle inched his way towards the door. 'You gave her a lift.'

'Is it a crime? She is my niece, after all.'

'She was drugged to the eyeballs.'

'She was. And perhaps you can see why she would call her uncle rather than her parents.'

'No, I can't,' said Boyle, pausing at the door.

'This is family business. I think it would be best if you didn't mention this to my brother or anyone else. Laura is a young girl who has had such a terrible time. You will only make matters worse – and if you make matters worse, then we will make life very difficult for you.' Salvador Clavaguera opened the door and gave a wave of his hand, as if to sweep Boyle out of his office.

Boyle slammed the door shut and kept his arm there to block the mayor's escape. The mayor's eyes widened. Boyle stared him down. 'Are you threatening me, Señor Clavaguera?'

The mayor gave a nervous laugh. 'Of course not, don't be silly.'

'Good,' said Boyle, as he took his time letting himself out.

As soon as Boyle entered Montse's office reception, he sensed something had changed. Then it hit him. He sniffed the air. It was tobacco-free.

Rosa came out of Montse's inner sanctum, yawning. She kissed him on the cheek. 'Montse's on the phone, Adrian,' she said as she collapsed onto the sofa.

'You stopped smoking?' asked Boyle.

'Yes,' she said, stifling another yawn. 'We haven't had a cigarette since last night,' she said, pulling off her jacket. She pressed against a nicotine patch on her arm, making sure it was in place. 'We have to quit. The ban becomes law soon. No more smoking in public places. But I'm so tired,' she said, stretching out on the sofa and laying her head down. 'My fifteen-minute lunch hour. I just want to sleep.'

'Everything alright with Manel Torres?' Boyle sat down in an upholstered chair and crossed his legs.

'Fine. He's home now. We still haven't found Cisco's phone.'

Montse shuffled out of her room, looking as bad as Rosa. 'Do you have a cigarette on you, Adrian?' she asked in mock desperation as she moved towards him, arms held out in front of her like a zombie.

'Haven't smoked in five years,' he said, getting up from his chair to greet her.

Montse put her hands on either side of his shoulders and kissed him on the cheek. 'How are you, *hombre*?'

Boyle looked at both of them. 'Did either of you know that Juanita Perez has not told her husband that her son is dead?'

Montse exchanged a look with Rosa.

'What is it?' he asked.

'We haven't told you this and I can only guess how it relates to what you just said. But I first met Juanita when she came to the refuge for battered women.'

'Her husband beat her?'

'Yes. Many times, from what she told Montse. One time she was even hospitalised,' said Rosa, sitting up. 'But she only reported it twice to the police. On those two times she pressed charges against him. Felipe was taken into custody but at the eleventh hour she dropped the charges and the "psycho" was released.'

This was certainly an unexpected twist but Boyle was uncertain what impact it had on the investigation into Cisco's death.

'We feared that Felipe would kill Juanita one day but thankfully, he had the stroke,' said Montse.

'It was the best bit of luck Juanita had for years, if you ask me,' said Rosa.

Back in his office, Boyle spent the next two hours looking through the plastic concertina folder containing Cisco's bills and receipts. He had done several murals for businesses in Barcelona and Girona, for which he had been paid generously. Over the past year he had been selling his drawings online and on top of that, Eduardo Clavaguera paid him a retainer of five hundred a month. Out of this, he paid his mother rent of three hundred euros a month and also gave her five hundred of the thousand euros he made on the family mural he painted for Eduardo Clavaguera. He was a generous kid and Eduardo Clavaguera was a generous patron.

10

'Hello, Señor Boyle?' said a woman with a silky voice.

Boyle was having a *bocadillo* and espresso in Café El Cisne. He didn't recognise the number.

'Yes?'

'My name is Señora Clavaguera, Eduardo's wife.'

'Hello, Señora.' She was the last person he was expecting to hear from. Eduardo seemed very possessive of his family.

'I wonder if you could meet me. I don't have much time. Is it possible now?'

'Of course, Señora. At your house?'

'No,' she said, giving a small laugh. 'At the Santa Nuria Horse Club.'

Presumably either Eduardo or Salvador had mentioned his investigation to her. Had Salvador said something that had prompted Tina to ring him? If he had, she moved fast. Boyle agreed to see her there in twenty minutes.

Taking the inland route from Sant Martí, Boyle became aware that he was being followed as he topped the ridge overlooking the town. It was a navy blue Porsche four-by-four, like hundreds of other SUVs clogging up the narrow roads along the Costa Brava. Turning into a side street, he allowed the vehicle to pass, but the tinted windows prevented him from identifying who was inside. After the car had disappeared from sight, he drove on. About a mile along, the SUV appeared behind him again and began to tailgate Boyle, in turns moving in, nearly kissing his bumper then backing up again. It wasn't a subtle undercover operation. They were trying to intimidate him. He memorised the number plate. Then the next time they moved in close, Boyle placed his foot on the brake and the SUV bumped him. They didn't like that and sped past him with a squeal of tyres.

A few minutes later, he drew into the car park at the stables. He scrawled the number plate of the SUV in his notebook. As he got out of his car, the blue Porsche SUV slipped into a spot across the road. He hurried across the road towards it but it sped off just as he reached out for the door handle.

He found Señora Clavaguera dressed in jodhpurs, boots, polo neck and gilet, leading a brown foal with a head collar and rope, the animal unsteady on its matchstick legs. Her spaniel was walking beside her. Boyle remembered seeing the dog with the man-eating pack at the Clavaguera estate and kept his distance.

When she saw him, she smiled and held out her hand. 'Señor Boyle?'

'*Encantado*,' he said as they shook hands. Close up, she was good-looking with her lightly tanned skin, no hint of makeup and her long hair pulled back into a ponytail.

'I'm taking him to see his papa,' she said.

Boyle followed her along a row of horse boxes, the horses with their heads out, curious to see who had arrived. She led the foal towards a dapple-grey stallion, ears alert, with a full black mane combed to one side of its neck. As the horse watched them approach, it lowered its head and whickered. The foal and horse touched noses, first tentatively and then they were nuzzling, the stallion whickering. The foal suddenly whinnied, high and sweet.

'You like your papa, don't you, *cariño*?' Tina said to the foal. 'See how he is?' she said, watching the stallion as it touched noses with its offspring. 'Yes,

Diablo loves to see his young. And the young horses always seem to know their papas,' she said smiling.

This seemed like a PR exercise to Boyle; first, Eduardo showed off his art collection at their *casa grande* and now it was Tina's turn with her horses. What were they trying to prove? What was it all in aid of?

'My husband is unaware that I am seeing you. But I think it is important that I do.' *So much for the joint PR exercise,* thought Boyle.

'Someone followed me here,' he said.

'Are you sure?' she said, frowning.

'Yes. Very sure. Navy blue Porsche SUV, tinted windows. Is it familiar to you?'

She thought for a moment then shook her head. 'No.'

Boyle had a hunch she was lying. 'They just tried to push me off the road.'

Tina looked alarmed. 'I'm sorry, I have no idea who it is, Señor Boyle.' The pitch of her voice rose, which alerted her dog. Her spaniel stared at Boyle, a low rumble rising from his belly.

'The report on Cisco's death said that your dog found the body. Is this the dog?'

'That's right, Nita,' she said. 'But I never saw the boy close up. As soon as I realised there was a body on the track, I went straight to Faustino's house. I couldn't bear to look.'

'Did you think it might be your own son?'

She looked shocked. 'Of course not. I knew Miguel was at home. I never thought for a moment it was my son.'

The spaniel was now sniffing at Boyle's feet. He could feel the pressure of the dog's nose pressing down on one foot, followed by a series of quick sniffs before moving onto the next foot, where the dog pressed down even harder. Boyle stayed rigid, afraid it would bite.

'Why did you ask me here?'

Señora Clavaguera took a deep breath. 'I know you went to see Salvador this morning. I must tell you, implore you, to leave my children alone,' she said, her voice breaking unexpectedly. Her dog made a low growl. 'My husband and I know about Laura's drug problems. This is personal, family business, nothing to do with you. I want you to promise me you won't bother them. Cisco died accidentally – that's what it was, an accident. Both my son and daughter have been traumatised by it. It is too…'

'So has Juanita Perez,' he interrupted.

'Of course. I feel sorry for her. The worst thing that could happen to a mother… to lose a child.' Tina closed her eyes for a moment then opened them. 'But my children had nothing to do with Cisco's death.'

'I'm sorry to say this, Señora, but how can you be certain of this?'

'My husband was home all day and he had lunch with Miguel and Laura.'

'I heard Miguel had spent the night in Barcelona.'

'That's right.'

'What time did he arrive at your house?'

'Eduardo said half past twelve.'

'The doctor says that Cisco died between 11am and 1pm that day.'

She gave Boyle a cold, hard stare. 'You can't possibly think Miguel had anything to do with this. Eduardo says that Miguel was calm and happy over lunch. Impossible to be that way if he'd just pushed his best friend to his death. He would have to be a monster to do that. And my son isn't a monster. My daughter Laura, just in case you're interested, Señor Boyle, spent the night at our house and didn't leave until well after lunch.'

Who said anything about 'push'? thought Boyle. He thought that the interview might be over, that perhaps he had gone too far with his questioning, but he continued.

'I hear Cisco and your daughter were an item?'

Tina looked confused.

'You know, boyfriend and girlfriend?'

'It was never serious.'

'You weren't thrilled about their relationship?'

'They were never right for each other.' They walked back towards the corral.

So, neither Cisco's mother nor Laura's mother was pleased about the relationship between their children.

'I never liked Cisco. I think he was a bad influence on my children. Four years ago he came into our lives, and from that point on everything seemed to go wrong. First, Cisco and Miguel were arrested for vandalism, and then we discovered that both of our children were on drugs. Miguel has given them up, *gracias a Dios,* but my daughter is still suffering.'

'Your husband liked Cisco.'

'Yes. He adored him. He could do no wrong in Eduardo's eyes. I think it was because he was the artist Eduardo always wanted to be.'

When Boyle got to his car, he discovered that all of his tyres were flat. They were clearly slashed. Incandescent, he contacted his local garage and while he waited for his friend Juan to change his tyres, he rang Rosa at the station and gave her the number of the licence plate of the Porsche SUV. She said she would look into it. After following Juan back to the garage in Sant Martí and paying the discounted amount of five hundred euros with his card, Boyle rang the *inmobiliaria* Fincas Deirdre several times, but there was only an answering machine and he decided not to leave a message.

Rosa rang back soon after. 'The licence plate on the SUV was from an Opel Vectra stolen two nights ago,' she said.

'What's going on?' he said.

'Could it be the anti-hunt people?'

'In a Porsche SUV? The only people who can afford a motor like that are the Clavagueras, Quimet Navarro and…'

'Faustino Duran,' said Rosa.

'He has money like that?' asked Boyle.

'Very wealthy. Barcelonan. He lives like a pig in the woods but there is plenty of family money there. They made millions in textiles.'

'Where is he hiding the SUV? It certainly isn't at Roca Alba.'

Boyle had been questioning whether or not Cisco had been pushed, murdered, up at Casa Cielo. There had been more than some doubt in his mind but despite that, he continued with the investigation mostly because Rosa and Juanita had asked him to and he had promised Juanita he wouldn't give up. But the SUV had banished the doubt. Something was wrong here. Who was so interested in the progress of his investigation that they would have him followed, try to threaten him and slash his tyres? Despite the promises he made to Juanita, he still had a choice. As a private detective, he could drop the investigation and go back to following delinquent husbands. But the funny thing with Boyle was that his interest in solving a crime rose with the threat level; the adrenalin was kicking in and it felt good. Whoever they were, they weren't going to scare him off.

On his way home, he drove by the *inmobiliaria*. The lights in the shop were out; it was shut up again. Not a total surprise since the few estate agents left since the property crash had irregular operating hours.

By the time Boyle reached the track to his house, the sun was already sinking behind the Pyrenees, casting a tangerine glow. He was forced to slow down because Faustino Duran was walking on the track, shotgun slung over his shoulder and hound close at his heels. Boyle caught up with him.

'Today isn't a hunting day,' said Boyle.

'Isn't it?' said Faustino.

'Can you at least use your own track? I don't like hunters on this road so close to my house.'

'No, it is not possible, sorry. This is a public track,' Faustino reminded him in his direct manner, never backward in coming forward, and although it aggravated Boyle, he secretly admired it. Boyle had had to work hard at learning to be forthright at the beginning of his policing career. It had never been easy for him to come out and ask, "Mrs Smith, did you murder your husband?"

Boyle hit the brakes and turned off the engine. 'Tell me. Do you own a Porsche SUV?'

Faustino stopped and moved up to the car, perplexed. 'What sort of a question is that? You've seen my SUV. It's a Kia.'

'Do you know anyone who owns one?'

'No, not that I can think of.'

'I'd like to ask you a few questions about Cisco Perez, if I may.'

'Who?'

'The boy who fell at Casa Cielo last week.'

Faustino approached Boyle's car and leaned on the door. Boyle caught a whiff of brandy. 'The Clavaguera kids and their friends were always at that house, drinking and taking drugs. An accident like that was waiting to happen. You saw what Cisco did to my house… and the cars.'

'We don't know if the anti-hunt slogans were done by Cisco. The police tend to think they were not, that they were most likely two separate incidents,' said Boyle, stretching the truth somewhat.

'¡*Que va!* Nonsense. It was done by that boy.'

'Cisco's mother thinks he was murdered.'

'Does she?' said Faustino.

'Can you tell me what you remember about the morning Cisco died? Was there anything unusual?'

'No, not really. I was with the hunters on the other side of the mountain.'

'When did you finish hunting?'

'When the body was discovered, we were all called back by the police. They told us there had been an accident. And when I saw what that son of a bitch did to my house, I was furious,' said Faustino. He paused as if remembering something. 'Although there was one strange thing. I did hear a scream. At first, I thought one of the hunters had been injured. It wasn't until much later, when I heard what had happened, that I realised that it must have been the boy falling.'

'Do you know what time this was?'

'It was just after twelve. I remember looking at my watch because I was hungry. I was disappointed because that meant it was two hours before lunch. I get ravenous when I hunt.'

'You didn't tell the police?'

'No, I forgot about it. And when the judge decided it was an accident, I didn't see how it could affect things one way or another.'

The hound emerged from a bush nearby dragging a small blue rucksack. He shook it and growled. Faustino grabbed him by the collar and ordered him to drop it, then kicked the bag out of the way, not interested. At that point Faustino's hound left the track, following the path down to the Roca Alba urbanisation below.

Faustino turned and shrugged at Boyle. 'Pardon, but I must feed my dog.' Faustino followed his dog down the path into the dark.

That was the longest conversation Boyle had had with Faustino and he wondered what had loosened his lips. The brandy, perhaps. There was a bit more information. Two people had heard the scream that day. It didn't tell Boyle that Cisco had been murdered, but it gave him an approximate time for his fall: twelve o'clock. Boyle got out of the car and picked up the bag. The chance of it having to do with the graffiti vandals was slim. This track was a popular trail across the Ardenya range. It must have been left by a hiker, but then that didn't quite make sense. What hiker leaves their rucksack behind?

Back at the house, Boyle placed the rucksack on the dining table. Although it was dusty, the bag looked new. He unzipped the main section. When he saw the contents, he felt a thrill as if he had found a hidden treasure. There were two unopened red spray cans, *Pintura Estrella,* the brand and colour used by the anti-hunt people. Had they planned to do more graffiti but been interrupted by something? What? Cisco's fall perhaps? Boyle put on surgical gloves and emptied the contents of the bag onto the table. First came the two cans of spray paint, then several pairs of unused surgical gloves like his own, and – also unused – a green face mask. Someone was concerned about the nasty paint fumes. There was a small, unopened bottle of water and two fig and coconut protein bars. There was a smaller pocket in the rucksack that he unzipped. Inside was a red envelope. Typewritten across the front was *Sres. Ferran I Valls*, just like the card he had seen at his in-laws' house.

11

Along the front, Boyle observed the small, messy graffiti tags sprayed here and there. Over the past forty-eight hours he had begun to notice the scribbles everywhere, in Sant Martí, Santa Nuria, Llagostera, on farm buildings, overpasses, walls, doors, traffic lights and the boarding around building sites – alienated souls, he guessed, crying "look at me".

The minute he stepped inside restaurant El Dorado, Carmen hurried over to him. 'Antonio has something to show you about Cisco,' she said, gently pushing him towards the door.

Boyle went to a side entrance of the building that led to three new flats above the restaurant. So rarely did he go there that he had to look closely to see which intercom button to press for Carmen's flat.

'*Bona tarda, Oncle,*' his nephew called through in Catalan, before buzzing him in.

Boyle climbed the shiny marble stairs to the first floor. Antonio was holding open the smooth oak door. 'I've found something you won't believe,' he said, wide-eyed.

'What is it?' asked Boyle as he entered the flat.

'On my computer,' said Antonio, rushing down the corridor.

Boyle paused before following and glanced at the door that led to Carmen's bedroom. He had seen it during the renovation of the building two years before, after Carmen's husband had left, but not since. Following Antonio through another door, he entered a massive rectangular living space, with kitchen, dining room and living room all in one. The space had high ceilings and three tall windows that overlooked the rambla. It was a mix of sleek, state-of-the-art kitchen and traditional furniture. Antonio's seventeen-year-old sister Isabella sat at the dining table, hunched over her homework with a worried look. Her long hair was tangled like a bird's nest, with wide, pink stripes running through it. Boyle smiled with amusement.

'Hello, Isabella.'

She looked up as if it were a chore. 'Yes?'

'What kind of a greeting is that?'

'My kind.'

'When did you do that to your hair?' It looked like a mangy animal.

'Last week. Mama hates it.'

'I'm not surprised.'

'At the moment she hates everything I do. We're not allowed to dye our hair at school. The nuns told me to wash it out. But it's permanent,' she said, lifting a strand and smiling at it with satisfaction. 'So, there's nothing anybody can do about it.'

'They can suggest you dye it back to brown and possibly, dare I say, comb it?'

She gave a throaty laugh. 'They can suggest that, but I won't do it. And it's against my human rights for them to force me.'

'More's the pity,' said Boyle in English.

Antonio grabbed Boyle by the arm and dragged him into his room, which was just off the living area. The walls of the room were covered with a collage of posters, graffiti and magazine cut-outs of skateboarders, rock groups and mountain climbers. Antonio sat in front of his laptop computer.

'Look at this,' he said to his uncle. Boyle took a seat next to Antonio and peered at the screen. It was a chaotic website, of which he could make little sense.

'What is it?'

'*Mundo Graffiti*, a graffiti website.' Antonio double-clicked the mouse. Boyle saw the title *Mundo Graffiti* in the top right-hand corner of the screen in red block letters. Antonio clicked the mouse again and at the centre of the screen, a grainy video clip began to play.

A man was standing on a red tiled roof facing the white wall of a Catalan tower. Despite the slope of the roof, he managed to turn around and, without so much as a wobble, bowed to the camera.

'It's Cisco,' said Antonio.

Boyle recognised him, and the roof and tower of Casa Cielo. In the film, Cisco turned back to the blank wall, picked up a spray can and started to paint. From this point, the tape sped up with time-lapse camerawork and Cisco popped in and out of the frame from one side of the painting to the other. In contrast to this frenetic movement, the painting seemed to develop smoothly, beautifully, before Boyle's eyes. It was the painting of the woman in the wicker chair holding a book. At one point, Cisco was spraying in the details of the reader's hands.

'They really do use spray paint for everything,' Boyle said, almost to himself.

Antonio looked at him, confused.

'Even for the hands, which must be difficult,' explained Boyle.

'What else would he use?'

'A brush, perhaps?'

'A brush?' scowled Antonio, as if it was an implement last seen in the middle ages.

The tape went back to real time as Cisco blocked in the trees behind the figure. Then suddenly, the film froze on Cisco and the unfinished mural. The screen faded to black and the words CISCO PEREZ, MURIO 09/09/10 appeared. The date he died. It gave Boyle an icy shiver, like walking over someone's grave. The clip then began to repeat itself. They watched it through again in silence. And then again.

Boyle wondered who had filmed Cisco. Was it one of the Clavagueras? Laura, Miguel, Eduardo or even the mother, Tina? Was it Cisco's other best friend Luis Sureda, to whom Boyle had yet to speak? He could work out where the camera was placed. He had studied the mural from the same spot in the garden. It was up against the stone balustrade that separated the garden from the steep drop to the gorge below. Cisco's clothes changed three times during the clip, which suggested to Boyle that it was filmed over three different days. On what would have been the third day of filming, Cisco was wearing jeans and a red sweatshirt, the clothes he was wearing on the day he died. Boyle couldn't be absolutely certain the last part was filmed on the day Cisco died. Perhaps Cisco had worn the same clothes two days running, or the filming could have been done the week before. But it did bring up the possibility that someone else was at Casa Cielo on that day, who had filmed him and was there when he fell.

When the clip ended, Boyle turned to Antonio. 'Do you have any idea when this was filmed?'

'No.'

'Can you tell when it was posted?'

'Yes, look.' Antonio pointed to the lower left-hand corner of the screen. Boyle read, "Two days ago." *About a week after Cisco's death. Whoever put this video up probably knew that his death had been ruled accidental and was confident the police would not investigate further,* thought Boyle.

'Whose website is this?' asked Boyle.

'I don't know.'

'Do you have any idea?'

Antonio shook his head.

'Is there any way I can find out who it belongs to?'

'It's difficult because some of the work is…'

'…illegal,' Boyle completed.

'Yes, and no one wants to get caught.'

Boyle wondered if the police could find out who ran *Mundo Graffiti* and made a mental note to ring Rosa.

'Let's look at some of the other clips. See if you can recognise any of the tags, possibly identify one of the artists.'

Antonio nodded, then from another selection of small boxes he clicked on another clip. Boyle wrote down the name of the graffiti artist – Yama. They spent over an hour viewing the different types of graffiti art, from simple tags to elaborate pieces. Any white public space, Boyle realised, was begging to be painted, along with buses, tube trains, lorries, buildings, bridges, walls and billboards. All the artists wore hoodies or baseball caps and some wore masks. They all had a graffiti name – or tag – which Boyle wrote down: Gordo, Doc, Diablo, Punki, Cara, Sueno, Remi, Make and Razk.

After viewing over a dozen – an endless bombardment of images, some executed, Boyle hated to admit it, brilliantly, some absolute rubbish – Boyle looked away from the computer screen to give his eyes a rest.

He perused the enormous collage of magazine cut-outs and drawings on the wall behind Antonio's desk. In amongst the images, he picked out a graffiti tag repeated over and over, drawn with markers. He wondered if it was his nephew's tag. It was written in black and white with round, puffy letters. Boyle studied the letters, trying to make out their meaning. Then it came to him. The letters spelt out 'LLEÓ', the Catalan word for lion. With all his nephew's talk about bravery, it made sense that he had chosen an animal representing courage, though it was odd how

Antonio had depicted courage with his tag – using white balloon-shaped letters that reminded Boyle more of marshmallows than the king of the jungle.

Boyle smiled to himself. He reckoned his nephew had really underestimated him when he allowed him into his room, without worrying what he might find there. Not wishing to alert the boy, Boyle turned his eyes away from the wall and looked back at the screen.

At the end of the search, Antonio said that he hadn't recognised any of the artists, or any of the work for that matter. Boyle gave him a sceptical look. 'I'm telling you the truth. I told you, writers keep their tags a secret. Their best friends know, maybe. That's it.'

'Whoever posted this must have been a friend of Cisco's, possibly someone who visited Casa Cielo frequently,' Boyle said.

'I'm surprised anyone went there,' said Antonio. 'I only went there a couple of times but Señor Clavaguera put me off. He only liked Cisco's work. He was even going to show some of Cisco's graffiti in his gallery in Barcelona,' said Antonio, frowning.

'What's wrong with that?'

'Graffiti in a frame? *Fatal*!' said Antonio. Boyle laughed, which brought a smile to his nephew's face. 'Graffiti's not meant to be framed for your living room, or in a museum. Museums are dead.'

'How do I find out who owns this site?' asked Boyle.

'I don't know. Honest.'

Boyle let it go. He didn't want to push his nephew too much and lose his confidence. 'Well done, Antonio, for finding this,' he said. He got up and patted the boy on the back. 'Keep this to yourself, alright?'

'Of course, Uncle.'

Boyle showed the tape of Cisco to Juanita and she confirmed that the clothes he wore on the final day of filming were the same ones he had worn on the day he died and that he had not worn them two days running; nor, in fact, had he worn them the week before – she was a good mother. She said that many people filmed Cisco, but especially his friends Miguel Clavaguera and Luis Sureda. Boyle had spoken briefly and unsatisfactorily to Miguel Clavaguera. And although he had left a message with Luis Sureda's mother, Luis had yet to return the call.

Boyle and Juanita Perez spent an hour and a half scouring all the clips on the website but Juanita recognised no one. It was tough identifying people who covered their faces when they worked. Afterwards, she looked so weary and mournful that Boyle insisted on driving her home rather than have her take the bus. They said nothing during the twenty-minute drive to Llagostera, but the atmosphere was heavy with grief.

She got out of the car and stood at the open door. 'Thank you,' she said. 'You will help me, won't you, Señor?'

'Of course I will. I said I would.' He was surprised that she would ask such a question when he had already agreed to investigate the matter for her.

'I mean, if it becomes difficult. If you have a hard time finding out who did it. You won't give up, will you?'

'I won't let you down, Señora.' He felt a certain duty to her to investigate. Cisco wasn't a saint but Boyle had investigated victims of every hue when he was with the Met. He felt it was the right thing to do if there were any doubts about the circumstances. Juanita walked to her door in a daze. Boyle sincerely hoped he could help her. As to whether he could get to the truth, that was uncertain. At least he was fairly sure that someone had been there at Casa Cielo the day Cisco fell. He had that to go on now. There was some progress.

12

'I have twelve points now,' said Narcis as he bent his knees to pick up the four boules from the pétanque pitch. Boyle was impressed with his father-in-law's strength and flexibility. In his late seventies, he did not resort to using a magnet on a string to pick up the balls, like many of the older players. Boyle went to the corner of the pitch, brushed out the number nine in the dirt and drew the number twelve with a twig. Twelve points to nine. Boyle was starting to feel mildly anxious, like he always did when he thought he might lose a game. His old friends from New Scotland Yard had moaned with derision when he told them he had replaced football with pétanque, it being what many people refer to as an "old people's game". But here in Spain and in France, the young joined in as well.

Narcis threw the orange cochonnet straight down the middle of the pitch. Then, holding the boule up in both hands, he squinted at the small orange ball in the distance and gracefully bowled the ball down towards it. It landed right next to the cochonnet – a perfect throw. Boyle then threw two in a row, missing the mark by a mile, and the game was over.

Narcis walked to a stone bench, picked up his anorak, fumbled in the pocket and drew out an envelope. 'We received another card this morning. It was not posted, just slipped under the door. Same as the first one,' he said, handing a pale yellow envelope to Boyle.

Boyle took the card from the envelope, holding it by the edges, careful not to contaminate it. It was another engagement card with a commercial photo of clasped hands on the front. "Congratulations" was printed on the inside, with the message "We offer our warmest congratulations to Montse and Rosa, the lovely brides to be." They kept the same message as the card that Boyle found. Boyle hadn't shown the rucksack to Rosa. He wouldn't do that until he had his father-in-law's permission to show Montse and Rosa the cards.

'I want you to take these to the police and Montse,'

Narcis said, then handed Boyle the first card. He stared at him with hard eyes. 'Esther is so upset, she missed Mass this morning.' It was customary for Montse and Rosa to accompany Esther to church at Solius every Sunday. 'She rang Montse and said she was ill. You can see how difficult it is for her to attend church with the girls now. The idea of facing them is abhorrent to her.'

Boyle walked quickly down a narrow street in Sant Martí that was lined with traditional terraced buildings, *una hilera de casas*, mostly shops with flats above. He had the rucksack over his shoulder. Montse and Rosa's house dated from Roman times and had been a garage before Montse had renovated it. It lay between a shoe shop and a baker. There were two massive windows at the front, one above the other, the lower including the front door and the upper including the French doors off the master bedroom, with a balcony just large enough for pots of geraniums, margaritas and wild rosemary. When he rapped on the door, Rosa answered almost immediately.

'Adrian. Are you joining us for lunch?' she asked, as she slipped on her flat shoes. Montse was standing behind her, car keys in hand.

There was an open invitation for him to lunch with them any Sunday in Tossa de Mar. That wouldn't happen today. Boyle held up the rucksack. 'We need to look at this first.'

'It can't wait?' Montse said.

'No, it belongs to the anti-hunt people.'

Boyle told them about the last film of Cisco found on the *Mundo Graffiti* website as they went inside to the dining room.

'So, someone must have been there when Cisco fell,' Rosa said. 'I knew it.'

'There's a possibility,' he said. He asked Rosa if she could find out who was behind the site.

'Give me a few days,' she said. 'The police in Girona handle the internet. I have a friend over there. I'll see what I can do.'

'My mother has a cold so we missed Mass this morning,' Montse said. They sat at the table. Boyle knew the real reason her mother was unable to attend Mass and soon, so would Montse.

After putting on gloves, they went through the rucksack. Rosa was excited by the find. She examined the spray cans. 'We have found several sets of prints on the cans we found at the scene. They've been sent off to Girona to run them through the system – so far, nothing.'

Boyle kept the cards until last. Finally, he took out the two envelopes that had been sent to Montse's parents. He gingerly took the card out of the red envelope and held it by the edges. 'Your parents received these,' he said to Montse.

Montse carefully took the first card. '*Vale*,' she said, giving him a worried glance. She opened the card, read it and put her hand over her mouth. 'Oh God!' She handed the card to Rosa, who read it and groaned. They then opened the second card that was sent to her parents.

'Who is doing this?' Rosa asked.

'I have no idea,' said Boyle. 'But it doesn't seem to be blackmail. No one has demanded money.' Boyle then handed them the third card. 'This one was found in the rucksack.'

Montse opened the card and froze. 'Who are these anti-hunt people?' Then, to Boyle, 'Why couldn't my parents just tell me about the cards? Why did they feel they had to go through you?' She seemed less worried about the connection to the anti-hunt demonstrators and more concerned about her parents' response.

'I'm sorry, Montse. Your mother is too distressed.'

'Yes, of course she is. She is only concerned about what her friends in Sant Martí will think. That is all that concerns her. Not me or Rosa.'

Rosa looked at the cards with puzzlement. 'Who would do this? Who knows about the wedding?'

'Only six people. The two of you, me, Carmen and her two,' said Boyle.

'Would Antonio or Isabella do this?' Montse asked him.

'Antonio does graffiti,' he said.

'Would he do this?' asked Rosa.

Boyle feared that Antonio might have some

connection. It would be a disaster for both Antonio and his mother. She had enough worries being a single mother, her ex-husband Pau now living in Madrid and offering no financial support, and she also had the responsibility of running the family restaurant on her own.

'But someone in our wedding party has said something,' said Montse.

'Not necessarily. It could be anyone,' said Boyle. 'The police. They seem to know everyone's business. Chief Inspector Marc Saldoni, for beginners.'

'I would pluck out my eyes before I would tell that bastard,' Rosa said, then she turned to Montse. 'I'm sorry, Montse, but I have told someone,' she admitted.

'Who?' asked Montse.

'My sister.'

'Maria Angels. Only the biggest mouth in the Vall d'Aro. You said you were not going to tell her,' said Montse.

'You know I have family too,' Rosa said, on the verge of tears. 'It's always about your family. She's my sister. I wanted to tell her about our relationship and that we were getting married. She promised she wouldn't tell anyone, not even her husband.'

'If you feel that way, you should invite them both to the wedding, *cariño*,' Montse said, placing her hand across the table onto Rosa's.

'I did. My sister said that her husband would

never agree to come. And that she wouldn't bother asking him.'

Montse stood up. 'I'm going to see my parents.'

'Is it a good idea to see your parents now?' asked Rosa.

'Yes. Today.'

'But your mother missed Mass. She is ill.'

'She's not ill,' said Montse, turning to Boyle. 'Is she?'

'No,' he said.

'I can't face your mother now, Montse,' said Rosa.

'Why?' asked Montse, perplexed.

'Why?' repeated Rosa, as if the answer were obvious. 'I'm embarrassed.'

Montse looked hurt. 'You mean embarrassed to be with me?'

Boyle squirmed. It was difficult enough that two women, both close friends of his, were getting married. He was just coming to terms with that, and deep down he wasn't sure he even understood.

'No, it's not that. I have pretended to be someone who I am not for the past three years. I won't be able to bear your mother's disappointment – or your father's, for that matter.'

'You're just afraid that my father won't flirt with you anymore,' said Montse, looking out of the window, trying to control her temper.

'You're being very unfair,' said Rosa. She was starting to become tearful and stood up.

Boyle took hold of her hand to stop her from leaving. 'Will you both keep quiet about the cards? Don't tell Carmen or the children, or anyone.'

The women agreed. Rosa put everything back in the rucksack. 'I'll check everything for fingerprints – see if we have the creeps on the database.'

Two days later, Rosa rang Boyle. 'There were no fingerprints on the cards themselves, except for the ones from Montse's parents. Several prints were taken off the cans and rucksack and those have been sent off to the database in Girona. Still no demand for money,' said Rosa.

'How did the meeting with Montse's parents go?'

'Only Montse went in the end. Disaster,' said Rosa. 'She ranted and raved when she came home. But in the morning, she was fine. That's what I love about her – she doesn't hold a grudge. But Montse's mother is different. She'll never, ever accept our marriage.'

'I'm sorry,' said Boyle.

'Look, there's some good news. We've discovered who runs the *Mundo Graffiti* site. His name is Jaume Cadero. He sells graffiti tools, cans of spray paint, stencils, markers; everything you need to be a proper graffiti artist. I don't have a phone number for him, just an address.' Boyle took out his notepad. 'He lives in Barcelona – in El Raval. Calle de Carme, number 60, flat B.' Boyle wrote it down and thanked her.

13

RATHER THAN TAKE THE TRAIN, BOYLE decided to drive down to Barcelona. It would be quicker taking the coastal route. He first drove through farmland, which eventually gave way to busy tourist towns along the sea. Arriving in just over an hour, he left the car in one of the underground car parks just off the main Rambla. From there, he walked west through the crowds of tourists on the Rambla, past La Boqueria food market and into El Raval, a neighbourhood that was more residential and quieter. Boyle remembered when this area was crime-ridden and impoverished but now, after much rejuvenation, it had become a centre for artists. He walked past the coffee bars, retro furniture shops and boutiques and turned into Calle de Carme. The address was one of three flats in a large, rundown turn-of-the-century building. He rang the intercom for flat B. No answer. He crossed the road and looked up at the windows of the middle floor of the three-storey property, where he reckoned Flat B was located. The curtains were open and there appeared to be no movement inside. He wondered if Jaume Cadero had a proper job or if he made his living running the graffiti site and selling paint. Boyle looked at his wristwatch. It was nearly 10.30. He decided to go for some tapas.

He found his favourite food bar in the open market, La Boqueria, and ordered three plates of tapas; *pollo croquetas, cargoles* and, for one of his five a day, *pebróts padron,* and, of course, *una cerveza* to wash it all down. After half an hour, he returned to the flat and rang the buzzer. Still no one home. He wasn't about to return to Sant Martí without seeing Señor Cadero but the thought did cross his mind that he might be away on holiday. He holed up inside a convenient coffee bar across the road. Picking up a used copy of *La Vanguardia* lying on one of the tables, he found a seat near the huge picture window, which gave a near-perfect view of the flat opposite, then ordered an espresso from a young, skinny waitress.

Two hours later, Boyle saw a scruffy man, who

looked to be in his early thirties, approach the door of number 60 and enter. Boyle paid his bill, crossed the road and rang the buzzer for flat B. It was answered immediately.

'I'm looking for Jaume Cadero.'

'Who are you?'

'My name is Adrian Boyle. I'm a private investigator working for Juanita Perez – the mother of Cisco Perez. I would like to ask you a few questions.'

'I don't know who you are talking about.'

'Yeah you do. You run *Mundo Graffiti*. And you are presently showing a video of Cisco Perez that was filmed on the day he died.'

'¿*Y que?* So what?'

'There are quite a few illegal postings on your site,' said Boyle. 'Vandalising trains, buses, buildings.' Jaume was silent. 'I don't want to get you into trouble,' Boyle added.

'Of course you don't.'

'Just a few questions. That's all.'

There was an audible sigh. 'Okay, come up,' he said as the buzzer went. Boyle took the wide stairs to the first floor. Jaume was standing at his front door. He wasn't going to let Boyle in. He had the pallid skin and the lumpy physique of someone who lived in front of a computer screen.

'What do you want?' Jaume snapped. He smelt of stale sweat and garlic.

'Easy. I want to know who gave you the tape of Cisco.'

'It was sent to me anonymously.'

'You must know who Cisco was.'

'I was aware of him.'

'I find it hard to believe that you don't know who sent you the tape.'

'I can't divulge my sources.'

'I'll make it very easy for you. Your address was given to me by *Mossos* Detective Inspector Rosa Pujol of Sant Martí. She will happily forget about you, give you time to clean up your website, if you tell us who sent you the tape. Otherwise she will close down your site immediately and arrest you.'

Jaume Cadero looked like he knew he was out-manoeuvred. 'Alright. His name is Luis Sureda.' The name was familiar to Boyle. He was one of Cisco's best friends.

'What is his tag?'

Jaume glared at Boyle. 'You said you just wanted the name.'

'Yes, and the tag. Then I will leave you alone.'

'I'll shut down my site before I give you his tag,' he said, rubbing his hand over his sweaty face.

'It won't make any difference to the police. You will be liable for prosecution for all the vandalism seen on *Mundo Graffiti*,' said Boyle, bluffing. He had no idea what the legal implications were.

'His name is *Punki*,' said Jaume.

As soon as Boyle got back to Sant Martí, he went to his office. He put a call through to Rosa and it went straight to messages. Opening his laptop, he logged on to *Mundo Graffiti*. He was interested in seeing Luis Sureda's graffiti work. If his work was painted in public places then Boyle had some power of persuasion over him. He clicked on one of the clips for *Punki* and it began to play. A male figure, dressed in a grey hooded sweatshirt, was spraying the side of a stationary train with blue paint. He worked quickly, waving his arm in wide arcs to block out the letters. Then, picking up another can, he expertly sprayed white onto the blue to define the tag, which even Boyle found easy to read. *Punki*, it said. He clicked to another video by *Punki*. Again, the hooded figure was spraying another stationary train with the same blue and white tag. Clearly it was all illegal.

Boyle rang Luis Sureda's number. His mother answered again. He identified himself. She said that her son wasn't in but that she would pass on the message. Boyle thought that, for whatever reason, she was lying. To make sure he got Luis's attention, he gave his number and name to her and then said, 'Tell him *Punki* is calling, will you?'

Five minutes later, Luis Sureda rang Boyle.

'What do you want?'

'I know you were there,' said Boyle.

'What do you mean?'

'When Cisco died.' Luis was silent. 'I've seen the video of Cisco taken on the day he died. It was on *Mundo Graffiti*. But you already know that, because you filmed and posted it,' said Boyle.

'No, I didn't.'

'Don't mess me about, *Punki*. I'm not in the mood for it.'

'I wasn't there,' said Luis, his voice cracking.

'If you don't tell me everything you know, I am handing these tapes and your tag over to the police,' said Boyle.

'*Vale*,' said Luis. 'I'll talk to you.'

Boyle met Luis in Bar Aurora at the top of the main, tree-lined rambla in Sant Martí. They sat outside. Dressed in tight black jeans and a tee-shirt, Luis sat hunched over the table. He had dark circles under his eyes and a thin, crooked mouth. Boyle speculated whether he had a drug problem.

'Why didn't you tell the police you were there that morning?' asked Boyle.

Luis took a drag of his cigarette and rubbed his goatee. 'I was frightened they would blame me for it,' he whined.

Boyle took out a notepad and pen and laid it on the table. 'Now tell me what happened that day.'

'I drove up to Casa Cielo to film Cisco. It was

about ten o'clock. Cisco was painting and I filmed him. That's all.'

Boyle paused, and planted a look of scepticism on his face. 'Did you see Cisco fall?'

Luis looked horrified. 'What! No, I would have said. I left before anything happened.'

Boyle kept up the pressure. 'What time was that?'

'At eleven fifteen.'

Boyle wrote it down. 'How can you be certain of the time?'

'I remember because I had to start work at eleven thirty.'

'Where do you work?'

'Oh God, you're not going to talk to them?' Idly, Luis scratched his head.

'Just tell me where you work.'

'At Computer World in Playa d'Aro. I did nothing wrong. Posting that tape was legal.'

Boyle gave a sarcastic laugh. 'But you're not telling me everything.'

'You can't treat me like a criminal. I had nothing to do with Cisco's death,' he said.

'But you are a criminal and I'm sure the police would be very interested in your tag and all the criminal damage you have done. It would take a bundle of money to repaint. And give you a nice criminal record.'

Luis said nothing. There was little eye contact.

Instead he watched the shoppers strolling on the rambla then allowed his gaze to wander over the walls of the café, focusing at one point on a poster that pictured a small, beautiful cove with turquoise water and high, rocky cliffs, characteristic of the Costa Brava. Boyle kept his eye on Luis. *He is definitely hiding something,* he thought. At that moment, Luis gave Boyle a furtive glance, clearly mulling over something. He was like an open book, hiding something and wondering if he should tell Boyle. *It would be easy if all suspects were this transparent,* thought Boyle.

'I'm going to the police if you don't tell me everything you know,' he said, concealing the fact that Inspector Rosa Pujol already knew all about the film clip.

'I've told you everything,' Luis insisted, his mouth forming a sour curve.

'I'll be honest with you. I'm not interested in having you arrested for graffiti. I'm investigating the possible murder of Cisco.'

'Murder? No way was Cisco murdered,' said Luis, appearing genuinely shocked.

'That may be, but I know you're not telling me everything,' said Boyle.

Luis sat there with his mouth shut tight and kept his head down as Boyle stood up to leave.

'You should ask Miguel Clavaguera about it; he was still there with Cisco when I left that day. He would know more about how Cisco died than I would,' said Luis, nodding his head, a look of relief already on his face.

After the meeting, Boyle went back to his office a couple of streets away. He rang Miguel Clavaguera's mobile but it had been discontinued. He then punched in Eduardo Clavaguera's number.

'Hello, Señor Boyle. How did you like Casa Cielo?' asked Eduardo.

'It was impressive, thank you. But that's not why I'm ringing you. Do you know that I have a witness who says your son was at Casa Cielo the day Cisco died?'

'That's impossible! Miguel hadn't seen Cisco for at least two weeks. I know that. I had lunch with him that day.'

'What time did Miguel arrive from Barcelona?'

'I don't remember exactly. Before twelve, I think.'

'Luis Sureda says Miguel was at the house when he left at eleven fifteen, forty-five minutes before Cisco fell.'

'I don't believe it. He came directly from Barcelona to the house.'

Boyle then told him about the video clip. 'I'd like to speak to your son.'

'Alright, but give me time. Let me talk to Miguel first.'

'If you don't let me speak to him, I am going to

hand this tape of Cisco in to the police,' he said, again not telling him that Inspector Rosa Pujol was already aware of the situation. Boyle was unsure what the full implications were on Rosa's side. He hoped that the warning would work and that Eduardo would let him speak to his son without involving the police. If Miguel was there when Cisco was filmed that day and possibly when he fell, why did he feel he had to lie? What was he hiding?

On the sofa in his office, the phone woke Boyle from a deep siesta. Through the blinds, he was surprised to see light from the streetlamps already on. In the semi-darkness, he made his way to his desk, switched on the Anglepoise and picked up the phone. It was Montse saying that she had some work for him. A suspicious wife worrying her husband might be straying.

'You'll never guess who it is.'

'Surprise me.'

'Quimet Navarro. His wife is Lola. Do you know her?'

'I've seen her around.' She was high maintenance, from what Boyle could tell; furs, jewels, nails, hair and the personality to match. He couldn't afford her.

'Every Sunday, he leaves the house at nine o'clock to play golf in Santa Nuria. Two weeks ago, his wife decided to surprise her husband and went to the club to meet him after his game. Only—'

'He wasn't there,' interjected Boyle.

'Not only that, but his friends hadn't played golf with him for two months.'

'What are they like?' said Boyle, although he had a pretty good idea.

'Selfish bastards. All of them.'

'So, you want me to find the girlfriend?'

'That's it.'

Boyle took down the address in Vespella and rang off. He was exhausted from the long day and decided to skip dinner out tonight and go straight home. On his way out of the door, his mobile vibrated and he took it out of his jacket pocket.

The caller was Rosa. 'I just had Eduardo Clavaguera in here with his son.'

Boyle went back into the office and sat on his desk. 'That was fast.'

'Yes. The concerned citizen bleating on about his son's innocence.'

'Did you interview Miguel?'

'Yes. He says he wasn't at Casa Cielo that day. We even picked up his friend Luis Sureda and interviewed him. Luis says Miguel was there, but Miguel is denying it.'

'No surprises there.'

'I think Miguel is a lying little rat. And so, I ask myself, why does he need to lie?'

'Did you arrest Luis for vandalism?'

'No. I've given him a second chance, since I think he's the one who's telling the truth. I've left the door open for him. Told him he can come back any time if he learns more. We will send copies of the interviews and the film of Cisco over to the judge Gabriel Llfranc, see if he will reopen the case. In the meantime, can you continue with the investigation?'

'Of course,' Boyle said. Though with what little he had to go on, he did wonder what the next course of action would be.

Boyle rang Eduardo, frustrated that he had taken his son to the police. After all, they had had a gentleman's agreement that Boyle would interview Miguel.

'I hear you were at *Mossos* this afternoon,' said Boyle, when Eduardo eventually answered the phone.

'Yes. I did not like your threat that you would take the matter to the police. I decided it was best that Miguel should go to the *Mossos* himself and tell them about the tape.' He had a frosty voice that was new to Boyle. 'And Miguel is not anywhere on the tape. So, it's just Luis's word that my son was even there,' said Eduardo.

'Yes. Luis is a witness.'

'Yes. He is a known drug addict and so not the most reliable witness. Miguel says that he was not there and I believe him. Furthermore, the police now have everything they need to know about that terrible accident and I doubt they will pursue a criminal investigation.' Before Boyle had a chance to respond, Eduardo said, 'By the way, is it possible for you to give me back my key to Casa Cielo? I have been expecting you to do so. Just ring before you come,' he said, and then hung up.

14

The next day, Boyle dropped off the key to Casa Cielo at the Clavaguera mansion in Santa Nuria. Naturally, he had made a copy in Sant Martí beforehand. He was made to wait outside the gate this time. There were fewer dogs to greet him, just the German Shepherd showing off his teeth again and a couple of the small, yappy dogs, hysterical at the sight of him. Gun shots boomed out across the valley and hills. *The other dogs must be on a hunt,* he thought. A young maid drove down to the gate and marched towards Boyle with the master's displeasure written across her face and, without a word, grabbed the key from him through the chain link fencing. He stared through it as the maid drove back to the house. In the far distance, he saw Pedro, one of the security men, with his automatic weapon held across his chest, walking in his direction. It was definitely time to leave.

As Boyle got into his car, his mobile rang. The caller spoke in English. 'My name is Gunnar Lundgren,' the man said. 'I am returning your call.' Boyle racked his brains. Who was he? Then he remembered the Swedish property developer. 'I'd like to see you, if I may – to discuss the problems you had with the graffiti artist Cisco Perez,' said Boyle.

The developer said he would be free in the afternoon and gave his home address.

From Santa Nuria, Boyle drove straight to Electronica, a special shop that sold surveillance equipment in Girona. With the help of a keen shop assistant, he bought the smallest camera on the market and then drove to his father-in-law's house. When Narcis let Boyle in, he did not mention his daughter Montse's visit. Instead, Narcis watched with great interest as Boyle set up the camera in the top corner of the main entrance to the house, with a perfect view of anyone going near the front door. DIY was easy for Boyle. It was something he had been taught in the children's home and was further developed with the police. After fastening the camera in the upper corner of the door with special tape, he stretched a fine wire through the door entrance and into the foyer and drew it up the side of the wall to a wooden cupboard, where he placed the receiver. He then gently tapped the wire into place with staples. He and Narcis studied the door from the outside.

'Well done,' said Narcis. 'You would never see it if you didn't know it was there.'

'Don't tell anyone about it. Not even Esther,' said Boyle.

Boyle drove to Santa Nuria for the second time that day. He moved slowly along the high street until he reached the sign marked *The Costa Brava Urbanisation* and turned left. Driving into the hills of the Ardenya, he wound past the large, modern houses and the manicured golf course of The Santa Nuria Golf Club, which was at the heart of the wealthy urbanisation. Beautifully coiffed umbrella trees, which brought to mind the image of Liberace's hairstyle, wound through the course, defining each hole. Gunnar Lundgren's house was near the top of the mountain, just on the other side of the peak from Boyle's house on Pedralta. Boyle knew there was a track that led from his house to this urbanisation because he and Ana had walked it many times.

The road and pavement were wet with droplets of water. There had been no rain, yet this north-facing side of the mountain was always damp. *Helpful for the gardens and golf course but murder on the bones,* thought Boyle. He parked outside a low-gated entrance and got out. The house was some distance from the gate. It was a huge, white, ultramodern bunker, set on a shoulder of the mountain that caught the sun. The house was modest compared to Eduardo Clavaguera's mansion but the money was there, more money than Boyle expected to see in his lifetime. He rang the buzzer on the gate, which immediately clicked open, and headed down the expensively paved drive that cut through a natural garden of ancient cork trees, umbrella trees and shrubs. Boyle paused when he heard the high barks of a little dog and froze when an ugly brown terrier shot out from the house straight up to him.

'Abbe!' a man yelled.

Boyle breathed a sigh of relief when the dog returned to the house, where a tall, grey-haired man with a moustache emerged from the double doors. He appeared relaxed, with his hands in his pockets and a friendly smile.

'Mister Boyle, nice to meet you,' he said as they shook hands.

'Please call me Adrian. Thank you for talking to me,' said Boyle in the stilted English he automatically fell into with people whose first language was not English.

'My name is Gunnar. And it is my pleasure to talk

to you, now I have the time. Although I don't know how I can help. Please come in,' he said, showing Boyle down the stone stairs into an immense, open-plan living space with floor-to-ceiling glass stretching around two walls. Boyle followed Gunnar into the kitchen area.

'My wife stayed behind in Sweden, visiting our daughter. Will you have an espresso?'

'That is very kind.' Boyle was curious as to why he had been invited to the man's house and not his office. Was Gunnar lonely because his wife was away?

'How do you take it?'

'One sugar, please.' Boyle stood at the marble-topped breakfast bar while Gunnar put two small cups under the espresso machine and pressed a button. 'What do you know about the death of Cisco Perez?'

Gunnar turned to him, a look of confusion covering his face. 'He died?'

'Yes, up at Roca Alba. About two weeks ago,' Boyle said, noticing what he thought was genuine surprise.

Gunnar looked away. 'I spent last month in Sweden. It's beautiful there in September. That is probably why I never heard. What happened exactly?'

'He fell off the roof at Casa Cielo. Straight over the cliff.'

'Was he doing his graffiti?'

'Yes.'

Gunnar shook his head slowly as he put the cups on saucers. 'Crazy boy.'

'Do you remember him?'

'Not very well. I only met him once. I can't even remember what he looked like. From what I heard, he was always doing that graffiti,' said Gunnar with a shrug.

'He did an incredible amount of damage to your property,' said Boyle.

'Oh yes, of course. I was really angry at first, but I forgot about it after Eduardo paid to have it repainted. So, what is your interest?' he asked as he handed Boyle his cup and directed him into the living area. Boyle sat on a cream leather armchair facing the sunlit hills of Les Gavarres across the valley. Lundgren sat to his side.

'His mother thinks he was murdered.'

'And you think I had something to do with it?' Gunnar asked with incredulity.

'You did tell Cisco that you would kill him if he ever damaged your property again,' said Boyle, sipping his espresso.

Gunnar laughed with unease. 'I cannot remember saying that. I may have, but I certainly didn't mean it literally, if I did.' Gunnar drank his espresso down in one gulp and placed the cup on the low glass coffee table. He got up and said, 'Come. Let me show you the views.' He slid open the patio doors and Boyle followed him across an expanse of fine lawn, portions of which had been ruined by the hooves and snouts of wild boar.

'I can see you've had the *jabali* here,' said Boyle.

'Yes. They have been here every night this past week, so my neighbours tell me. The *ayuntamiento* has given us permission to shoot them if they come onto our property. So, tonight I will take my rifle and climb up into that tree,' he said, pointing to a massive umbrella pine on the perimeter of the property. 'And I will wait. And when I see them – bang!' he said, laughing.

They walked to the edge of a swimming pool that overlooked Santa Nuria. On the right, in the distance, lay the high-rises stretching along the beach of Playa d'Aro, and to the left stood the majestic Pyrenees, layered on the horizon, reminding Boyle of a Japanese watercolour.

'It is a beautiful view you have here,' said Boyle.

'Thank you. I've known Eduardo Clavaguera for nearly forty years and in all that time, I could never get him to sell me any of his land over there in Sant Martí. That is where I originally wanted to live. So, I bought land here in Santa Nuria instead. See the cranes?' asked Gunnar, pointing at Santa Nuria nestled below.

Boyle counted three perched above the village, looking like colossal stick insects. 'Yes,' said Boyle.

'I'm building forty more flats down in the village.'

'I thought it was a bad time for selling property.'

'They're all sold. It is social housing, workers' flats. Beautiful, functional and reasonably priced. I will tell you something,' said Gunnar, leaning close to Boyle, about to tell him a secret. 'When Eduardo sold that land along the bypass in Sant Martí to Quimet Navarro, I was really upset. Quimet built that huge complex there. You know the one?'

Boyle nodded. 'How can you miss it?'

Gunnar laughed and started back towards the house.

'When did Eduardo Clavaguera sell the property to Quimet?'

'Six or seven years ago. But how Quimet Navarro could afford it, I have no idea. He started out with nothing. How does a man with no money accumulate so much, so quickly, and become so rich? Thank God I didn't buy that land because Quimet is in trouble now. No one is buying property. The apartments were completed two years ago and in those two years, he has only sold a few flats. But I think it is his fault. A two-bedroom flat for four hundred euros, in this economic climate – ridiculous.'

'How does he survive?' asked Boyle.

'Who knows?' Gunnar picked a few weeds from a large planter.

'You don't like Quimet?' asked Boyle.

'Don't trust him. Never have.'

'Are you familiar with Casa Cielo, where the boy died?' asked Boyle, trying to get Gunnar back on track.

'I know the Roca Alba urbanisation, but I am not familiar with a house by that name.'

'It's Eduardo Clavaguera's old house. You know, at the edge of the cliff?'

Gunnar squinted. 'Oh, that house. Yes. It used to be called Casa Teresa. You would think that after Eduardo's first wife had been killed there, he would have torn it down.'

Boyle stared at Gunnar. So Eduardo had been married before? And she died there. He held his face still to hide his surprise. His time in the police had taught him to do that, but the Swede still noticed something.

Gunnar laughed. 'You didn't know that, did you?'

'No, in fact, I didn't.'

'That house is unlucky,' said Gunnar, shaking his head with conviction.

'How was she killed?' Boyle asked.

'Accidentally shot by a hunter.'

'When did it happen?'

'In the late seventies.'

'Who shot her?'

'A hunter named Felipe Puig. He went to prison for eight years. He was a worker on the Clavaguera estate. I was part of the hunting party, so was Eduardo.'

'How did it happen?'

'Although Felipe was a good shot, he was still a novice. But he had a powerful Finnish rifle, a Tikka – much too powerful for him. The hunting around here is incredibly dangerous. The paths are narrow and the place is full of boulders where the bullets can ricochet. That's what happened. The bullet from his rifle ricocheted and hit her. Her name was Teresa. She was a lovely young woman.'

'Was Teresa hunting with you.'

'No. She never hunted. She was at the house, sitting there on the terrace – you know, the high terrace off the *torre*?'

Boyle nodded, guessing what was coming next.

'Teresa was always reading. That's what she was doing when the bullet got her, straight through the heart,' said Gunnar, tapping his chest with his finger. 'It upset me so much that I only ever hunt in Sweden now.'

She was reading on the terrace, exactly like the woman in Cisco's mural, thought Boyle. 'How well do you know Eduardo Clavaguera?'

'I met him thirty-five years ago when my wife and I first moved down here. His wife Teresa helped us with our Spanish. Eduardo and I became good friends because we both liked to hunt. We don't see each other much anymore. I hear he hasn't touched a rifle since the accident.'

'Who else was part of the hunting group that day?'

'Eduardo's brother Salvador, Faustino Duran and Quimet Navarro.'

Boyle decided to look into the shooting of Eduardo's first wife. It was strange that there were two accidental deaths at the same house, even though thirty years apart. But not only that, the two deaths seemed to be connected through the same mural that Cisco had painted. Why did he paint it? Was there a real connection? And what was the link between Cisco and Eduardo Clavaguera's first wife, Teresa?

15

'I had no idea that Eduardo Clavaguera's first wife had been killed on Pedralta,' Boyle said to Carmen, as she set his starter of marinated cod salad down on the table.

Carmen looked thoughtful. 'I haven't thought about that in years,' she said, resting her elbows on the table and her chin on her hands. Her low-cut white top now revealed a hint of cleavage. This was new. Normally she wore higher necks. Boyle tried to keep his eyes on her face. 'It happened so long ago. I was about nine or ten but I remember when she died because it was the biggest thing that had happened in Sant Martí.

Everyone was talking about it; it was so awful. They say Eduardo never got over her death.'

'Who was she?'

'Teresa Duran. Faustino Duran's cousin, I think.'

Carmen's sleek laptop beeped and she quickly checked her email, then closed it with a sigh. Boyle ate a slice of the fish, which was marinated in olive oil and lemon. It melted in his mouth.

'Keeping track of Antonio?' Boyle asked.

'That's becoming impossible.'

'Eduardo's second wife – how did he meet her?' he asked.

'I don't know exactly. I do know that Tina was a chef in Barcelona when they met. This was unusual at the time. I mean, it was more than twenty years ago. She's amazingly good. Papa tried to get her to work here but she told him she had retired.'

'No need to work.'

'What an old-fashioned man you are,' she said, with a teasing smile.

'Nothing old-fashioned about it. If I met a woman who had enough money to keep me in the style to which I had become accustomed, I'd stop working too. I'm all for equal rights.'

'You, stop working? Never.'

His laugh gave him away. 'I tell you what, though. Tina Clavaguera makes great *bunyols*.'

'She is famous for her pastries.'

'How long ago did Eduardo marry her?'

'After his wife died, he was single for years. People said he was too depressed to consider another marriage. But nothing stops these Catalan mothers. They threw their daughters at him one after the other. But once Eduardo saw Tina, he knew she was the woman he would marry, straight away.'

'How can you possibly know that?' asked Boyle with mock cynicism. How Carmen's romantic slant on things coexisted with her hard-nose business sense was a mystery to Boyle.

Carmen shrugged and pouted. 'It was just part of the story that went around. Anyway, they married soon after they met. Over two hundred people packed into Sant Elm church for the wedding, and the reception was held at the Hotel Els Pins, overlooking the bay at Sant Pol. It was a happy ending to a tragic time for Eduardo,' said Carmen, as if she too was hoping for better times.

'And then they had Miguel?' Boyle asked.

'No. That was another thing, I remember now. Eduardo and Tina desperately wanted children, but at first she was unable to conceive. I used to hear my mother discussing it with her friends. There was talk that Tina might be *esteril* – the women pronounced that word with such heaviness, as if she was dying, as if it was the worst thing that could possibly happen to a woman.'

'It was for Ana,' said Boyle, remembering the years of heartache when he and Ana had tried for a child.

Carmen laid her hand on top of his and closed her eyes. 'I'm sorry, *cariño*, I wasn't thinking.'

Boyle felt an ache in his chest, unsure if it was due to Carmen's touch or a longing for Ana. The fact that Carmen looked so much like her sister was disconcerting. 'No. It's alright,' he lied. 'Go on.'

'After five years of trying, Tina finally gave birth to Miguel. And then, about two years later, they had Laura.'

'Eduardo still lived at the house on Roca Alba?'

'No. I think he left that house after his wife was killed there.'

'Was that when he moved into the estate in Santa Nuria?'

'Yes. Eduardo's father had died, I forget when, so he took over the family house. He refused to sell the house at Roca Alba though. It was all closed up but, of course, like everywhere else in those days, not locked. I remember when I was a teenager. We all used to drive up there. It was so hidden. The perfect place to drink and party,' she said, looking sad for a moment, then smiling. 'That was where I first met Pau. It was so easy to meet guys then. Now it's difficult.'

'How do you mean?'

'It's different, obviously. Now I have the children to think about. When I'm not working, I'm upstairs with them. It's not easy to bring a new man into my life. Sometimes I feel it is impossible,' she said, looking straight at Boyle with a vulnerability that confused him. Was she hinting at something? It made Boyle uneasy and he swiftly changed the subject.

'The hunter who shot Eduardo's wife was named Felipe Puig. Do you know anything about him?'

Carmen shook her head. 'I can't remember, but he went to prison for years.'

'Do you have any idea where he is now?'

'No.

In the modern library, just off the Carretera de Girona near the centre of Sant Martí, Boyle found the back copies of *El Periodico* on microfilm. He took the box of film reels for the whole of 1978, '79 and '80 from an old filing cabinet and wondered how many people made use of this technology today. At the projector, he pulled out the tray from underneath the lens, placed the beginning of the film onto the spindle and threaded it through to the take-up reel. Pushing back the tray, he rolled through the film, focusing on the hunting seasons from October to March. He found it quickly. The accident happened on 10 November 1978. The story had been reported the following day. The headline *Accidente Cazarando* was splashed across the front page of the paper but there was not much information.

> *Yesterday, Maria Teresa Duran, aged 25, the wife of Eduardo Clavaguera, was shot and killed by a hunter at her house on Pedralta. Her husband is the eldest son of the late Fernando Clavaguera. The police gave no further information, only to say that the incident is being investigated.*

There was a large, old-fashioned studio photo of the victim with her hand behind her head, dramatically looking up at the camera. The style was different from the way Cisco had painted her, but he had nonetheless painted an incredible likeness, with her handsome, sculpted face and large, dark eyes. She was definitely the same woman Cisco had painted on the day he died, no doubt about it, but Boyle could not understand why. Why would Cisco Perez paint Eduardo Clavaguera's dead wife? And could it have something to do with his own death? Teresa had died long before Cisco was born. What possible interest in her or knowledge of her could he have had? But the one person they both had in common was Eduardo Clavaguera. Boyle wondered if he had played any part in both the killing of his wife and the death of Cisco.

He came upon an article dated 24 November 1978, two weeks later – the amount of time it must have taken to check the ballistics. It was front page news again.

> *The police have named the hunter responsible for the death of Maria Teresa Duran, wife of*

Eduardo Clavaguera. He is Felipe Puig, age 25, a worker on the Clavaguera estate and resident of Santa Nuria. The hunter was arrested and will stand trial early next year. Maria Teresa was shot on the terrace of her house two weeks ago. There is growing concern that such an accident could have happened. There are calls for the qualifications of hunters to be reviewed and made more stringent so that nothing like this ever happens again.

Boyle zoomed in on the article and printed off the page, then continued to roll the microfilm through the months. On 5 October 1980, the trial began. It lasted three days, but there was not much information in the paper. Felipe had pleaded guilty of causing death by negligence and was sent to prison for eight years, two of which he had already served waiting for the trial. Boyle made a note to ask Montse to obtain a transcript of the trial.

There was a photograph of the hunter at the bottom of the article. The young, strikingly handsome face was familiar but Boyle was unable to place him. He zoomed in to get a better view and it struck him like a thunderbolt. Under the photograph, he read the name Felipe Puig. So that was his original family name, Puig, but the man Boyle saw in the photograph, he knew as Perez, Felipe Perez – Cisco's father and Juanita's husband.

16

'EDUARDO WAS MARRIED TO SOMEONE BEFORE Tina?' asked Rosa.

'Yes, it was thirty-two years ago,' said Boyle.

'It was before your family moved here,' Montse said to Rosa, who was originally a farm girl from Tarragona. They were in Montse's office having their afternoon break. Montse moved up closer to Rosa and read the newspaper clipping with her.

'I was just six,' said Montse, taking copies of the articles Boyle had made at the library.

'Notice who shot her. On the second page,' said Boyle.

Rosa flipped the page and they stared at the photo.

Montse's eyes widened. 'She was shot by Juanita's husband?' Even Rosa looked surprised.

'Yes, Felipe Puig – aka Felipe Perez,' he said. 'Didn't she tell you about it when you applied for an autopsy of Cisco?'

'No, she said nothing at all,' said Montse.

'You would have thought that Eduardo Clavaguera would have been the first person she would point her finger at for the murder of her son,' said Boyle.

'And she didn't say anything about it when Felipe was brought in for assaulting her either,' said Rosa.

'He is using his wife's name now. Perez instead of Puig. I wonder how long Felipe has used that name and if the police are even aware of his former identity,' said Boyle.

'He might have changed his name to Perez after leaving prison,' said Rosa. 'That could explain why the *Mossos* never brought it up when Felipe was brought in for the assault.'

'Could you obtain a police report on the shooting for me?' Boyle asked Rosa. It took place on November the tenth, 1978.' Rosa wrote down the date in her notebook. Thirty years ago, the Catalan police, the *Mossos d'Esquadra*, had barely existed. Before Franco's death in 1975, the Guardia Civil would have investigated the shooting. Nowadays there was an office in Girona with three desks; one for the *Mossos d'Esquadra*, one for the Guardia Civil and another for the National Police. It was here that they swapped information.

Boyle looked over at Montse. 'The trial of Felipe Puig began on October the fifth, 1980. Can you obtain a court report from the trial?'

'Yes, but don't hold your breath. The new courthouse was built twenty years ago. The old transcripts were moved and no one seems to know where they put them. But I will give it a try.'

Rosa paused at the door and looked at Boyle before she left. 'Will you go and see the investigating judge Gabriel Llfranc and tell him about the new developments? See if there's a chance he'll reopen the case?'

'Certainly,' said Boyle, pleased that Rosa was getting behind the new developments.

'Of course, don't mention my name,' she said. 'I can't approach him again because it might cause problems at the *comissaria*; not enough evidence, wasting police time, etcetera, etcetera. Not to mention my ex-husband, who would love to see me fail.'

After Rosa left, Boyle drew up a chair to Montse's desk and asked her how the meeting with her parents had gone.

'Mama was hysterical in her own delightful way. She felt that she had been hoodwinked. She no longer wants Rosa and me to go to church with her. As you can imagine, she thought our attendance at church sacrilegious,' she said with amused contempt.

'Eventually she will get used to the idea and come around,' said Boyle.

'She told me that if we go ahead with the marriage, that she and Papa will no longer see us.'

'You'll go ahead?'

'Of course,' she said, with a look of surprise that he should even ask the question. She leaned in close to Boyle. 'I care about Rosa and I want to make sure that she is provided for should anything happen to me.' She then told Boyle that there were no prints found inside the engagement cards, except two sets of prints belonging to her parents. 'So, no luck there.'

When Boyle got back to his office, he rang Juanita Perez, who said that she could see him that afternoon at her flat. He did not want to discuss the new information concerning her husband over the phone. He then rang the office of Gabriel Llfranc. His assistant said that he was out for the day but that she would make an appointment for Boyle the following morning.

With three hours to spare before his meeting with Juanita, Boyle decided to drop by Fincas Deirdre to see if it was open. Approaching the sales office in Calle Joan Marigal, he saw there was someone inside. He walked into the cool and contemporary reception area. Although there were several properties advertised in the window, complete with photos and details, most of the space was taken up with the display of Quimet Navarro's apartment complex, with two large, freestanding boards featuring colourful photos of the apartments on offer.

'May I help you?' asked the receptionist, who was getting her bag out, looking as if she was preparing to leave. It was Laura Clavaguera, Eduardo's daughter. She appeared to recognise Boyle and smiled with embarrassment. 'Hello,' she said.

'Hello. I'm just looking. Is that alright?' asked Boyle. 'You're not closing, are you?'

'Not for another five minutes, but don't worry, take your time.'

Appearing to have undergone a personality change, Laura Clavaguera was quite agreeable, nothing like the arrogant, drugged-up girl he had met at Casa Cielo. Picking up a brochure, he discreetly watched the girl. With one elbow on the desk, she was doodling on a notepad, a curtain of long, glossy hair covering her face.

At that moment, a Mercedes SLK pulled up outside and parked up on the narrow pavement, blocking it.

He recognised the woman with the red hair who stepped out of the car. It was Deirdre Clavaguera, Salvador's wife. She was probably in her late forties, slender and sophisticated, and wearing a power suit in muted colours. Although she had an air of confidence, her eyes exposed a sadness within. *A fellow traveller,* thought Boyle. He could spot it a mile off. On a scale of one to ten, one being depressed and ten happy, he would give her a four.

Boyle introduced himself in English when she came through the door.

'Hello, Mister Boyle,' she said offering her hand. 'I think we've met before.'

'Yes,' he said, shaking her hand. 'A couple of times.'

'What can I help you with?'

'I'd like to buy a flat.'

She brightened up considerably. 'Are you going to sell your lovely house on Pedralta?'

Boyle paused, taken aback that she knew his house.

'I know practically every house in the Vall d'Aro. I've been in this business longer than you can imagine,' she said, answering his unasked question.

He glanced over at Laura, who appeared to be listening to them, a confused look on her face as she tried to follow the conversation in English.

'Yes, I want to sell. It's too much upkeep for me on the mountain. Not only the house, but constantly having to clear the surrounding woods for the council,' Boyle lied easily. It was part of the job. He had absolutely no intention of selling his house.

'Tell me about it. We have the same problem with our property. It's like the Forth Bridge. Once you finish painting it, you have to start all over again. It never ends.'

Boyle smiled. He liked her. 'You're so right. I'd like to buy something here in town that I can lock up and forget about when I go to England.'

'Would you like to see our new flats?' she said, gesturing towards the freestanding boards.

'Yes,' he said, approaching the display.

She glanced at her watch. 'Do you have a few minutes now?'

'As a matter of fact, I do.'

She went to her desk, pulled open the drawer and took out a ring of keys.

Deirdre drove Boyle to the flats, which were perfectly placed at the top of Sant Martí, overlooking the harbour. It was only when they got out and wandered amongst the six peach-coloured buildings that Boyle realised what an enormous development it was.

'Each building has eighteen flats,' she said.

It was bleak, the whole place feeling like a ghost town. All the white shutters were closed and the balconies empty, suggesting to Boyle that few of the flats had sold. Worst of all, a few homemade "For sale" signs hung from the balcony railings of the owners who already wanted to move on.

'There aren't many people around,' said Boyle. 'I take it that not many of the flats have sold?'

'I won't pretend. We expected to have shifted them all by now but, as you know, the property market is slow. *El Crisis* has hit us hard. But we have sold half of them.'

'Half?' said Boyle, not believing a word of it.

'Yes. Really. Many of them belong to weekenders from Barcelona. Or foreigners, like you.' She looked at him and gave a wistful smile. 'I do envy you living part-time in England. The older I get, the more I miss it.'

'Don't you visit?'

'I have no family there now,' she said, making no attempt to hide her gloom.

A bit like myself, thought Boyle. 'How long have you lived here?' he asked.

'Twenty-seven years. I was nineteen when I came here on holiday. I met Salvador. You know my husband?'

'Of course,' said Boyle. He kept a straight face to hide his contempt for the man.

'We married the next year and soon after had our two sons. And that was it,' she said in a manner that suggested it hadn't been enough.

They came to the entrance of one of the blocks and she punched four numbers into the keypad. 'This building is very secure.' The door buzzed open, revealing a pale marble foyer that reminded Boyle of a crematorium. On the first floor, two maids in pale blue emerged from a flat, carrying bags of rubbish. Boyle recognised the maids, having seen them at Eduardo Clavaguera's *masia*.

'That flat belongs to my niece, Laura,' said Deirdre. 'She loves it. It's safe, comfortable and, of course, has the wonderful views.'

The flats may be comfortable and have nice views but they definitely aren't safe, thought Boyle. He knew a bit about locks. The lock Deirdre was now opening to the show flat could be opened by any self-respecting burglar, it was so simple. 'Those maids work for your brother-in-law, don't they?'

'Yes.'

'I recognised them from his estate.'

'You've been to his house?' she asked. So Deirdre had no knowledge of his visit to Eduardo's estate.

'Yes.'

'Oh, you are privileged,' she said, with a hint of sarcasm.

'Surely you've been there?'

'My husband has been there several times but poor me, just the once since he had the work done. After the renovations, he had a cocktail party to show it off. Eduardo is a bit of a show-off, of course. I'm not telling you something you don't already know. What did you think of the house?'

'What can I say? It was beautiful.'

'Eduardo has definitely got the Midas touch.

Unfortunately, his brother, my dear husband Salvador, has the opposite effect. Everything he touches turns to *mierda*.' She opened the door and put her hand across Boyle's back to guide him into the flat.

Boyle was surprised that she should confide in him. Women did not usually make disparaging remarks about their husbands to strangers. It was hard to imagine Tina saying anything negative about Eduardo.

'I was under the impression you had pots of money,' he said.

'Eduardo has, but the rest of us are struggling.' Boyle was unsure exactly what that meant. Everyone's idea of 'struggling' was so different. She drove a brand new SLK, he, a clapped-out Rover, and many of the African immigrants in the area rode around on old push bikes.

Deirdre then gave him a tour of the vastly overpriced flat. He hated the shiny floors and would rather live in a tent, but he played along, waiting for her to reveal more titbits about cosy family relations with the Clavagueras. After the comment about her money difficulties, however, she stayed away from anything confidential.

Before they parted at Fincas Deirdre, she arranged to come to his house the following day to take photos for the display window at Fincas Deirdre. *I must be mad to play this game,* he thought. He adored his house, but anything for an inside scoop. Besides, nothing was selling in the Vall d'Aro, or anywhere else on the Costa Brava.

17

As Boyle approached his car, he had the overwhelming feeling that he was being watched. He looked around discreetly, not wanting to give anything away. He was hesitant to get into his car, reminded of his royal protection days with the Met, when you always checked underneath beforehand. He reached into his pocket, dropped a coin and, while picking it up, scanned the undercarriage of the Rover. Nothing dodgy there.

While driving to Llagostera, he realised for certain that someone was on his tail. It was an old blue Astra steadily keeping pace two cars' distance behind. At great speed, Boyle left the autovia at the exit to Panedes and, rather than follow the narrow road up into the hills of Les Gavarres, he took a sharp turn. With a great squeal of tyres and a cloud of dirt, he pulled into the drive of a farm he knew and hid behind an outbuilding. Moments later, after the dust had settled, he saw the Astra speeding past on the narrow road winding up into the hills.

Boyle arrived at Juanita's house carrying a manila folder. The lock to the main front door was still broken so he went straight to Juanita's flat. Juanita answered the door, looking agitated. 'Señor Boyle, will you help me please? There's been an accident.'

Boyle heard Felipe shouting, '¡*Largata!* ¡*Largata!* ¡*Largata!* You bitch!'

He hurried and upon entering the kitchen caught the foul, sweet smell and knew immediately what kind of accident it was. Felipe had messed himself. He was lunging from side to side in his wheelchair, howling at Juanita.

'Follow me.' Juanita moved the wheelchair out of the kitchen, while Felipe continued to scream, '¡*Largata!*', twisting his head around to target her.

'¡*Cállate!*' Juanita finally bellowed. Felipe stopped screaming.

They entered a small bedroom with dark furniture. There was a massive crucifix above the bed and there were several statues of saints on the bedside tables and window ledge, which Boyle, however much he tried to fight off his Catholic past, found comforting. Juanita placed a rubber sheet on the bed, then Boyle helped her pick Felipe out of his wheelchair and lay him on the bed.

'Will you make sure he doesn't fall?'

'Of course,' said Boyle, taking her place at the head of the bed.

She left the room and entered the bathroom. Felipe's face had softened and was turned towards the door that his wife had just disappeared through with an anxious stare of devotion, like that of a dog left tied up outside a supermarket. Felipe then turned to Boyle, his eyes expressing a clarity of mind he had not yet seen.

'Is Cisco coming home for lunch?' Felipe asked.

'I don't think so. He's in Barcelona looking for work,' Boyle said, using Juanita's stock answer.

Felipe frowned, perplexed. 'Isn't Cisco at school?'

Juanita came back with a large plastic bowl of soapy water and a towel over her arm. 'No, *cariño*,' she answered for Boyle. 'He's left school already, you remember? He's looking for work now.'

Boyle sat with Juanita in the living room, the manila folder on his lap, drinking a strong cup of her South American mate tea that she told him she couldn't live without. She explained how pleased she was that it was now sold in a shop in Llagostera. Juanita looked relaxed. Boyle hated to break the peaceful interlude.

'A hunting accident happened here thirty-two years ago. Eduardo Clavaguera's wife was accidentally shot and killed by a hunter.'

'How terrible!'

'You never heard about it?'

'No. I thought Tina was his first wife.'

Revealing life-changing information to loved ones was never easy for Boyle. He paused, taking a slow breath. 'Were you aware that the hunter who shot her was your husband?'

Juanita looked mystified. 'No. I don't see how he could have. Felipe never met the Clavagueras, not even Laura or Miguel. And he's never fired a gun in his life.'

Boyle handed her the manila folder. She opened it and glanced inside. She flipped through the copies of articles, taking out the one with Felipe's photo and reading the caption. 'Local Hunter Accidentally Kills Woman.' She gasped with dismay. 'It can't be!' Boyle nodded with sympathy. She read the article, squinting to see the words. 'He went to prison! *No puede ser!* It's impossible!' she said, covering her mouth with her hand.

'I'm sorry, Señora. I'm going to look into this further, to see if it could be related to Cisco's death in any way.'

'It was Eduardo's wife who was killed.' Juanita looked away, staring at nothing as she tried to take it all in. 'Then Eduardo must have killed Cisco.'

'Don't jump to any conclusions,' said Boyle.

'No, you are right. Eduardo could not hurt Cisco. He loved him like a son.'

Here was another point that Tina Clavaguera and Juanita Perez agreed on: that Eduardo loved Cisco like a son. 'Can you think of anyone else who might have wanted to hurt your son?'

She dropped the folder and shook her head violently, as if to rid herself of the bad thoughts. 'I don't want to talk about it now. Please go.' She buried her head in her hands.

Through the window, Boyle checked the road outside Juanita's flat for any suspicious cars or people and then left. He sat in his car for a few minutes and thought about Juanita. What was going on? How could she be unaware that something so monumental had happened in Felipe's life? And then he remembered what his sister-in-law Carmen always liked to say to him: that the woman is always the last to know. Carmen's husband Pau had denied all along that he was having an affair. It wasn't until Pau's girlfriend had given birth to his child that he finally admitted it to Carmen. And how many times, as a policeman, had he come across men who had other families, both families totally unaware of the other's existence? Felipe could easily have kept his past a secret. Although he was from the area, his parents now lived in the south. Why was that? Were they too embarrassed to face their neighbours after their son had gone to prison? And he didn't marry a local girl either, who might have heard about his past. No, he had married a South American and taken her name.

Driving out of Llagostera, he decided he would go and talk to Faustino Duran up on Pedralta. Carmen had told him that Faustino was related to Teresa Clavaguera – a cousin, she had said. Gunnar Lundgren had mentioned that Faustino had participated in the hunt the day Teresa was shot. Perhaps he might be able to fill him in on what had happened all those years ago.

Boyle parked his car in the woods of Roca Alba and walked towards Faustino's house, Can Bosc. The air was crisp and the dry twigs crackled underfoot. As he came upon the back of the house, he could see that the red graffiti left by the anti-hunt group had been painted over. It looked like the whole house had been repainted. Faustino's maroon SUV was parked in the drive. The day had cooled down considerably and there was smoke coming out of the chimney. Faustino answered the door before Boyle had the chance to knock and came outside, closing the door behind him.

'Yes?' He said it as a greeting.

'As you know, I have been investigating the death of Cisco Perez. And I read that your cousin Teresa was accidentally shot and killed at the same house.'

'What has the death of the boy got to do with Teresa?'

'I don't know yet. I was hoping you might tell me something about the day Teresa Clavaguera was shot. You were there that day, I hear.'

'Yes, I was. And I can see you have been doing your homework, but you have got something wrong already. Teresa was not my cousin; she was my sister.'

Boyle was surprised. That put Faustino at the top of his suspect list for killing Cisco. 'I am very sorry.'

'Why sorry? You didn't know her. For all you know, she could have deserved it,' said Faustino with a bitter smile.

Boyle paused, taken aback by Faustino's comment. 'I hear that Felipe Perez, the father of Cisco, went to prison for the crime.'

'Yes, I know nothing of how the boy died but I do know that, in my sister's case, it was Felipe's rifle that fired the shot that killed her.'

'Two accidents in the same place, both connected by Cisco's last painting. That strange portrait of Teresa on the *torre* at Casa Cielo.'

'What are you talking about?'

'Haven't you seen it? Cisco's last painting was of Teresa on the day she was shot.'

Boyle led the way down to Casa Cielo to show Faustino the painting. As they approached the front of the house, Faustino groaned at the sight of the dense graffiti and asked Boyle what possessed people to paint such junk. Boyle had no desire to get into it with him. Instead, he directed him around to the back garden to see the painting of Teresa, but when Boyle looked up at the *torre*, he saw that the painting had disappeared under a fresh coat of white paint.

'Did you have this painted when you had your house done?' asked Boyle.

'Of course not. I don't have the money to go around painting other people's houses,' said Faustino.

'That's not what I heard,' said Boyle.

Faustino jutted out his chin. 'You British are very nosy people and, I am sorry to say, you have no class.' Faustino then turned and walked back onto the track. Boyle followed close behind. He took out his smart phone and brought up the photos he had taken of Cisco's last mural.

'Look, I have it here,' he said, moving under the shade of an umbrella pine for clarity.

Faustino followed him and leaned in to focus on the image. Boyle tried to read his response but the man was a sphinx. 'Have you seen this painting before?'

'Never.'

'It's a painting of your sister, no?'

Faustino threw up his hands and hurried on. 'I have no idea who it is.'

Boyle didn't believe him. Even he recognised that the painting was of Teresa Clavaguera. Why would Faustino not admit it?

'Have you seen any workers down here?' asked Boyle as he caught up with Faustino.

'No. Besides, there is no question. Eduardo Clavaguera is the only person who would touch this monstrosity. It's his house.'

18

'YOU'RE WASTING YOUR TIME COMING TO ME. There is nothing to suggest that the death of Cisco Perez was anything but an accident,' said Gabriel Llfranc, the investigating judge, in his cramped office near the market square. Boyle was standing in front of Llfranc's desk. There had been no offer to take a seat. 'The kid was crazy. He hung from buildings and cranes like a monkey. I'm not surprised he fell.' Llfranc was a busy man. There were thick manila folders stacked everywhere – on the desk, on shelves lining the walls, even some on the floor. Boyle wondered if this was why the judge closed the case of Cisco Perez so quickly. Was it the pursuit of easy targets? Even so, Boyle hadn't finished.

'Are you aware that Cisco wasn't alone when he died?'

'Yes. I got the report from *Mossos*. I read it. Luis Sureda claims he was there earlier in the day filming Cisco Perez with Miguel Clavaguera and says he then left, leaving them both behind. But Miguel Clavaguera was brought in for questioning and denies he was there. And I hear you have been bothering Eduardo Clavaguera.'

'Questioning, yes.'

'You have questioned him enough and now you must stop.' Boyle never read the manual that stated you were only allowed to question a witness once. He could see straight away that for Gabriel Llfranc, the feelings of Eduardo Clavaguera were more important than finding out what actually happened that day.

Boyle then told Llfranc what he had discovered about Cisco's father accidentally killing Teresa Clavaguera. 'Were you aware of that?'

That gave Llfranc pause for thought. 'Interesting,' he said. 'I vaguely remember hearing about the original event but I had no idea that the hunter was the boy's father.' He paused again and Boyle hoped he might consider the new findings and reopen the investigation. 'It doesn't change anything though. It is simply an awful coincidence,' Llfranc concluded.

'If there was one thing I learned in the Met, it was that there is no such thing as coincidence.'

Gabriel took in an audible breath. 'Yes, but regrettably you are no longer with the London Met. You are in Catalonia, in a small town, just a lowly private investigator. I know you are looking into this accident for Juanita Perez but, you must understand, it's partly her fault that her son died. She has to take some responsibility. She was the one who encouraged him with his graffiti.'

'That is a bit hard,' said Boyle.

'I'm sorry she lost her son, I am. But I remember her from before, when Cisco was arrested for vandalism. Cisco was actually remorseful, but not the mother. She was self-righteous. She seemed to think that whatever her son touched turned to gold. It didn't matter whose property he defaced, she thought that he made it more beautiful and that they should be grateful.' Llfranc shook his head, his mouth tight. 'There is no way that I'm going to reopen this case.'

Boyle wasn't going to let him off that easily. He proceeded to go over the case in minute detail, giving him information from the reports and witness statements. Llfranc made no attempt to hide his boredom and, in the end didn't budge or offer him any help, ending the meeting after glancing at his watch and saying. 'It is my lunchtime. This meeting is over, if you don't mind, Señor Boyle.'

Boyle did mind. He hated being dismissed and felt like telling Llfranc to piss off, but instead, he politely thanked him and left. Better not burn any bridges. He might need Llfranc's help in the future.

Boyle hurried back to his house to meet Deirdre Clavaguera, who was coming up to photograph Casa Ana. She was all business, refusing the coffee Boyle offered, insisting she had no time to dawdle. Boyle wondered what kept her so busy. It cannot have been her property company; nothing was selling, just like he knew his house, Casa Ana, would never sell. But as she expertly snapped each photograph, she projected an attitude of optimism that someone would buy his house.

Boyle had tidied the place as best he could; having done all the housework since Ana died, he was used to it now. Montse had suggested he hire a cleaner but he had balked at the idea of someone invading his and Ana's private space. And now a stranger was photographing it. At one point, while Deirdre was photographing the bedroom, Ana's overstuffed wardrobe opened, the colourful sleeves of her garments bursting out as if in protest. Deirdre smiled sympathetically at the sight of his dead wife's clothes. Boyle was conscious that he would have to clear out Ana's things at some point, but not just now.

When Boyle arrived back at his office, he found Juanita Perez in the corridor, waiting for him. She said that Dolores from the council was watching Felipe at home. She apologised for having thrown him out the day before and said that, after thinking about what he had told her, she had come to some conclusions.

Boyle suggested they talk in his office. He wanted to avoid confrontations like the one she had had with Quimet Navarro in the café. Also, there were fewer distractions here. Juanita was perched at the edge of her seat, opposite Boyle, with a tissue in her hand prepared for any tears. Boyle poured a glass of water for her and himself. He wasn't going to offer her whisky, which was the only other beverage he had, though she looked like she could use it.

'When you showed me the photo of Felipe with the rifle, I was shocked at first. But when you left, it stayed with me and I realised how little I knew my own husband. Now things are beginning to make sense.'

Boyle took a biro and a pad of paper from his desk drawer. 'What "things", exactly?'

'Felipe and I were close, but there was always something there, some barrier between us. I thought it was maybe because I was Colombian and not Catalan. The Catalans are family people… but then he never saw his family. I have never met or spoken to any of them, and even when Cisco was born, their own grandchild, Felipe told me they didn't want to see him.' She looked at Boyle with bewilderment. 'Felipe is so confused now. I don't want to tell him I know about his time in prison. What should I do?'

'Don't tell him,' Boyle said.

She nodded her head slowly. 'You know, when my son was a boy, he was closer to me. It was always, "Mama do this, Mama do that, Mama, Mama, Mama", which I liked. But as he grew up, he and my husband began to get closer and I felt I was being pushed aside. Many times, after I would go to bed, I could hear them talking late into the night. It made me jealous.'

'Do you think Cisco knew about his father's past?' asked Boyle.

Juanita took a deep breath. It looked like acceptance. 'It's possible.'

'Can you remember any names Felipe might have mentioned over the years?' Boyle picked up the biro, ready to write.

'No, he said he didn't like people and he always discouraged me from making friends.'

Boyle put down the pen and leaned forward. 'You don't know any of your neighbours or your customers?'

She closed her eyes and slowly shook her head. 'Not really. They would invite us over but Felipe always had an excuse not to go. I know it sounds strange.' Her lips trembled. 'But Felipe always told me that all he needed was Cisco and me. Some men are loners, I think.'

Yes, and some men are abusers and it suits them to keep their women emotionally imprisoned, thought Boyle. He settled back into his chair and put his feet on the desk. 'What did your husband do for a living?'

'He worked with me, washing and ironing the clothes I mended. I even taught him how to use the sewing machine.'

'How did you meet?'

She brightened a bit and relaxed into her chair. 'I was working at the Sunday market in La Bisbal selling fruit and vegetables. He was working on the *kiosco* next to me. We talked and laughed. We were definitely attracted to each other. I couldn't wait for Sundays to come around when I would see him again. I had just arrived from Colombia and only knew other South Americans. I was lonely. Felipe was the first Catalan I made friends with. He was so good-looking and charming and he paid so much attention to me, it made the other girls jealous. Well, one Sunday he didn't show up. The man running the *kiosco* said Felipe had quit, just like that. I was devastated to tell you the truth because I thought Felipe and I had made that special connection, you know?' She looked at Boyle to see if he understood.

Boyle nodded and, to his shame, thought of his relationship with his sister-in-law Carmen rather than his dead wife as the "special connection".

'Two Sundays later, as we were closing the

market, he turned up. Apart from the day that my son was born, that was the happiest day of my life,' said Juanita, stopping a moment, as if to remember. 'We married four months later.'

'Did you continue with your job?'

'No. Felipe had lots of ideas about what we could do together. Once he knew I could sew, he encouraged me to start my own sewing business from home. But I realised soon after we moved in together that Felipe was lazy. He wanted an easy life. He was happy for me to do most of the work.'

'He took your name. Didn't you find that strange?'

'No. He said he hated his family. After we married, he changed it legally. Now I know why. He didn't want anyone to know who he was. It all makes sense now.'

'Do you know that Cisco's last painting was of Teresa Clavaguera?'

'The woman who was shot?'

Boyle nodded. 'How did Cisco know who she was?'

Juanita looked confused. 'Felipe must have told Cisco. But my son never said anything to me.' She set her mouth firmly. 'I want you to continue with the investigation into the death of Cisco.'

'Of course,' said Boyle. She had paid him for forty hours work and he had already done thirty-five. He also felt that if he didn't delve further into the investigation for Juanita Perez, then no one would.

How were the two accidents at Casa Cielo related? He felt Cisco knew how. And so did Felipe.

That night, the wild boar kept him awake. It sounded like a dozen of them. He heard the heavy knocking of their hooves on the stone drive as they moved over towards the wooded area at the side of his house, in search for the mushrooms that covered the hillsides at this time of year. The loud crunching sounds they made as they gorged on the acorns from the oak tree, and all the snorting and squealing, amused him. Thankfully, Boyle had no lawn for them to dig up. The mess the *jabali* made was easy to spot; it was random, chaotic, quite unlike an evenly tilled field or neatly dug garden. Something about the pigs tugged at his heart.

Early the next morning, Boyle received a call from Rosa.

'Are you awake, *guapo*?' asked Rosa.

'Two hours ago.'

'The police from Llagostera just rang me. Felipe Perez died last night.'

19

Rosa told Boyle that Felipe had died of natural causes. Boyle rang Juanita but there was no answer. He left a message of condolence and said if there was anything he could do, that she must contact him. In Spain they try to bury or cremate people within forty-eight hours of dying. Juanita was busy preparing to bury her husband.

It was Sunday, so Boyle would see what Señor Navarro was up to when he wasn't playing golf. At ten to nine, he turned into Calle Pablo Picasso in the coastal resort of Vespella. He parked near the security entrance to the exclusive Vespella Nou urbanisation, where luxury houses covered the headland, overlooking the sea. At nine o'clock, a burgundy Lexus saloon moved through the gate. Navarro waved to the guard and then turned left, inland. After a few moments, Boyle pulled out and followed at a distance. The Lexus took the autovia near Castell d'Aro and got off at the exit to Santa Nuria d'Aro. When he got to the bottom of the off ramp, he saw the Lexus take a right turn at the roundabout towards Santa Nuria village, which so far was the same route Señor Navarro would take if he were on his way to the golf club. On the verge to Boyle's right was a *Mossos* police car with an officer in the passenger seat. Another officer stood outside the car. Boyle didn't recognise him; possibly he was a new recruit. He looked at Boyle's Rover and the British registration and frowned as he waved him over. Boyle drove onto the verge, irritated by the interruption to his surveillance.

The *Mosso* approached the car with confidence and leaned down to talk to Boyle. 'I would like to see your driver's licence, please,' he said haltingly in English. Boyle realised he had just been stopped so the officer could practise his English. Many of the Catalans, when they weren't speaking their own language, preferred to speak English rather than Spanish. Grandparents and great grandparents had told their families about the violence, deprivation and injustice during the Spanish Civil War. They associated these dark memories with the Spanish language. As the old people died off, the young Catalans remembered for them.

Boyle handed over his British driving licence, which the officer read with great solemnity.

'And there is my tax disc,' Boyle said, pointing to it on his windscreen. He had lost his trail on Señor Navarro; he would now just go with the flow.

The officer read it. 'January,' he said. 'It is nearly time to make new one.'

'Yes, it is nearly time to renew it.' Boyle enunciated every word.

'Renew it,' repeated the officer with a smile.

'That's right,' said Boyle, who wasn't looking forward to the drive all the way back to England in his rickety car in icy cold January just to have it MOT'd.

Boyle arrived at the church of Sant Feliu in Llagostera for Felipe's funeral mass and immediately zipped up his Barbour jacket against the cold of the damp stone. These old churches were freezing. Inside were mostly elderly women, *las señoras mayores*, sitting at the back of the church, hunched over their shopping baskets on wheels. Boyle sat at the front with the straggly funeral party, recognising few of the people there. Eduardo Clavaguera gave Boyle a friendly smile and then continued his quiet conversation with Quimet

Navarro and his pretty wife Lola, who was enveloped in a fur coat. Boyle also spotted the balding, portly bar owner from Santa Nuria, Alfonso Serra, and his wife Maria. He had no idea that Alfonso and Maria knew Felipe. There was a woman crying, who he guessed to be Felipe's helper, Dolores. He had not spoken to Juanita since Felipe's death but he had sent a card and flowers. He wondered how Juanita was going to cope with both her son and husband dead within a month. She had lost everything.

The casket, topped with a bouquet of white lilies, appeared just after ten, rolled in by two young funeral workers. Juanita followed behind, dressed in a black trouser suit. Father Vall, an elderly priest with a grey pudding bowl haircut, appeared at the altar in his requiem white and purple robes. Before Juanita took a seat near the casket, she gave a sad, thankful smile to each of the mourners.

Boyle tried to follow the mass but it was punctured by the constant slamming of the church door as the Catalan women left to do their shopping and then again as they returned, just in time for the communion. Boyle then heard them, as the mass drew to a close, attempting to whisper with their loud, croaky voices, comparing the price of fruits and vegetables. *They'd never get away with that in England,* he thought, holding back a smile.

After the service, the funeral party walked to the

cemetery behind the hearse. Father Vall and Dolores walked on either side of Juanita, helping to keep her upright. People stood at the side of the road to show their respect as they progressed through the town. Eduardo Clavaguera edged his way over to Boyle. He was sombre but friendly and Boyle wondered if he was the sort of person who didn't hold a grudge, a bit like his sister-in-law, Montse.

They talked in low voices about Juanita and Felipe and then Boyle said, 'Why didn't you tell me that Felipe had shot your first wife?' He was uncertain whether he was still on the case or not but out of habit, his mind still worked on the puzzle.

Eduardo reeled around. 'The problem with private detectives – and the police in general – is that you often try to make something out of nothing. You have too much time, too much imagination and not enough evidence. A dangerous combination.'

'Why won't you answer my question?'

'It didn't even occur to me to tell you about the shooting. I admit, I hated Felipe at first, but that was thirty years ago. Felipe served his time in prison. And now the poor man has just died. I have tried to move on.'

'Tried to move on? From what?' asked Boyle.

'My wife's death.'

What, Eduardo Clavaguera still mourns his first wife?

Eduardo looked at Boyle with a certain empathy, as if he knew exactly what he was thinking. 'You and I have something in common. We have both lost someone we love, tragically early,' said Eduardo, his voice cracking.

'But you are happy with your wife now, aren't you? You have children together.'

Eduardo shrugged and lowered his voice. 'It does not make one bit of difference. I still think about Teresa, every day. I love Tina, don't misunderstand. She is a wonderful wife and has given me two lovely children, but she will never be to me what Teresa was. No one could ever take Teresa's place.' There were tears in Eduardo's eyes. 'The death of Felipe brings it back even more.'

What Eduardo is telling me is giving him even more motivation for killing Cisco, thought Boyle. *But then again, everyone – including Eduardo – keeps saying that Cisco was like a son to him.* 'How did you find out that Cisco was Felipe's son?'

'That was very interesting. It was about two years ago. He was working on a family portrait. It was the one with his mother and father and Cisco as a baby. Do you know it?'

Boyle nodded, remembering the mural of Cisco's family from Casa Cielo.

'I was watching Cisco's technique with the spray can,' continued Eduardo with growing excitement.

'He was detailing the man's face. I had noticed this face in other portraits of Cisco's. You know how some artists seem to paint the same faces over and over? Usually they are of family or a lover. Well, this face was eerily recognisable, but I was unable to place it. Cisco was working from a photograph he held in his hand. I asked him to show me the photograph. When I looked at it, it just clicked. The man was Felipe Puig.'

'Did Cisco know what his father had done?' asked Boyle.

'No.'

'Did you tell him?'

Eduardo looked away from Boyle. *Is it guilt?* Boyle wondered.

'Yes. I don't know if I should have. But when I became certain he knew nothing about what his father had done, I told him. I thought it my duty to tell him,' said Eduardo.

'What was his reaction?'

'He was devastated. But then he said it all made sense. It explained how secretive his father was. Cisco had never met any of his father's family. They were mortified by what he had done and all moved to Andalucía after he was sent to prison.'

They turned a corner and saw the *cementerio* at the end of the road. Boyle thought about what Eduardo had said. Was it right for him to tell Cisco about his father? Perhaps he did it to get back at

Felipe for killing his wife. 'Did you ever tell your wife or children about this connection?'

'No, of course not, and I don't think Cisco told his mother or father either. She hasn't mentioned it. It was just between Cisco and myself.'

That did not quite add up. Boyle thought about what Juanita had told him; that Felipe and Cisco constantly confided in each another. Surely Cisco would have told his father what he had found out. It would have been a vital piece of information. Perhaps that is when the father and son became close. Either way, Cisco knew exactly who Teresa was and also that his father was responsible for her death.

The *cementerio* was enclosed by high white walls, which they entered through an archway. The place was empty and the air still. A buzzard hovered overhead. The burial sites, *los nichos*, were in the main walls of the cemetery, stacked four rows high and covering most of the interior wall, the walls deep enough to take a full casket. Boyle shuddered. He loathed cemeteries. The burial service was short. When Boyle was asked to help with the coffin, all he could think was, *God give me strength*, as he, along with Eduardo and the funeral men, and the help of a ladder, struggled to lift Felipe Perez to the top tier of the wall, four flights up, to his final resting place. He would need a drink after this.

When Boyle exited the cemetery with the funeral

party, he saw flashing blue lights. There was a *Mossos* squad car waiting outside, along with an official hearse. Juanita was approached by two policemen. The priest asked them why they were there but he was pushed aside. It all happened so quickly. One officer handcuffed Juanita while the other told her that she was being arrested for the murder of Felipe Perez. She screamed and kicked out, hitting both officers. Boyle moved towards them. The officer behind Juanita grabbed her under the arms and the one in front lifted her by the legs and began to advise her of her rights. She continued to kick wildly. Boyle followed them as they carried her to the police car. She looked at him with panic and screamed, 'I would never hurt Felipe. Why are they doing this?'

'I don't know. But you must be quiet, stay calm. You must relax or you could get hurt. Just go with them. I'll ring Montse. We'll sort everything out.'

She obeyed Boyle and relaxed as the police placed her in the back seat.

'Where are you taking her?' Boyle asked the arresting officer.

'To Girona.'

Juanita watched in horror as two men from the coroner's office entered the cemetery. There was a collective sigh, no one in any doubt that the coroners had come to take away Felipe's body.

Boyle rang Montse on his mobile. She told him

that she would go straight to the *comissaria* in Girona and would ring him after she had spoken to Juanita and the authorities. He then rang Rosa on her mobile and left a message. He feared it would do little good ringing her this time anyway. She knew nothing. She was with the Sant Martí police and they had no jurisdiction over Girona.

20

Boyle sat at the family table in the El Dorado restaurant, drinking a glass of beer before lunch. He kept his smart phone on the table, waiting to hear from Montse. Carmen was doing last-minute checks on the tables, looking radiant in a deep red dress. By the time she was able to sit down with him, he was already on his main course – one of his favourites, *arroz parellada*. Boyle thought about Juanita. Could she have killed her husband? Was it possible that when Juanita heard that Felipe was responsible for Teresa Clavaguera's death, which possibly led to her son's death, it tipped her over the edge? If so, how did she do it? And most confusing of all was that if the police did think it was murder, then why did they release the body for burial in the first place? Carmen was shocked when Boyle told her that Juanita had been arrested for the murder of her husband. She asked what the funeral was like.

'Sad. Juanita has no one now.'

'*¡Pobrecita!*'

'I had a long talk with Eduardo Clavaguera. You know, he told me that he still misses his first wife.'

'I suppose you never get over something like that.'

'It just surprised me to hear him say it. I thought he was besotted with Tina.'

Carmen leaned across the table towards him. 'Well, you know I don't like to gossip,' she said with a cheeky smile.

'Not much,' he said.

'But the rumour is that Salvador Clavaguera and Tina have been having an affair for years. There is even talk that Laura is his daughter.'

Boyle was staggered, not certain whether to believe another of Carmen's "rumours", but he said, 'That would explain why Salvador and the girl are so close. And if Eduardo is still in love with his first wife, it gives Tina motivation to stray,' he said. 'How old is Laura?'

'About eighteen,' she said. 'They had been married several years before Laura was born, plenty of time to cheat. Personally, I find it difficult to believe that Tina ever had an affair with her brother-in-law. Every time I see Eduardo and Tina together, they look so happy. I saw them at Fiesta Mayor this year and they looked totally devoted to each other, holding hands...' she said, glancing at the door for customers.

Eduardo had told Boyle that he had adored his first wife and that Tina could never mean to him what his first wife did. But that wasn't how Carmen was now describing it.

Carmen turned her warm brown eyes to Boyle. 'I think that Eduardo and Tina are soulmates. And I consider myself a good judge. I can read people.'

Boyle glanced down at his glass of *vino tinto*, hoping she was unable to read him, and wondered how she could have married a shit like her ex-husband, if she was such a good judge of people.

'They are like you and Ana,' said Carmen. 'They are a couple who are truly at one with each other. And that's hard to find.'

'Yes,' said Boyle, thinking that he had managed the impossible, that he might have found the same *simpatico* with Carmen that he had had with Ana, if only Carmen would realise it. He heard the front door to the restaurant open behind him as a customer entered.

Carmen smiled in such a way at the customer that Boyle knew with certainty that her recent transformation into this sensuous being had nothing to do with him and everything to do with the man who had just walked through the door. His stomach sank. He didn't look up.

'*Bona tarda*, Carmen.' The man spoke with a deep, rich Catalan voice.

'*Jordi, bona tarda*,' said Carmen as she rose to her feet, a bit flustered, Boyle now forgotten.

Boyle wanted to see the man who inspired her enchantment but once again, he pretended great interest in the dregs of his *vino tinto*, raising the glass, swilling and drinking it down. Once they had passed, he looked up and saw Carmen lead him to a table on the far side of the room. Jordi looked to be in his late forties and was definitely shorter than him, he thought with satisfaction. He looked like a socialist politician with his overly long hair, jeans and brown leather jacket. Where had Carmen met him? He hadn't noticed him in the restaurant before. *So much for Carmen having no time for a social life,* he thought with resignation.

By the time Boyle had finished with his lunch, he still hadn't heard from Montse or Rosa and he had seen enough of Carmen's lovesick smile as she waited on Jordi personally and they flirted quietly. What was worse, the rest of the customers looked on with broad smiles of encouragement, happy for the lovebirds. Boyle slipped out without saying goodbye.

Driving down the track to his house, he noticed Tina Clavaguera's Land Rover and Salvador Clavaguera's grey Mercedes sedan parked below in the woods. He heard shouting; someone was having a row. He pulled over, got out of the car and from behind an umbrella pine watched Tina and Salvador approach their vehicles, dressed in bright hunting jackets with rifles slung over their shoulders. Salvador was doing most of the shouting, clearly giving his sister-in-law a piece of his mind. They were too far away for Boyle to understand most of it, but he did hear Laura's name mentioned once. Tina ignored Salvador, opening the back of her SUV and laying a brace of rabbits inside. Salvador was raising his finger, pointing at her, to emphasise what he had to say. Finally, she lifted her palm to his face.

"¡*Cállate la boca!*" she yelled. Fuming, he got into his sedan, slammed the door and backed out in a cloud of dust. Tina watched the car disappear, then took out her mobile and made a call.

Is there any truth to the talk that Laura was Salvador and Tina's daughter? Boyle thought. *Could they be arguing about her drug addiction?* Laura appeared to be sober when Boyle saw her at the *inmobiliaria*, but that didn't change the fact that she was paralytic the day before and still had a huge drug problem. Were Tina and Salvador at odds on which way to help Laura? They may have been lovers in the past but it didn't look like that now.

Boyle settled down on his terrace with a bottle of beer and watched the swifts and swallows fly through the air, feeding on mosquitos. It was the time of day he loved best, when everything was bathed in a golden light particular to the Vall d'Aro, light that Ana told him had given the valley its name. The wait was soon over. Montse rang as he started on his second bottle.

'They've formally charged Juanita with the murder of her husband.'

Boyle had thought as much. 'What proof?'

'There is a burn on Felipe's nose consistent with suffocation. A pillow was placed over the face. They say he fought hard.'

'Why was the body released?' said Boyle, with an anger that surprised him.

'A trainee *forense medico* missed the burn. When the boss got back from holiday and saw the photos of Felipe's face, she was furious and immediately ordered the body back.'

'What does Juanita say?'

'That she didn't do it.'

'Do you believe her?'

'Yes. You know she genuinely loved her husband. There is no doubt about that, although it is hard to believe, after all the times he beat her.'

'What about bail?'

'There's a court hearing on Monday. There is something interesting though. Juanita says she felt drugged when she woke that morning. At first, she put it down to the fact that Felipe had died and didn't mention it to anyone. But in retrospect, she thinks it was a severe reaction to a drug the murderer had given her; she had headaches, nausea and joint pain. I was thinking possibly a gas of some sort...'

'Chlorophyll?'

'Yes, something like that. It has been used in many of the burglaries around here. Also, she woke at 11am, which is unusually late for her. And had it not been for a customer ringing the bell to pick up her clothes, she might have slept much later still. But that fact is working against her at the moment. The detectives don't believe she was drugged and are asking why she waited so long to call the police when Felipe had clearly died in the middle of the night.'

'They should give her a blood test as soon as possible.'

'I have asked for it.'

'And ask the *forense medico* to check Felipe's body for gas inhalation.'

'Okay.'

'Have the forensic team gone over Juanita's flat?'

'As we speak.'

As Boyle drove to Llagostera, the glare of the sun hurt his eyes as it set behind the Pyrenees. A white forensic van was parked outside the block of flats. The windows from Juanita's flat glowed brightly, moving shadows of the police inside. The entry phone pad to the building showed eight flats. It was not functioning along with the door to the block. The door was closed to flat 1, which belonged to Juanita, and had yellow and black police tape across it. The lock on the door was a simple spring-latch one, easily opened with a slim piece of metal, like the one Boyle carried in his wallet. Juanita didn't have to keep her door unlocked, or even open, to invite in unwanted guests. Of the seven neighbouring flats, Boyle spoke to people in four of them. They were, for the most part, older and told him they had heard nothing on the night Felipe was killed. In flat 2, opposite Juanita, a young chatty mother told Boyle that she was away at her parents' house that night and also informed him that the elderly woman in flat 3, the one next to Juanita, wasn't answering her door because she was in Trueta Hospital in Girona. When Boyle asked what day she had entered the hospital, she said that she was unsure but Señora Deulofeu was still there when she went to her parents' house. He wrote down the name of the elderly woman: Maria Rosa Deulofeu.

As Boyle stood outside the block of flats, the hair prickled on the back of his neck. Was he being watched? The temperature had dropped and he raised the collar of his jacket. He glanced over at the windows of the residences opposite. They were dotted with people staring out at the police activity. In the shadows across the road, behind the neighbourhood dumpster, stood a man, his gaze focused on Boyle. He was well-built and wearing a hoody. Boyle took off towards him at a brisk walk and the man ran off at great speed between two buildings. Boyle hurried after him. When he reached the back of the buildings, he saw the man running in the distance, towards the edge of town. Boyle followed. The man took a quick right and slipped on the damp cobblestones, not quite falling but allowing Boyle to close the gap between them. They raced up a dark street of small terraced houses, Boyle gaining on him. Boyle could hear a powerful car engine rumbling behind him. He glanced back. The navy-blue Porsche SUV was just turning into the road. Suddenly it gunned its engine, took off, and came straight for Boyle. There were no gaps between the houses, which were flush with the pavement. Boyle flattened himself in a doorway and the car squealed towards him, mounted the pavement and then turned sharply, missing him by inches. Boyle had no doubt that if the car could have hit him without hitting the house, he would now be dead. The hooded man at the top of the road glared at him. Boyle showed him two fingers. The SUV came alongside the man, he jumped in and they sped off.

21

The following Sunday morning, at ten to nine, Boyle parked outside the Vespella Nou urbanisation and waited for the burgundy Lexus of Quimet Navarro. Hopefully today he would find out where Navarro was spending his time when he was supposed to be playing golf. Boyle was driving a blue Corsa that he often borrowed from his father-in-law. He thought it was a better surveillance car than his British registration Rover but even so, over the years he had come to realise that many people up to no good had no idea who was tailing them. You could follow them in a Churchill tank and they wouldn't notice.

Twenty minutes later, near the golf course in Santa Nuria, Boyle parked around the corner from the cul-de-sac that Señor Navarro had just pulled into. He took a rucksack from his car and ran up the road. The Lexus was parked outside one of two houses normally rented out for the summer and now shuttered up. Navarro got out of the car. He was humming to himself as he opened the gate, walked up the path to the door and let himself in. The chimney was puffing smoke. Someone had lit a nice fire for Señor Navarro.

Boyle crept to the far side of the house next door and into the back garden and followed a path up the steep hill, through the scrub, cork and umbrella pine to the top of a ridge. He sat down under a small tree that overlooked the house. The wooden shutters behind the house had been folded back, and on the terrace, a small table with two chairs had been made ready with a setting for two. Taking a pair of binoculars out of his rucksack, he trained them on the house but the reflection made it impossible to see inside. He poured himself a coffee from the thermos he had packed. He knew he could be in for a long wait. Every Sunday, Navarro told his wife that he played a leisurely game of golf with friends and afterwards had a drink and a plate of pasta in the bar. That could be five hours.

Over the following two hours, as the temperature rose, the smoke from the chimney dwindled to a wisp.

In all that time, no one had come outside. The sun had moved over the house, lighting up the back garden. Boyle took off his sweatshirt, enjoying the warmth. He liked the meditative nature of surveillance; he could sit still for hour after hour. A basic truth of some sort often emerged. That simple truth is what drove Boyle. He didn't understand God or the universe. He hadn't a clue. But he could usually identify who had done what to whom and sometimes even figure out why.

There was movement in the living room. The French doors opened and Señor Navarro stepped out wearing a dressing gown, carrying a bottle of wine and two glasses. A woman followed, holding a tray with two bowls of food, possibly pasta... pasta? Wasn't that what his wife said he had after a game of golf? Perhaps there was some truth to what he was telling her after all. Long dark hair over her shoulders, barefoot and dressed in nothing but a white gossamer shift, she glided up to the table. Señor Navarro watched her every step of the way. She looked familiar. Boyle lifted his binoculars. Of course she was familiar. But what was she doing with Quimet Navarro? Over a leisurely, intimate lunch, Boyle caught the scene on camera and several good close-ups of Quimet Navarro with his mistress – the lovely Tina Clavaguera. Boyle wasn't an expert on male attractiveness, but he knew for certain that if he put a hundred women in a room and asked them to choose between Eduardo Clavaguera and Quimet Navarro, that Eduardo Clavaguera would win hands-down. What was Tina Clavaguera doing with Quimet Navarro? Looks weren't everything, but Quimet had a face only a mother could love.

Boyle went home, showered and changed his clothes and headed down to his office in Sant Martí. After downloading the photographs, he examined them on his laptop and deleted the bad shots.

Then he went for a walk. The Sunday market in Sant Martí was closing down; just a few of the fruit and vegetable sellers were there, packing unsold food into the back of vans. He stopped outside the El Dorado and debated on whether he should join Carmen and her children for lunch. Normally, everyone in the Ferran family had their own plans for Sunday lunch. Rosa and Montse would be on their way to Tossa de Mar, Narcis and Esther would be at Can Salvi on the front, and Carmen would be with her children at El Dorado. As for Boyle, he usually kept to himself on this day. It had been different when Ana was alive. They used to all meet up at El Dorado then. But after her death, the family had split somehow and now made separate plans for the day.

As he peered through the glass wall of El Dorado, he decided to change that and have lunch here; they were his family, after all, his only family. The restaurant was full. Waiting customers crowded the reception area and obscured his view of Carmen and her children at their table in the far corner. He was surprised to catch a glimpse of Narcis and Esther sitting there with Isabella and Antonio, and there was someone else there as well. Isabella was sitting next to a girl who looked unfamiliar. *She must have brought a friend from school,* Boyle thought. And then, like a jolt, he saw Jordi at the bar, taking a tray of drinks from Carmen. It felt like a gut punch. Boyle then watched Jordi carry the drinks over to the table and serve them, something he always used to do. Everyone appeared to be in good spirits, which only worsened Boyle's own. He would rather lunch with the seagulls at the tip near Solius than eat here.

Boyle drove inland. Thirty-five minutes later he pulled into the carpark at the Josep Trueta Hospital in Girona. He went to the enquiries desk and asked for Maria Rosa Deulofeu, and was sent to the orthopaedic ward.

The corridor in the orthopaedic ward was noisy with visitors crowded round the doorways. The room had two beds, friends and family surrounding each one. It was easy to guess which one was Rosa Maria Deulofeu. In one, there was a young woman with her leg in traction, and in the other, an elderly person who looked to be in her seventies with a bruised face and an arm in a long cast. She was sitting up in bed while a middle-aged woman held a drink through a straw to her mouth. In chairs surrounding the bed were a man drinking a bottle of Estrella Damm and two teenage children with their eyes glued to the screens of their smart phones. Boyle stood at the end of the bed, introduced himself and said that he would like to speak to Maria Rosa Deulofeu, and then added the little lie that he was helping the police.

The woman wiped the face of the patient and went up to him. 'Maria Rosa is my mother,' she said with a low voice.

'I'm sorry about her injuries.' They both turned and stared at her mother. 'They look quite severe. Can you tell me what happened?'

'She was found outside her flat on the floor, early in the morning. The door was wide open. She had fallen; we don't know when.'

'What day was this?'

'The twentieth of September.'

The same day Felipe died. Boyle thought the injuries severe for a fall; she must have gone down hard. 'Have the police spoken to her yet?'

'No, a neighbour found her and called an ambulance. No one rang the police – not that I'm aware of, anyway.'

'Is it alright if I speak to her?'

'Of course. But you must keep in mind that they just operated on her arm and she is never in her right mind after an anaesthetic. I don't know how helpful she's going to be. Mama, this man wants to ask you about your fall,' she said. Boyle sat down and faced the woman. She smiled.

'Are you the police?'

'I'm helping the police. I'd like to know why you were outside your flat on the morning of the twentieth.'

'I heard some noise. I always wear my hearing aid to bed because I'm frightened if I can't hear. There are so many break-ins in the neighbourhood.'

'Then what happened?'

'I opened my front door and saw two robbers coming out of Juanita's flat. I demanded to know what they were doing. They said nothing but one of them walked up to me and pushed me forwards onto my face. The next thing I remember, I was here, in hospital.'

'Why do you say they were robbers?'

'Because they were carrying big bags. They had stolen things from Juanita and Felipe – I'm sure of it.'

Or were carrying gas paraphernalia inside. 'Do you remember anything about these men? What they looked like?'

'They were big. Dressed in dark clothes – jeans, sweatshirts. One had curly hair.'

Boyle turned to the daughter. 'Why didn't you call the police?'

'We just heard about it this morning and didn't

believe it. After her last anaesthetic she thought the nurses were trying to kill her. She gets paranoid. She's been operated on several times. They've tried different drugs to put her to sleep but she is always the same. It only ever lasts a few days, *gracias a Dios*.'

Boyle told them he would have the police come over to take a statement from Maria Rosa and requested that the daughter mention nothing of her mother's post-operative paranoia.

First thing Monday morning, Boyle went into the office, printed off the photos of Señor Navarro and Tina and wrote up a report. Montse was attending a court hearing for Juanita Perez in Girona so would not be back until midday. With time to spare, he wandered through the *calles* of Sant Martí thinking about Cisco Perez. A case that had begun as an investigation into the death of the graffiti artist now included two other people, Teresa Clavaguera and Felipe Perez. The deaths were all related, Boyle was certain of that. The problem was that Juanita was in prison and Boyle was unsure how to proceed. Unable to let go, he mulled over them – at least it kept his mind occupied and prevented it from wandering towards Carmen. He was sitting on a bench in the Rambla gazing up at one of the jacaranda trees when Montse rang and asked him to meet her at the office.

'Juanita was refused bail, but we never expected her to get it,' said Montse, sitting behind her desk. 'But it went as well as could be expected from a system with a four-year backlog.'

'How is she doing?'

'Looking a bit thinner. And alright considering that if it doesn't go her way, she could spend the next ten years in prison.'

'I don't think she did it,' said Boyle.

'I agree, but try and convince the judge of that.'

He then told her about the neighbour who he interviewed in hospital. Montse was encouraged by the news and immediately called the Police in Llagostera and asked them to go to the hospital and get a statement, pronto.

'By the way, I have something for you,' he said. He took the photographs of Señor Navarro and Tina Clavaguera with the report from his briefcase and laid them out in front of her. He had wondered, since Navarro was one of the people he was investigating, if he should keep the photos back to be used later as possible leverage, but had decided against it.

Montse looked through the photographs, muttering "*madre mía*" several times. 'What is she doing there?'

'You'd think you would be used to it by now,' he said.

'Never.'

'Do me a favour. Don't let Lola or Quimet Navarro know I was investigating this. And can you wait until this case is over before you reveal Tina Clavaguera as the mistress?'

Montse nodded. 'Don't worry, it can all wait. Telling Lola Navarro that her husband is having an affair with Tina Clavaguera will cause an earthquake in their social circle.'

Boyle had decided not to bring up the subject of Carmen's new boyfriend, but it didn't take long for Montse to bring him up.

'Carmen has been off with the fairies since she met him,' she said. 'It's about time she found someone. *Ojala!* I hope it works out. She has pined over that jerk Pau long enough.'

'I hadn't noticed Jordi in Sant Martí before,' said Boyle, feigning disinterest.

'He's from Barcelona. Forty-five years of age. Divorced, but it is an unusual situation because his wife left him for someone else.'

'It can't be that unusual, surely?' Boyle wanted to discredit this usurper in any way he possibly could.

'I assure you, Adrian, it is. How many bad wives have you investigated for me?'

'Not many.'

'Try zero. He has a teenage daughter,' said Montse.

Who must be the girl I saw yesterday with Isabella.
'What does he do?'

'He is a professor of languages at Barcelona University, specialising in English,' said Montse, pursing her lips, clearly impressed. 'And he spends his free time giving free Spanish lessons to Moroccan immigrants.'

A goody-goody, thought Boyle, *the worst sort of creep.* He hated himself for being so mean-spirited but there was no way he could feel positive about this man. 'How did they meet?'

'Over the internet, on a site called *Las Parejas. com*,' she said.

Boyle looked at her with astonishment.

'It is a perfectly acceptable way to meet someone,' she explained. Moving closer, she added. 'In this century, anyway.'

Boyle took a notebook and pen from his jacket pocket. 'What's his full name?'

'*Hombre. Tranquillo.* I have already done an internet search on him.'

'Then there is no harm in putting his name through the police system, which I think might be slightly more accurate than the internet.'

Montse gave him a knowing, sympathetic smile. 'His name is Jordi Tura I Herrero. Professor.'

When Boyle got back to his office, he called Rosa on her mobile. She was unavailable so he left a message asking her to put a check through on Carmen's boyfriend. As soon as Boyle hung up, Deirdre Clavaguera rang.

'I've got some very good news for you, Adrian. I have someone who wants to buy your house.'

He paused, caught off-guard. He hadn't expected much interest in the house, let alone offers to buy; people he knew were taking up to seven years to sell. 'It's so soon. When did they see the house?'

'He already knows it.'

'Who is it?'

'Quimet Navarro. He remembers when the house was first built in the fifties. Says he's always loved it. He's willing to pay you the asking price. Four hundred and fifty thousand.'

That surprised Boyle. Why did Quimet Navarro want his house? He had a mansion on the posh Vespella Nou estate overlooking the sea. Was it to be used as a love nest for his affair with Tina Clavaguera? The asking price of four hundred and fifty thousand had been a joke price that Boyle had thought he would never receive. His mind raced. There were many things he could do with that kind of money. He had no mortgage. He could move back to England; he had no family there, but there were still friends. Or he could buy a flat in Sant Martí. Or buy a boat and go fishing; not that he had fished – or even sailed – much, but he could start.

'It's too soon,' he said finally. 'I'm not ready to leave this house.'

'He'll be very disappointed. Just think about it. Alright, Adrian?'

'Yes, alright,' said Boyle, certain that nothing would change. He wasn't about to sell. It surprised him. Until that moment, he had not realised just how attached he was to his tiny house on Pedralta.

Father Vall, the priest who had said Felipe's funeral mass, turned up at Boyle's office after lunch. He was dressed in a black suit and dog collar. Boyle welcomed him in and gave him a seat. The priest told Boyle that Juanita wanted to thank him for his help in finding Maria Rosa Deulofeu – so far, the only witness in Felipe's murder case. But rather than asking Boyle to follow on with that investigation to get her out of police custody, Juanita asked that he continue with the investigation into Cisco's death; she thought Cisco's and Felipe's death were committed by the same people. Boyle thought the same and told the priest that he was back on board.

Father Vall then told Boyle that the exhibition of Cisco's paintings in Barcelona, at the Clavaguera Gallery, was going ahead and that Juanita wanted Boyle to go in her place. Boyle thought that it would be a good opportunity for sleuthing.

The priest handed Boyle an envelope. 'That should keep you going for a while.'

Boyle glanced inside. There were ten one-hundred euro notes.

'Whose money is this?' he asked, laying the envelope on his desk.

The priest hesitated before answering. 'It is from friends who are trying to help her.'

'Juanita told me that she had no friends.'

'She has more friends than you know. She may not know it, but many people care deeply about her, including me. She is a good woman. She did not murder her husband.'

22

Bar Can Rui d'Or was set behind the petrol station on the main road through the village of Santa Nuria. Boyle parked beside a dirt-covered area at the front, shaded with tall plane trees. In between the trees were red plastic tables, kept outside all year round. He passed the huge grill near the door. Ana had loved coming here for breakfast on Saturdays. You went inside to choose whatever meat you wanted, then came back out and threw it on the barbeque.

He had seen the owner of the bar, Alfonso Serra, at Felipe's funeral and wanted to know how they were connected. Juanita had described her husband as a friendless man, so perhaps Alfonso was one of Felipe's few friends. Boyle was curious as to whether he had been in contact with Felipe post-prison.

Inside, Alfonso was sitting behind the bar, smoking and reading *El Punt*. 'Adrian, nice to see you,' he said as he closed the paper, eased himself off the high stool and went to the espresso machine. '*Cortado*?' he asked with his raspy, forty-cigarettes-a-day voice.

'Yes, please.'

Alfonso set down a small glass of espresso and topped it off with steamed milk. He brought up the subject. 'I was surprised to see you at Felipe's funeral. Did you know him?'

'I know Juanita. I have been investigating their son's death.'

'She's loco! Smothering her poor husband like that. What kind of wife does that?'

'How well did you know her?'

'I never met her before. It's no wonder Felipe didn't want me to meet her.'

Boyle knew the reason Felipe kept his wife away from his friends – he was afraid she would find out about his prison term. He thought that if the jury for Juanita's case was going to be as generous as Alfonso, then Juanita had better prepare herself for a long stay in prison.

'How did you know him?' Boyle asked.

'We grew up together. As kids, we used to play all over here.' Alfonso waved his hand around, indicating. 'In the river, up in the hills, all over. He was born in Can Roca; it was a small farm that Felipe's family rented from the Clavagueras. This was before the Clavagueras ruined everything and sold the land to build the urbanisation and golf course – but don't get me started on that! It was all farmland then. Beautiful. Now, with all this building, it's too much. Fifty years ago, there were eight hundred people in our village, now we have nearly five thousand. Everyone tells me the people have got to live somewhere. But I say. "Why don't they go and live somewhere else?" They don't *all* have to live here in Santa Nuria. And the foreigners!' He caught himself, realising who he was talking to, and laughed. 'I always forget you're a foreigner, Adrian. You were married to Ana for so long, you became a Ferran. Anyway, I'm half Basque. You're probably more Catalan than I am.'

Boyle gave a rueful laugh, knowing that however long he lived here, no matter how well he spoke Catalan, with his pale hair and eyes, he would never be thought of as anything other than *extranjero*.

'So, when was the last time you saw Felipe?' asked Boyle, getting back to the subject.

'Two years ago, maybe three. I hadn't seen him since he went to prison. I tried to visit him there but he wouldn't see me, he wouldn't see anyone. Then one day he just walked in here.'

'What did you talk about?'

'Nothing really. He just said he wanted to say hello to me and Maria Dolores. He didn't look too good. That shooting accident ruined his life.'

'This was presumably before his stroke?'

'I knew nothing about the stroke until the day of his funeral. I figure that's why he stopped coming in.'

'He came in often?'

'Three, maybe four times.'

'So, was he alone?'

'Yes,' said Alfonso, and then he looked up as if remembering something. 'No, that's not right. The last time he came in here he was with someone.'

'Who was that?'

'Quimet Navarro. The big man,' he said, puffing his chest out in imitation.

'How do you know him?'

'We grew up together, Felipe, Quimet and me. The three musketeers. But Quimet was the ambitious one. He's done very well for himself.'

'I hear he hasn't sold a flat in months,' said Boyle.

'Serves him right. He is greedy. But he's worked hard for everything he's got. Not like Eduardo Clavaguera, who had it all handed to him on a silver platter.'

'Eduardo has built up quite a collection of paintings,' said Boyle, fishing.

'Paintings? Bah! I'm not interested in that stuff. That's not work.'

A fierce wind was forcing white horses across the sea. Fincas Deirdre was still open. Through the window, Boyle could see Laura Clavaguera behind her desk. When he entered the shop, Laura got up and rushed to him.

'I heard that Juanita was arrested for killing her husband.'

News travelled fast in the Vall d'Aro. 'Yes, isn't it terrible? But unfortunately, I know nothing about the circumstances,' Boyle lied. He was not going to discuss the case with Laura. He was here to talk about her relationship with Cisco.

'It's so awful. Unbelievable,' she said, wide-eyed. 'How could she do something like that?'

'I don't know. It is truly a dreadful situation.' Boyle paused a moment to let Laura know that no other information on Juanita would be forthcoming. 'Laura, I'd like to ask you a few questions, if I may.'

'About Juanita?'

'No, Cisco and you.'

'Of course. It's nearly closing time anyway.' If Laura was worried, it didn't show. She closed the shop and they went to the coffee bar across the road and minutes later were both sipping *cortados*.

'Señor Boyle, I am really sorry about the way I

behaved last week. I had a relapse after Cisco died. I was feeling sorry for myself and took lots of downers and some cocaine. I had been off drugs a year. But when he died, I found it impossible to cope.'

'Are you attending a self-help group?'

'Yes. Narcotics Anonymous. Do you know it?'

'Yes,' said Boyle. When he was a detective, he became familiar with most of the twelve-step programs through his work; alcohol, drugs, sex and gambling – and that was just the police. 'Is it helping you?'

'I get comfort from it. I realise there are people with problems like mine. I don't feel so alone,' she said. Her face was pale and tense.

'It will get easier. But you need to give yourself time.'

'Cisco has been dead less than a month,' she said to herself. Then she looked at Boyle. 'Sometimes it feels like no time at all, and then it can feel like it's been forever.'

Boyle nodded. He knew that feeling.

She put her elbows on the table, cupped her chin in her hands and looked him straight in the face. 'No one is interested. My family seem to be glad that Cisco is gone. The police aren't interested. And here you are, taking the time to look into what actually happened to him.'

'Do you think it was more than an accident?' asked Boyle.

'I don't know.'

'What car do you drive?'

'A silver Clio. But Eduardo took my car away when he caught me driving high on cocaine last year. I haven't driven since.'

Boyle remembered seeing the car at the Clavaguera estate. There was a possibility it was the silver car that sped through the woods just after Cisco died. 'Is there a reason you call your father by his Christian name?'

She shrugged and smiled. 'Probably because some of my friends call their parents by their first name.'

'Because it's the thing to do?'

'Yes.' She gave him another sweet smile. 'You know, you are a funny man.'

'In what way?'

'Perhaps it's because you are English, perhaps that's it,' she said, leaning her head to one side as she gazed at him, positively beaming. Laura Clavaguera did have charm after all, and she was trying to use it on Boyle.

'I'm sorry to ask this Laura, but where were you when Cisco fell?'

Her smile dipped and she lowered her face. 'I was at my parents' house with my brother and father,' she said.

'Your brother was in Barcelona that night.'

'That's right.'

'What time did he arrive at your house for lunch?'

'Eleven or so. I know it was in the morning. It could have even been earlier.'

So, Eduardo, Miguel and Laura all had alibis. They were together at the family *masia* in Santa Nuria. 'Were you having lunch with your father and brother?'

'Yes. If I had been at Casa Cielo, Cisco never would have died.'

'How so?'

'I wouldn't have let anyone touch him. Or, if it was an accident, I would have been there watching him, telling him to be careful.'

'Did he take chances?'

'Too many. It frightened me when he stood on the roof. I told him that it wasn't necessary to paint every part of the house. But he always wanted to paint the most difficult parts to reach, as well as the easy.'

'Are you going to Cisco's exhibition tomorrow?' asked Boyle.

'I plan to,' she said, her eyes suddenly becoming glassy. 'But I don't know if I'm up to it…' She took a deep breath. 'I miss him, you know.'

'I know you do,' said Boyle.

The tears came. She took a tissue from her bag and dabbed under her eyes. 'But no one cares about Cisco.'

'I do. Now I'm investigating his death,' said Boyle.

'Is that true?'

'Yes. I see how his mother and you are suffering and I want to find some justice for him.' She dried her eyes and smiled at him. 'There are a few things that bother me, though,' he said.

'What things?'

'Luis said that when he left Casa Cielo, your brother was there.'

'He's lying.'

'Why would he do that?'

At that moment Laura's mobile vibrated and she answered. 'Mama,' she said. Then, informing Tina where she was, she put the phone into her bag. Less than two minutes later, a silver Peugeot pulled up outside. Tina Clavaguera was driving. Laura's small white terrier was seated in the passenger seat.

'¡*Cariño!*' Laura called to it, suddenly choked with emotion. The dog saw her and began to bark, frantically scraping its claws on the window. 'I must go,' she said, taking a card out of her bag and writing down a number. 'Here's my mobile number.' She handed him the card. 'If there's any way I can help, please call me. If Cisco was murdered, I want you to find out who did it.'

'Do you think he was murdered?' He handed her his card.

'I have no idea,' she said, her eyes brimming with tears.

Boyle saw Laura out and watched her get inside the car, where she wrapped her arms around the little dog, now hysterical and yelping with delight as he licked her face. In the driver's seat sat Tina, watching Boyle with a stony "if looks could kill" stare.

23

Back in his office, the first thing Boyle did was take a bottle of whisky from the battered filing cabinet and pour himself a generous measure. The golden liquid slipped down easily, warming his throat. There was nothing like it. The sound of children's laughter and banter drifted up from the *calle*. He parted the blinds. The mothers were herding their offspring back to school after their two-hour siesta. Ah, the comfort of routine. Taking another sip, he sat down on the sofa and thought about Tina Clavaguera's hard stare. Why was she so against him speaking to her children if she was convinced they were blameless in Cisco's death? Was there some doubt on her part? He got the impression that Laura was desperate to talk about Cisco but that her family blocked any mention of him.

He took the manila folder containing the notes on Cisco's death and read through them again. There were several unanswered questions. Why were his mobile and sketchbook missing? Who had dumped his motorbike? Had it all been a simple case of robbery gone wrong? Although Boyle thought it unlikely that Cisco was an anti-hunt advocate, there was the possibility that the anti-hunt people went to Casa Cielo and robbed him. Why was the packet of cocaine found near his body when there was absolutely no trace of drugs or alcohol inside his body? Both Gunnar Lundgren and Quimet Navarro had motives to harm him because he had vandalised their property. There was also the possibility that Miguel Clavaguera was lying when he claimed not to have been at Casa Cielo that morning, if Luis Sureda was to be believed and if Laura and Eduardo Clavaguera had been untruthful about Miguel joining them for lunch that day. That would place Cisco's two closest friends there on the day he died.

He poured another drink and read the notes and newspaper clippings on Teresa Clavaguera's death. Eduardo had told Boyle that he had been deeply in love with his first wife – so much so that it eclipsed the love he had for his second wife, Tina. But Carmen had told him how much Eduardo appeared to adore Tina, which did not add up. And what sort of relationship did Faustino Duran have with his sister? He seemed dismissive at first when Boyle spoke to him about her. But the most important question was, why was Cisco painting that portrait of her on the day he died? The two deaths were not only brought together because they happened in the same place, but most importantly because Cisco was painting a portrait of Teresa that depicted the moments before her death. Unlikely to be a coincidence. Some of the men hunting on the day Teresa died were also there when Cisco fell to his death; namely Quimet Navarro, Faustino Duran and Salvador Clavaguera.

And then he thought about the possible murder of Felipe. What was that all about? Was someone trying to shut him up? But why? The moments of clarity for Felipe had been few and far between, but perhaps that was enough for him to reveal something damning enough to threaten someone. Or was Juanita lying? Was she so angry that Felipe had hidden his former life from her that she put a pillow over his face and smothered him? He found this scenario the least likely. He didn't believe that Juanita was a killer.

Boyle's mobile rang. It was Montse. 'Come by the office now, if you can,' she said. 'We have some information on Quimet Navarro.'

When he entered the office, he saw Montse and Rosa pouring over some papers laid out on Montse's enormous desk. Rosa looked up at him and smiled.

'We have had some luck,' she said, gathering up the papers, placing them in a manila folder and handing it to him. He opened it. Inside was a copy of the title deeds, the *escritura de propiedad*.

Boyle looked up at Rosa. 'What is this?'

'Quimet Navarro has bought one hundred and twenty hectares of land on Mount Pedralta from Eduardo Clavaguera, which includes all of the Roca Alba urbanisation below you and then some.'

'Even Faustino's house?' asked Boyle. Faustino's place was the only privately-owned house on the urbanisation besides Boyle's own, which was accessed on a higher track than the urbanisation and not actually part of it. The rest of the houses on the mountain were owned by Eduardo Clavaguera.

'Yes,' said Rosa.

'Why would Faustino suddenly sell? He isn't someone who comes and goes like others on the mountain. He has lived there for years.'

'Perhaps he wants to be nearer his family in Barcelona,' said Montse.

Boyle scanned the page for a date. 'August sixteenth, two thousand and ten,' he read. 'That was over a month ago,' he said with disbelief. Why hadn't Deirdre Clavaguera told him about this? Obviously, this was why Quimet wanted to buy Boyle's house, of course it was.

'There was never a deposit. Quimet just paid for it all outright,' said Montse.

'How much did it cost him?'

'We're not certain,' said Rosa. 'All I heard was that he got it at a very cheap price. It appears that Eduardo Clavaguera was anxious to get rid of the land.'

'Why? He's certainly not desperate for money,' said Boyle.

'Who knows?' said Montse.

'And look,' Rosa said, unfolding a large map of the mountain and placing it down in front of Boyle. 'The land has been re-classified from rural to urban, all set to build. These are the plans for fifty plots. The luxury development will be called Marvista.'

Boyle lent over and examined the topographical print of the mountain. 'Marvista?' he mumbled with derision. Drawn on the map were the proposed plots, fifty large ones. The new urbanisation would border his property then fan out to engulf the woods below, and would stretch down to include some of the higher farmland. Boyle was staggered. It would ruin the mountain. Over the years there had been several people interested in developing a new urbanisation on Pedralta – the views over the whole valley and up the Costa Brava to Palamos were stupendous. But Eduardo had refused to sell. What had changed his mind?

24

It was already dark when Boyle reached the town of Caldes de Malavella. He left his Rover on the dirt stretch of the dimly-lit car park and checked to see if he was being followed. No one drove in after him. Buttoning his tweed jacket up against the chill, he walked fifty yards up the road towards the newly renovated train station. The tiled lobby was cold and empty. After buying the ticket, he exited onto the platform and crossed the tracks to catch the train to Barcelona.

The modern Renfe train to Barcelona pulled in and Boyle climbed on board and managed to find a window seat. As the train accelerated out of the station, progressing south through the foothills, the farmland shrank as the villages and then towns took over, lighting up the landscape. At stops along the way, more passengers boarded. Most of them were joyful couples who appeared to have the same idea as those who had entered the train at Caldes de Malavella – a night out in Barcelona. Boyle imagined they would go to dinner, then possibly the theatre or the cinema or perhaps a concert at the Palau de la Música, and finally for the couples *jóvenes* who had the energy to stay up after midnight, the clubs. Boyle wondered if Carmen had visited her new friend Jordi in Barcelona.

Boyle got off the train at the Passeig de Gràcia station and headed down the Avinguda del Portal de l'Àngel. Turning off into the intimate narrow lanes near the Barri Gòtic, he gazed up at the antique street lamps lighting the way. He had often wandered these streets with Ana, who would point out the intricate, exquisite ironwork on the windows and balconies. He walked past the Els Quatre Gats where Picasso had had his first exhibition, now a restaurant bar for tourists.

The Galeria Clavaguera was set in a grey stone, art nouveau-style building, which was one of many properties the Clavaguera family owned in Barcelona. A sign at the front read *Cisco Perez* in huge type. Boyle gazed through the window of the gallery, where arty types dressed in blacks, browns, denim and furs stood in tight clusters, holding glasses of cava. He heard the din of their voices from outside. Waiters wearing bow ties circulated, carrying trays with canapés and flutes of cava. In between the people, the rich colours of Cisco's paintings radiated through.

Boyle squeezed past some of Cisco's fans who had spilled out onto the pavement, and entered the gallery. He glanced around the room at Cisco's work, curious to see what the artist had done in his last few months of life. Twenty oversized paintings were evenly placed along the walls of the high-ceilinged room. The images were varied; some abstract, others almost photorealistic and the rest filled with dense calligraphy, all with Cisco's distinctive style, now so familiar to Boyle. Lacking the intimidation he normally felt in art galleries, he viewed each painting like an old friend.

Boyle moved through the crowd to see if there was anyone he knew. A waiter offered him a glass of cava and Boyle thanked him as he took it. He sipped the drink. It was dry and expensive. The first person he recognised was Salvador Clavaguera, chit-chatting with one of the guests. That was what Salvador was, Boyle decided, a chit-chatterer, incapable of any deep conversation. Salvador glanced his way and Boyle gave him a small wave, which Salvador pretended not to see. Boyle moved towards him anyway. After the "hellos" were out of the way, Boyle got straight down to business.

'I have just seen plans for an urbanisation on Pedralta. Fifty houses. Why didn't you tell me?'

'Roca Alba is below your house and has nothing whatsoever to do with your property,' said Salvador. Then he gave Boyle a contemptuous smile. 'But there is good news. The road up the mountain will be resurfaced, starting in two weeks.'

'The development will ruin the woods.'

'There is no pleasing you, Señor Boyle. First, you complain about the crumbling road up to your house. Then, when we decide to fix it, you moan about the proposed urbanisation. You can't expect a nice new road for just you and a hanging rock.'

'The houses won't sell. Nothing is selling.'

'Oh yes, they will,' Salvador said with a laugh. 'The plots are huge and the views are tremendous. It will be a gated community with twenty-four-hour security. Perfect for our wealthy Russian friends. We have sold some off plan already,' he said with a satisfied smile as he walked off after sighting his wife Deirdre.

Salvador was right. The Russians loved the Costa Brava and they brought millions of desperately needed euros into the area, albeit much of it dirty money, so Boyle had been told, transported in suitcases hidden in the boots of luxury cars. They liked the big, modern houses with sea vistas, and safety was definitely high on their list. The new urbanisation would be perfect for the Russians, but a disaster for Boyle and the mountainside.

Boyle observed Salvador, Deirdre and Laura contemplating one of Cisco's paintings. Laura looked distraught. Hardly surprising. Laura was an emotional girl; tonight would be difficult for her. Tina went straight to her daughter. Out of her horsey gear and wearing slightly more than a negligee – a tight red dress and a touch of makeup, she scrubbed up well, thought Boyle. She put her arm around Laura and disappeared with her into a back room. Deirdre said something to Salvador that made him grimace and he walked off.

Glancing to the side, Boyle saw Eduardo Clavaguera staring at him through the crowd. He walked up to Boyle and held out his hand.

'Juanita asked me to come along in her place,' said Boyle, shaking hands with him.

'How is she?' asked Eduardo.

'Incredibly well, considering she's been locked up for something she didn't do.'

'I am sorry for her. Hopefully, if she is as innocent as you say, she will be released soon,' Eduardo said. 'So, what do you think of the exhibit?'

'You have done a beautiful job,' said Boyle.

'It is all my son's work. He did everything. It is the first exhibition he has put on on his own, and so poignant that it is the work of his closest friend.'

'Cisco's work is growing on me.'

'Look at the turnout,' said Eduardo, glancing around at the people. 'You can see what a popular artist Cisco was.'

Boyle stepped closer to Eduardo and with a low voice said, 'But it's a bit quick, isn't it?'

There was a flicker of anger in Eduardo's eyes and Boyle thought for a moment that he would lose his temper, but he remained calm and asked, 'How do you mean?'

'So soon after Cisco's death. Within a month.'

'Yes. We thought the same at first and discussed changing it, waiting a few months to give Cisco's friends and family more time… But from the beginning, Cisco's mother has insisted we go ahead. "It is what Cisco would have wanted," she said.' Eduardo pronounced the cliché while attempting to hold back a tear. Either he was genuinely saddened by Cisco's death or he was a great actor.

'Now Cisco's paintings will be worth so much more,' said Boyle, gazing at them.

'Why? Because he is dead?'

'Yes,' said Boyle. 'Isn't that what normally happens when an artist dies?'

'We are celebrating his work here tonight. I hope

you understand the importance of that and don't try to sully it with your cruel insinuations.'

'*Me disculpo*,' apologised Boyle. It was a mistake to start questioning Eduardo now. At a party, Boyle usually waited until people had loosened up with a few drinks before questioning them. Unfortunately, Eduardo's hands were empty, and since Boyle had been talking to him he had already turned down an offer of cava from one of the waiters. He would probably stay sober all evening; perhaps he was even teetotal. Eduardo struck Boyle as a man who needed to stay in control.

'Your apology is accepted. Anyway, if we had waited to have the exhibition, let's say a year from now, then the paintings would have been worth a whole lot more.'

'Of course.'

Eduardo then suggested Boyle have a look at the back gallery, where there was more of Cisco's work. 'I defy you to have a dry eye after seeing it,' he said, becoming tearful as he spoke. Boyle entered the gallery. He was not sure if Cisco had been murdered. He was now just following the clues; nose to the ground, picking up the scent, sometimes weak then becoming stronger. He kept moving, one foot in front of the other, *poco a poco*, bit by bit. He would not stop following the scent until he was satisfied one way or the other.

The back gallery was darker with just a few people inside. There was a sign on the wall, softly lit from the ceiling, which glowed, *CISCO PEREZ, 1989-2010*. The funereal feel of this gallery contrasted greatly with the vibrant exhibition up front. About thirty small paintings lined the walls; some were in colour, some in black and white. They were the exact same size and each was spot-lit. As Boyle wandered, he recognised the script *El Cazador* in varying luminous colour schemes. Sketches for murals Boyle had seen at Casa Cielo were on display, including the one Cisco did of his family – mother, father and baby Cisco – in the village square. Even on a smaller scale, the painting was powerful. Boyle swallowed hard; the tears gathered at the back of his eyes. Eduardo was right. For the first time, he understood the enormity of Cisco's death; all that potential wiped out. The familiar faces of Felipe, Juanita and even Laura stared out from many of the paintings with mournful expressions, as if to say, "Where's Cisco?"

Something nagged at Boyle, something not right. Each piece had a card below. The dark frames made them look larger but they were marked 210 × 297 mm, sketchbook size. Were these from the sketchbooks that were stolen from Juanita's flat? Did Miguel steal them?

Back in the crowded front gallery, a girl in a grey mink coat and ripped jeans pointed Miguel out to Boyle. He was skinny, dressed in a black leather jacket and tight jeans. Leaning against the front desk, he was laughing with Quimet Navarro, the proverbial "bad penny". Boyle waited for Navarro to disappear.

'Miguel Clavaguera? We haven't had the opportunity to meet. I'm Adrian Boyle,' he said, stretching out his hand. Miguel turned to him and offered him an unenthusiastic, limp handshake. 'Congratulations on Cisco's exhibition. You've done an excellent job.'

'Thank you, Señor Boyle.'

'There is something that troubles me in the other gallery,' said Boyle. Miguel frowned with curiosity.

There were only a couple of people in the back gallery; it seemed that people preferred the liveliness of the large colourful paintings up front. Boyle stood in the centre of the room and indicated. 'These drawings were taken from Cisco's sketchbooks.'

'That is correct. So?' said Miguel with a shrug.

'Who gave them to you?' It came out more as an accusation rather than a question.

'Cisco,' Miguel backed away from Boyle as if he might make a run for it.

Boyle realised he was starting to badger him and softened. 'When?'

'About three months ago. I needed time to have them framed.' Miguel walked up to one of the sketches and made an infinitesimal move to straighten it.

Boyle joined him. 'There's a problem here. Cisco's

mother told me that his sketchbooks were stolen from her flat after he died.'

'That's nonsense. These are from his sketchbooks, but they were not stolen. He gave them to me.'

'All of them?'

'Yes. Except the last one he was using the day he… died,' said Miguel, averting his eyes from Boyle.

'So, I don't get this,' said Boyle, pausing. Miguel brought his attention back. 'Why would Juanita tell me that they were taken?'

'I have no idea. Ask her! The police asked me the same thing several days ago. We showed them the contract Cisco had signed. My father had insisted there was a contract before we did any work on the exhibition. Cisco never told his mother but she found out about it then.'

Boyle was confused. It seems as though the contractual arrangements had already been agreed when Eduardo had taken his son to the police. Why had Juanita kept this information from him? Why had she lied to him? And why did Eduardo fail to say anything about it when he interviewed him at his *masia*? He remembered mentioning the stolen sketchbooks then.

'Your father seemed to imply that you were not getting on with Cisco.'

'You must have misunderstood him. Cisco and I quarrelled, sure, and didn't see each other for a while, but we made up many months before he died. When I gave up painting and the competition between us had gone, it made it much easier being friends. We were always friends.'

'When you sell these paintings…'

'We have sold a third already,' said Miguel with a smile.

'What percentage will Juanita receive from the profits?'

'Sixty percent.'

'You'll make sure of that?'

'Of course. It's in the contract.'

'And then you'll return what's left of the books to her?'

'I will, although what she will do with them in prison, I have no idea.'

'Do you know what happened to the last sketchbook, the one Cisco was using the day he died?' asked Boyle, ignoring Miguel's unkind comment.

Miguel ran his fingers through his hair and then scratched his neck. 'No.'

'But you were there that day. Weren't you?' Boyle was certain Luis was telling the truth when he said that he saw Miguel at Casa Cielo.

Miguel strained to keep the emotion from his face, trying not to give anything away. He glanced at the door through to the front gallery, as if to escape. 'No. I was not there.'

'Luis says you were,' said Boyle, remaining calm, which seemed to agitate Miguel even more.

'I had nothing to do with Cisco's death,' he snapped.

'That's not what I'm asking.'

'I wasn't there. Luis is lying.'

'Why would he lie?'

'I don't know. Maybe he pushed Cisco.'

'So you think Cisco was murdered?'

Miguel looked perplexed. 'I never said that…'

Something made Boyle turn towards the door. Eduardo was standing just inside the room, expressionless. 'Are you quite finished, Señor Boyle? I think my son needs to get back to work.'

'Of course,' said Boyle as he moved off to view more of the sketches.

'Not that way, that way,' said Eduardo, pointing to the entrance to the galley. 'It is time you left.'

Boyle paused for a moment, taking in what Eduardo said. He had been physically removed from pubs before when he was young, drunk and involved in fights, but not since then had he been kicked out of any establishment. Unusual for a private detective. He was surprised at how angry it made him feel and left immediately.

On the street just outside the gallery, someone said in English. 'What do you think of the paintings, Adrian?' Boyle turned around and saw Deirdre Clavaguera leaning against the wall. They were on a first-name basis now, were they? She was holding a glass of cava, one hand around the glass, the other on the stem. He recalled hearing somewhere that she had a reputation for drink. He said hello and was surprised when she kissed him on both cheeks. She was wearing a rich, musky scent and Boyle had the overwhelming urge to bury his face in her neck.

'The paintings were powerful, but I've managed to make myself *persona non grata*.'

Deirdre laughed. 'Welcome to the club.'

'What did you do?'

'Just being myself is enough. I don't have to do anything.'

Boyle laughed. It was another way of saying, "My husband doesn't understand me." But in this case, Boyle thought that she was speaking the truth.

'I have a question for you,' said Boyle.

'Yes?' she said, with a hopeful sigh.

'I've heard that Quimet Navarro is developing a new urbanisation on Pedralta.'

Her face dropped with disappointment. 'I thought you were going to ask me something interesting.'

Boyle ignored the way the conversation was going – dangerous territory. 'Were you ever going to tell me about the urbanisation?'

'I thought you knew. I assumed that was one of the reasons you wanted to sell your house.' A seductive smile followed. 'You won't reconsider selling?'

'So, my property would have fitted in nicely.'

'On the top of the mountain – the cherry on the cake,' she said. 'And after all, it was you who put your house on the market. No one twisted your arm.'

She was right and, to make matters worse, Boyle was deceitful. He had never intended to sell his house. It was just a way to get close to Deirdre and question her. Boyle couldn't blame her for doing her job. Now, he needed to do his. 'Did you know Cisco Perez?' he asked.

'Of course. He was Laura's boyfriend. Salvador and I knew him very well – too well. It's a shame, what happened to him, but it didn't surprise me,' she said with a regretful smile.

'Why was that?'

Deirdre looked behind her before she spoke. Boyle saw with dismay that Salvador was hurrying over to claim his wife, a fake smile plastered across his face.

'*Cariño*,' Salvador murmured to Deirdre, as he took the empty glass from her and set it on the window ledge. 'We're going now. Excuse us, Señor Boyle.' He grabbed her by the arm and pulled her away. She smiled back at Boyle, her eyebrows lifted, and there was even a slight puckering of her lips – a kiss?

Before catching the 10pm train back to Caldes de Malavella, Boyle stopped off at the Café Fiorentino in the Passeig de Gràcia and had a *café solo* and a large *boccadillo de jamón*. As nice as the canapés at the art exhibit were, they were not enough to fill him. There were a few people in the café, mostly stragglers on their way home from work. As he ate, he wondered why Juanita Perez hadn't told him the truth about Cisco's sketchbooks; that she knew all along they hadn't been stolen and were being used as part of the exhibition. Why did she lie to him? He was convinced that the deaths of Cisco Perez and Teresa Clavaguera were interconnected in some way.

He saw two men come in and sit down near the entrance. Both were dressed in jeans. The thinner one was wearing a leather jacket and a buzz cut, and the other, curly-haired, bigger, heavier one, a sweatshirt. They were staring at him openly. He recognised the curly-haired one as the man he had chased outside the flat of Juanita Perez. If he were a betting man, he would say that they were the same two men who had followed him to the stables when he had interviewed Tina Clavaguera. Did they kill Felipe? The odds were favourable on that one too. Didn't the neighbour of Felipe and Juanita, Maria Rosa Deulofeu, say that one of the men had curly hair? Could they be Manel and Pedro, Eduardo's security men?

25

THE TWO MEN WERE WAITING FOR BOYLE IN the busy underground tunnel as he went to catch the train home. Rather than avoid the thugs, Boyle flowed past them with the crowd but when the men pushed towards Boyle, the people scattered, and once the tunnel was empty, the one with the curly hair swung a punch that Boyle ducked. Boyle then gave him a punch under the chin that sent him flying. Once he had regained his balance, the attackers split up, one to the back of Boyle, one to the front. The bigger one pulled Boyle into an arm lock from behind as the skinny one punched away, first at his face, then stomach. Boyle had little chance to recover his breath before the next punch was delivered. The thug continued to pound him, clearly enjoying himself. His expressions brought back memories of the beatings Boyle had received in the care home; the looks of determination, anger and sheer joy on the faces of the carers as they gave you "a good hiding". It was nothing as posh as a caning – in the care home they preferred fists, boots and belts. The man had his fist up ready to punch Boyle again when Boyle kicked out with fury, his leg landing in the groin of the attacker, who doubled over in agony. The bigger one loosened his arm lock slightly and Boyle shot around and elbowed him in the face. The wiry man recovered quickly. He went for Boyle's throat, trying to strangle him. Boyle grabbed his arms, trying to pull the hands off his throat as they did a peculiar backwards-and-forwards dance in the tunnel, Boyle trying not to black out. The other man was still on the floor. Luckily for Boyle, after a few seconds he heard him say that someone was sure to alert the police and the tunnel could be blocked at both ends. He spoke Spanish with a definite Catalan accent, thought Boyle. He took off. Wanting to continue his fun, the skinny one swore at his partner with a soft Spanish accent, and Boyle knew at once that he was Galician. The man threw Boyle to the ground. Boyle rolled into a foetal position, holding his arms around his head as the Galician gave him a farewell kick to the kidneys before following his partner.

Boyle moved up into a sitting position. He leant against the cold tiled wall to catch his breath but was overcome with wooziness and nausea so laid back on the floor, where he was quite happy to spend the rest of the night. The Galician thug was clearly highly trained, having moved with an expertise that Boyle thought came from an army background. He remembered that Eduardo Clavaguera had said that one of his army-trained security men was named Pedro. Did Eduardo order his men to attack Boyle? Was he so threatened by the idea that Boyle might find something out? Boyle's stomach was already sore but he knew it wasn't bad; the Galician was strong, he could have killed him if he had wanted to. Did Eduardo send them out just to scare him? The tunnel remained empty and silent. Boyle had difficulty keeping his right eye open and lifted his hand to feel it. His hand was streaked with blood. He pulled out his mobile and rang the police.

Later, he heard the siren of the police car arriving above on the Passieg de Gràcia, followed by the echo of footsteps as the police hurried down to the underground. One officer asked him who he was, and he gave his name and told them that he had been mugged. They called for an ambulance and the second he was laid on the gurney and rolled into it, he relaxed. At the hospital, he listed his next of kin as Montse Ferran. His only family was the one he had married into – it was at times like this that it hit hard. While he waited to be seen by a doctor, the police took a statement from him. They were surprised that his wallet, watch and smart phone had not been stolen and said that perhaps the motivation for the attack wasn't robbery, and they asked Boyle if there was any other reason these men might have attacked him. Boyle said he had no idea at all, that he had never seen the men before. The last thing he needed was the Barcelona *Mossos* nosing about in the Vall d'Aro. Boyle suggested that the men had intended to rob him but that he had resisted and that the robbers must have run out of time. The police both nodded their heads in agreement but their expressions remained sceptical.

A young, sombre doctor checked him over and ordered a CT scan of his head because Boyle was still experiencing dizzy spells. When everything checked out okay, the doctor said that it would be better if he spent the night in hospital just to be sure. Boyle could have resisted but the idea of taking the train to Caldes de Malavella, picking up his car, driving to Sant Martí and then up to Pedralta made him feel worse than he felt already. He was wheeled into an empty two-bed room, tucked into bed and given a sleeping tablet because he was too wired to sleep. Twenty minutes after stretching out in the cool, clean sheets, he was asleep.

The next morning when Boyle woke up, he saw an older, plump nurse opening the blinds. The sun streamed through the windows straight into his eyes. The nurse, whose name tag said Nuria, took one look at Boyle's face and winced.

'Is it bad?' he asked, feeling two Steri-Strips on his right eyebrow.

'Yes.' She slapped his hand away from his eye, then took a closer look and pulled a face. 'You English men like to fight, no?'

'I was mugged, actually. It happens a lot in Barcelona.' Boyle felt defensive about his nationality and Barcelona was, in fact, the mugging capital of Europe.

'Funny muggers. They didn't take your things,' she said, pointing to his bedside table where his phone, watch and wallet lay. He sat up to get out of the sun and faltered, stretching and twisting all his sore muscles into an agonising concert of pain. It was his turn to wince.

Nuria uttered, 'Harrumph,' as if he deserved it and left the room.

Anxious to get away, Boyle passed on breakfast. After Nuria had cleaned and dressed his face and the doctor had released him, he made his way down the corridor to shower, carrying his clothes and his dirty, bloodied tweed jacket. With a mop and bucket and stinking of bleach, it was more like a broom cupboard than a bathroom. He had a good look at his face in the mirror. There was a brilliant shiner forming over his right eye – and there was bruising that stretched across his midriff. With his fingers, he brushed his hair forward to the right side to help cover the bandage strips on his brow.

Outside, it was sunny and the air was brisk. As Boyle was approaching the entrance to the train station, Diedre rang him.

'How are you, Adrian?' Her voice was both vulnerable and seductive.

He couldn't understand why she was calling. Was she going to invite him to a hotel? For a tryst? Impossible – he could barely move. Boyle tried to quiet his mind. 'I'm fine. Well, apart from being attacked and spending the night in hospital.'

'Oh Adrian, I'm so sorry. Are you hurt?'

'No, I'm fine. Deirdre, why are you calling?'

'It's about my niece, Laura. You saw her last night?'

'Yes, she looked an emotional wreck.'

'Well, she took an overdose last night. She's in a coma.'

He felt incredibly sorry for Laura but he couldn't say he was shocked. 'Where is she?'

'In Girona. At the *Clínica*.' By which she meant the *Clínica Girona*, the exclusive private hospital.

'How is she doing?'

'She's in intensive care. That's all I know.' Her mood lowered. 'Salvador, Eduardo, Tina and Miguel are all with her. They don't need me.' She was sounding miserable.

'Are you busy?' asked Boyle.

'What are you suggesting?' she said, her mood brightening.

'Lunch?' he said. She accepted. They agreed to meet at one o'clock, at bar Cal Nap in the spa town of Caldes de Malavella.

26

Boyle's train arrived at Caldes de Malavella a few minutes before one. He got his car, changed from his bloodied tweed jacket into a waxed jacket and drove to the restaurant, which was situated just off the quiet main square.

As he entered the restaurant, Boyle eyed several air-cured haunches of Serrano ham hanging from the bar. His stomach growled. Deirdre Clavaguera was seated at a table facing the front door. She was wearing a silky, low-cut white dress with a blue flowered pattern and a skin-tight blue cardigan to match. Again it crossed his mind that she might make a pass, but he dismissed the thought; he had been wrong about Carmen's intentions and hopefully wouldn't make that mistake again. Besides, Deirdre was married. She gave him a big smile when she saw him and was out of her seat, kissing him twice on the cheek like old friends.

'You poor thing,' she said as she looked over his bruised face, lips pouting with concern, the pleasant smell of gin on her breath. 'Let's get you a drink.'

Boyle edged down into his chair, keeping his back as straight as possible. The pain in his ribs was moderate. The waiter came over and took her empty glass and replaced it with another gin and tonic. Boyle ordered a *cortado* and to eat, *jamón* and *pan con tomate*. She asked him if he would like something stronger to drink but he declined. Coffee was enough.

'How is Laura?'

She took a sip of her drink. 'Awake, thankfully.'

'What did she take? Did she say?'

'There was a Valium packet near her when they found her in her bedroom. She was at her father's house. She says she took a hundred milligrams. Plus who knows how much drink. She couldn't stop drinking last night.'

'Was it because of Cisco?'

'Of course. Last night she told me she couldn't live without him.'

'Do you think that she had anything to do with his death?'

'Of course not. I don't always like my niece, but she is definitely not a murderer. Anyway, enough of that. Sleeping beauty woke an hour ago and now everyone is happy,' she said, biting her lip as if fearful she might say too much.

'It sounds like you're not particularly happy,' said Boyle, leaning in towards her. 'Why is that?'

She gave a small unconvincing laugh, then folded her hands on the table and looked down at them. 'I have a lot to be unhappy about.'

'Like what?'

'It's such a bloody mess.' A sad smile formed on her lips.

'What is it?'

She dropped her head. 'I don't know how to say this. I'm really sick of the whole affair.' Then she shook her head. 'Silly me. I can't possibly tell you.'

'Does it have anything to do with Cisco's death?'

'Yes and no.'

Boyle's bruised head was beginning to ache. 'You're winding me up, Deirdre.'

'I'm sorry,' she said and burst into tears. 'Everybody hates me. I can't do anything right.'

Boyle reached across the table and held her hand. 'I certainly don't.'

She smiled at him, got a tissue out of her bag and dried her tears. 'My husband speaks Spanish, my children do. I'm tired of living in a place where I can't hear my mother tongue every day. Aren't you?'

'Not yet,' said Boyle, fearing that one day he would get to that point and have to return to England, like all of the rest of the homesick Brits. But return home for what? 'Would it help you if you told me what's been bothering you?'

Deirdre nodded her head. 'Probably.' Boyle squeezed her hand then let go. 'If I tell you this, you must never say where the information came from. Promise me.'

'Of course. You have my word.' Boyle decided to take a stab. 'Did your husband have an affair with Tina Clavaguera? Is Laura his daughter?'

'You are right about one but not the other. They have never had an affair. My husband and Tina are not interested in each other. Anyway, Tina loves her husband too much. In fact, I don't think that Tina and Salvador even like each other.' She leaned forward and lowered her voice. 'Besides, Salvador is a dreadful lover.' Her laugh was wicked.

If Tina Clavaguera loved her husband so much, why was she having an affair with Quimet Navarro? Happy people don't stray, do they? But one thing was becoming clear to Boyle – Deirdre Clavaguera had a deep loathing for her husband.

'But Laura is Salvador's child?'

'Yes, and so is Miguel. Eduardo was unable to have children, so Salvador became the sperm donor.'

'Why bother to tell me this?'

'I know about your investigation, that you have been asking questions about the family.' Her eyes filled with tears again and she turned away from Boyle. He cupped her hand in his and waited. A piece of the puzzle was about to reveal itself. He was certain of that. She wiped the tears away.

'What is upsetting you so much, Deirdre?'

She sat back and sighed. 'Isn't what I've told you enough?'

Boyle shook his head and regretted it immediately; the pain was excruciating. 'There has to be more.' He took a blister pack from his pocket and pushed out a tablet of ibuprofen. Deirdre poured water into her glass and handed it to him. He downed the medication. 'Thank you.'

She took another sip of her gin and tonic. 'Do you know Sal and I have two sons of our own?'

'Yes, you mentioned them before.'

'Well, we had our children before Tina had hers. But the moment Tina's children came along, Salvador seemed to fall in love with them. The totally devoted *oncle*. Big gifts on birthdays, the lot... What's worse, they never bothered to ask me if it was alright for my husband to father their lousy children. Salvador never discussed it with me. Can you believe that?'

'I'm sorry. What a terrible situation to find yourself in. When did you discover this?'

'Six years ago. It was Laura who worked it out. She was good in science at school, wanted to be a nurse, if you can believe it – before she became a full-time slacker. They were studying blood types, families and blood types. Turns out that Laura has blood type AB and so does her brother. Her mother has type B but poor Eduardo has type O. There is no way he is the father. When Laura confronted her parents, it all came out. Eduardo wasn't her biological father but good old Uncle Sal, with bloody blood type A, was. Our families didn't speak for weeks. Of course, I had to be told… eventually. The last to know – story of my life. Even the servants knew before I did. Eduardo was furious that the knowledge was out, but Sal was delighted. The generous, fertile brother. Good for his ego. It certainly explained why he doted on Laura and Miguel so much.'

'Your children, do they live with you?'

'No, they took off about three years ago. Jordi is a Spanish teacher in the US, in Virginia, and Enric is a gaucho on a ranch in Patagonia; he's amazing with horses. They both know. I think my sons left because of their father's infatuation with Miguel and Laura.' She hung her head, fighting back more tears. 'I visit them once a year. Salvador has yet to accompany me. Too busy with Miguel and Laura.' She took a swig of her gin and tonic. The waiter came and set the food and coffee on the table. 'Will you have a wine or beer with that?' Deirdre asked.

'No thank you, Deirdre. This is great.' He was dying for a cold beer but there was no way he would have a drink. It would only encourage her. And at the rate she was chugging her G and Ts, she would need to be carried home. Boyle picked up a piece of tomato bread, placed two slices of *ibérico* ham on it and offered it to her, to soak up some of the alcohol.

She waved it away. 'No, thank you. I hate the stuff.'

Boyle took a bite. The ham practically melted in his mouth. After a few moments he asked about Laura. 'How did she react to finding out who her biological father was?'

'She began to fight with Eduardo. It got so bad she came to live with us.'

That explains why Laura calls Eduardo by his first name, thought Boyle. 'How did Tina feel about her daughter living with you?'

'She went mad with jealousy. Dropping by all the time. She even accused me of encouraging her daughter to stay with us. As if I wanted all that drama. It was Salvador's doing.'

'When was this?'

'About a year and a half ago, perhaps two years. She had just started going out with Cisco. They were both taking cocaine and, as the final crowner, Cisco began spending nights at our house.'

Boyle remembered that Salvador had insisted he didn't even know Cisco. Why did he feel the need to lie?

Deirdre smiled and gave a small laugh. 'Of course, Sal made them sleep in separate bedrooms but you know what they're like. At it like rabbits. Laura insisted she was a virgin and Sal actually believed it. What a liar she is. A manipulative little liar. And then when she became pregnant…'

Boyle set his ham and bread back down on the plate and stared at her.

'Yeah,' said Deirdre, nodding and laughing. 'When the little virgin Mary became pregnant, Sal was a bit surprised to say the least.'

The ham was salty. Boyle finished the water in his glass and thought about how complicated some people make their lives. What compelled Laura to be so reckless? Was it finding out that Salvador was her biological father? Is discovering that your uncle is in fact your father enough? Boyle had never met his father, he didn't even know the man's identity, so there was a lack of understanding on his part. Deirdre took the pitcher of water and filled his glass again. 'Are you sure you won't have something stronger?'

'I shouldn't with the medication.' He took another long draught of water. 'What happened with the pregnancy?'

'She had an abortion at nine weeks.'

'That's a bit late, isn't it?'

'Nearly two and a half months. Yes. But Cisco was dead set against an abortion.'

'What was his reaction when he found out about it?'

'She told him it was a miscarriage.' She hesitated and gave him an uneasy glance. 'It was for the best. Laura couldn't take care of a guinea pig, never mind a baby. She was still taking drugs while pregnant. She is the most feckless individual I have ever met.'

'She works for you.'

'That was Sal's doing, not mine. Only eight to fifteen hours a week, when she feels like it. But she's bone idle. Her father's maids do everything in her flat; cooking, cleaning, walking her dog. She doesn't even wash her own hair, for goodness' sake. She goes to the hairdresser three times a week to have it done.'

'How has Salvador reacted to Cisco's death?'

'I think he's secretly delighted. He tries to hide it from Laura, but he has told me that it was the best thing that could have happened.' Deirdre stopped suddenly, appearing to have run out of steam.

Boyle asked. 'Have you told anyone else about this?'

'When I first found out, I confided in Lola, Quimet's wife. She is probably my closest friend, but she isn't known for keeping secrets. Anyway, I never said "don't tell anyone". A few people must know by now.'

'You think she told her husband?'

'Of course. He was most likely the first person

she told. But I don't care. Part of me wants everyone to know.'

Boyle wondered if it gave Quimet Navarro any power over Eduardo, knowing that Eduardo's children were not biologically his but his brother Salvador's. Would this have helped Quimet Navarro in purchasing Eduardo's land for such a reasonable price? Would that be enough pull?

27

AT THE BACK OF THE CEMETERY IN SANT MARTÍ there were four rows of large family tombs. The *panteón de las familias* was where the wealthy buried their dead. Each *panteón*, the size of a large room and surrounded by wrought iron railings, contained the tombs, and stone statues of saints. Boyle had difficulty finding the Ferran tomb and felt guilty. What widower abandons his newly deceased wife in the cemetery and fails to visit her all year? Boyle – he loathed cemeteries. After searching for five minutes he finally discovered it, filled with tombs and plaques going back two hundred years. A large plaque on a granite plinth read, *Familia Ferran I Vall*.

Towards the front in a new, creamy marble was Ana's own plaque. This was the first time he had seen it. It was hard to believe a year had passed. He was pleased to see there were several bouquets of colourful flowers laid out. Opening the small gate, he laid his roses next to them. He bowed his head. He often spoke to Ana, sometimes out loud, although over the past few months he had been less communicative. What did he have to tell her anyway? That he had not been to the cemetery once since the burial? Or worse – that in those twelve short months he had fallen in love with her younger sister Carmen? He tried to picture Ana's face but Carmen's kept getting in the way.

In the corner of the *panteón* there was a life-sized *pietà* in worn, moss-covered stone, which he had failed to notice the year before. He must have been truly dazed not to see it. Mary was folded over the body of her son, her hands wrapped around him tightly, desperately trying to hold him up but defeated by his dead weight. In this *pietà*, she was not looking at her son with the typical expression of Mary – one of sadness and peace and, most importantly, the acceptance of God's will. No, Mary's eyes were glaring heavenwards, her mouth open and twisted, expressing fury and anguish, as if she were screaming, "Why did you take my son? Why did you do this to me?" Boyle immediately thought of Juanita Perez and the loss of her son. He couldn't begin to imagine the power of the grief she felt over Cisco. Boyle's own mother had died of an overdose when he was five and there was no memory of any grief at all – he just felt the absence of her. Even with the death of his wife, there was simply a dullness and a void that he only now realised he had conveniently filled with Carmen. Juanita Perez, on the other hand, was in the grip of an emotion that would never end, one that he would probably never understand.

While exiting the cemetery, Boyle bumped into Montse on her way in. She was carrying a bouquet of mixed flowers. When she saw the bruising on Boyle's face, her mouth opened in surprise. '*Hombre*, what happened to you?'

Boyle brushed his hair forward to help cover his black eye. 'I was mugged in Barcelona on the way back from Cisco's exhibition. I fought them off.' He decided not to say that the culprits were Eduardo's thugs. They approached a stone bench and Montse motioned for them to sit down. 'I'd rather not,' said Boyle, holding his hand up to his ribs.

Montse eyed him with compassion. 'Did the police catch them?' she asked.

'They are working on it.'

'Ah,' said Montse. 'Before I forget – the *Guardia Civil* have lost the records of the shooting of Teresa Clavaguera. There is nothing there.'

'Well, that's convenient,' said Boyle.

'Records go missing all the time, Adrian,' said Montse. 'I am still waiting for a transcript of the trial of Felipe Perez. Hopefully we'll have better luck with that. But I'm not so sure that digging around in the past is going to benefit anyone. Juanita should worry about her own case first, put all her energy into her defence.'

Montse was right. Releasing Juanita from prison was top of the list. She told him that the police had taken blood samples from Juanita and also from her neighbour Señora Deulofeu, and from the body of Felipe. They were testing all blood samples for the nitrous oxide gas. 'It will take a while. But Felipe was murdered. I have no doubt about that.'

Boyle agreed. The case of Teresa Clavaguera, on the other hand, would never be investigated if he didn't do it. And the one thing he was certain of was that the killings of Cisco, Teresa Clavaguera and Felipe Perez were all related in some way. He then asked Montse if she could arrange for Juanita to ring him.

'Where is Carmen?' asked Boyle, trying to mask his disappointment at not seeing her.

Montse scrutinised him. 'She's not coming. But

that shouldn't surprise anyone; Carmen is unable to deal with death. She nearly stayed away from Ana's funeral claiming *el gripe*.' She shrugged. 'She deals with death in her own way. A bit like you, *hombre*.'

'At least I came here today,' he said.

'By the way, her boyfriend is coming to the wedding,' she said.

More good news, thought Boyle. 'Is it wise to invite someone you hardly know?'

'Don't be so negative. He seems good for her. I like him. I think it is serious already,' she said.

'Rosa checked him out?' Boyle was astonished.

'Of course. He is everything he claims to be,' she said.

'In my opinion, it is all happening too quickly,' said Boyle.

'Adrian, Pau left Carmen two years ago. And the bastard is working on his second child with that horrible bitch. How long does Carmen have to wait to find some happiness?'

'I mean she hasn't known Jordi long enough,' he said.

'You have a thing for Carmen,' said Montse, leaning forward and looking him straight in the face. 'You cannot hide it from me.'

'It is just a little brotherly concern,' said Boyle, lying through his teeth and in the process trying to convince himself it was true as well.

'Anyway, Carmen is not right for you. My sister will never be right for you,' she said in her matter-of-fact manner. 'But it is understandable that you should be drawn to her.' Montse placed a comforting hand on Boyle's arm. 'I know it's difficult for you, Adrian. Carmen looks so much like Ana, it's eerie at times – but that is where the similarity ends, *hombre*. Carmen is nothing like Ana.'

Without admitting it, Boyle agreed with everything Montse said. He gave her a small smile. They heard loud squawking and both gazed skyward. High up, a flock of geese were moving through the wispy clouds southwards and he wished his desire for Carmen would fly away with them.

28

Juanita rang Boyle from prison. He was seated at a rustic wooden table on the terrace at his house having his morning coffee when the call came through. It was a cool, clear morning with views all the way up to Palamos. He had been gazing across at the sunlit hills of Les Gavarres and thinking how lucky he was to live in such a beautiful place. *Not for much longer, if Quimet Navarro has his way and builds his luxury urbanisation.*

Juanita and Boyle discussed her case briefly. He took a sip of his coffee then asked her about the "missing" sketchbooks. A long pause ensued.

'Yes… I found out that they were not stolen. It was just ten days ago. Miguel told me about it. He showed me the contract that Cisco had signed.'

'Didn't Cisco ever mention it to you?'

'No, he never told me.'

'Why not?'

'Maybe because he knew how much I loved his sketchbooks, so he didn't want to disappoint me. The sketchbooks had to be ripped to pieces to sell. I hated it…' she stopped, suddenly choked with emotion.

He deliberately softened his tone. 'You could have told me.'

'I didn't want to give you any reason for dropping the investigation. I am very sorry.' She paused for a moment and said. 'Please don't give up. Find out who killed Teresa.'

'Don't worry, I won't give up,' he promised her.

'My son painted that picture of her. It is so strange. I feel Cisco must have known his father was in prison. I want to know what happened. For Felipe, now.'

'What about your case?'

'I don't care about that. I have lost my son and husband. My life is over now.'

He tried to change her mind, saying he wanted to assist with the investigation into Felipe's death, to get her out of prison, but she refused any help.

After he put down his mobile, he observed his two feral cats sprawled out on a boulder, sunning themselves. One black, one ginger, he envied their ability to relax. They had first appeared at the house just after Ana died. He had done what you were never supposed to do: feed them. Now, they were here to stay. His mobile rang again. It was Rosa.

'I've got a hit on those anti-hunt people. He's the ringleader – Gabriel Osorio. Twenty-five. An asshole, from the sounds of it. A couple of our men interviewed him yesterday but failed to ask anything about Cisco. Talk to him, if you would.'

'Of course.'

Boyle met Rosa in the Plaça de Mercat, where she handed him a typewritten report of the interview with Gabriel Osorio, his phone and address.

Boyle read the report in his office and, for the first time, he felt like he might be getting to the truth of what actually happened that day.

He took the autovia heading north to Palamos on the coast, a town famous for its *gambas*. He decided not to ring first. The element of surprise was sometimes best.

Boyle reached the two-storey block of flats before 9am. It was a typical eighties' brick building with what looked like two balconies for each flat; one for sitting out on, and the other for the washing machine and a rack for drying clothes. Carrying a large backpack, he approached the front of the building and pushed the button for flat 2B.

'Yes?' answered a woman.

'My name is Adrian Boyle. I'm a private detective. Is Gabriel Osorio there?'

'No,' she snapped.

'Señora. He's not in any trouble. I thought he might be able to help me with something.'

'You're not with the police?'

'The police have sent me here,' he lied, hoping she would respond favourably to a hint of police backup.

'The police where?'

'At Sant Martí. Chief Inspector Marc Saldoni,' he said, using the name of Rosa's ex-husband. If it hadn't been for Montse's relationship with Rosa, Boyle would still be friends with Marc.

The woman took a deep breath. 'Come up,' she said, as the buzzer went.

A young white man with dreadlocks answered the door. He had an air of self-righteousness that made Boyle want to punch him. 'Gabriel Osorio?'

'Yeah?' he said, and smirked when he saw Boyle's face. The Steri-Strips had come off his brow, but the black eye was dark and colourful.

'I'd like a few words.'

'I already spoke to the police.'

'Look, I'm not interested in what you did at Roca Alba, but what you possibly might have seen.'

'Like what?'

'May I come in?'

Gabriel opened the door and showed Boyle into an impeccably tidy open-plan living-dining area with traditional dark wood furniture and shelves full of knick-knacks. Gabriel, with his torn jeans, woolly hair and several rings in his face, looked totally out of place. The boy sat down, cross-legged in a wing-backed chair, like the maharaja of bloody Jaipur, and left the sofa to Boyle. The mother came in from the kitchen and wiped down the breakfast table. An attractive woman, she smiled at Boyle. It took him a second to clock that despite the black eye, she liked what she saw. Boyle smiled back somewhat self-consciously and wondered if there was a husband somewhere.

'Would you like a coffee, Señor?'

'No thank you, Señora.'

'Everything's okay, Mama,' Gabriel said with a dismissive wave of his hand. She disappeared into the bedroom. Boyle guessed that Gabriel never lifted a finger in the house.

'You say you arrived at Can Bosc in Roca Alba at ten fifteen that morning and were gone by eleven.'

'So?' he said with a shrug. There was no eye contact.

'We have another witness who says that when he left Casa Cielo – that's another house on the complex – at eleven fifteen, he saw no sign of vandalism. Why did you lie to the police?'

Gabriel was glaring at Boyle, not liking to be caught

out. 'Okay, maybe I lied about when I was there. I had read about the graffiti guy dying up there and I didn't want the police to think I had anything to do with it. Because I didn't.'

'So, you didn't know Cisco Perez?'

Gabriel Osorio looked straight at Boyle. 'No. I never met him.'

'Good, alright… I believe you. So, tell me, when *did* you arrive and leave?'

'I got there at eleven thirty-five and left at about five or ten past twelve. I can't remember exactly.'

That was enough for Boyle. 'Did you see or hear anything during the time you were there?'

Gabriel twisted his hands nervously and nodded. 'You know what happened?'

'No, I don't. Tell me.'

'I was nearly finished when I heard the weirdest scream. I froze, wondering what it was. I'd never heard anything like it. It wasn't till I heard about the guy falling that I knew what it was.'

'Then what happened?'

'When I heard the scream, I started to throw my cans and stuff into the car to get the fuck out of there.'

'Did you see the car?'

'No, what car?'

'Oh, come on. I heard and saw the car myself.'

'Then why are you asking me?'

Boyle gave him a stern look.

'Okay, I heard a car but I didn't see it, I'm telling you. I hid behind a tree.'

'Were you alone?'

'Yes.' Gabriel looked away as he said it. Boyle thought he was lying.

'Are you sure?'

'Yes, I am sure.' Another furtive look. Of course he was lying.

Boyle then took the small blue rucksack out of his backpack. Gabriel looked at it with suspicion. Boyle held up the rucksack. 'Have you seen this before?'

'No,' he answered a bit too quickly.

Boyle opened the back and took out the evidence: the spray cans of red paint, food, and lastly, the red card. 'Normally I would wear gloves when dealing with evidence like this. But the police have already taken prints off these cans and the card. Guess whose prints they are?'

'Whose?' said Gabriel.

'Yours.'

'The police never said anything yesterday. You can never trust the pigs. How do I know they didn't put them there to frame me?'

'That's not what concerns me at the moment. There was another set of strong prints on the spray cans and on this card as well. Do you have any idea who they belong to?' Gabriel shook his head. 'Someone else was with you that day.'

'No. It was just me.'

'All that graffiti from just one person? I don't believe it.'

'Well, believe it, old man.'

That comment made Boyle fume. Boyle took out Montse and Rosa's engagement card and handed it to Gabriel. Gabriel opened the card, read it and laughed.

'Have you seen this before?'

'Never,' said Gabriel as he handed it back.

Boyle was certain that Gabriel was protecting someone. Possibly someone who had seen who was driving the car out of Roca Alba that day. He wasn't finished with Gabriel Osorio.

When he arrived at his office, Boyle rang the property developer Gunnar Lundgren and asked for a meeting to talk about the death of Teresa Clavaguera. The Swede sounded happy to hear from him and invited him over for lunch. He said his wife was still in Sweden visiting grandchildren, and that he had taken some moose meat out of the freezer and was making a stew. Boyle pulled a face at the mention of moose for lunch but he accepted the invitation with gratitude.

Gunnar Lundgren served lunch on the terrace. After all the laughs about Boyle's bruised face were out of the way, Gunnar placed a steaming bowl of moose stew in front of him. Boyle's stomach turned from the extra strong smell of game, which he had never liked.

Boyle took a small forkful of the stew. Gunnar's dog Abbe sat at Boyle's feet, staring mournfully at the fork as Boyle lifted it to his mouth. Gunnar waited, eager for his response.

'It's delicious,' Boyle lied. He then had to sit through a blow-by-blow description from Gunnar of how this particular moose was felled in a Swedish forest, and the importance of having a quiet hunting dog like Abbe.

'You upset the animal if your dog barks. The stress hormones make the meat tough.' Boyle glanced down at the dog, who was gazing at him, licking his chops hopefully. 'Abbe did a good job,' said Gunnar as he got up and walked to the kitchen to fill the water jug. Quickly, Boyle slopped half of his portion of food onto the terrace floor, which the dog mopped up in seconds.

Later, once they were nearly finished, Boyle began to question him. 'I didn't know that Teresa Clavaguera was Faustino's sister. Faustino must have been devastated.'

'Yeah, sure, but not as much as you would think,' said Gunnar. 'I don't think they got on that well. They were always bickering and competing for their parents' attention.'

'Do you believe her death was an accident?'

'Yes. It was an accident waiting to happen. All my fears were realised that day.'

'How do you mean?'

'About the safety of the place. I have already mentioned this to you. I don't like to hunt here because the tracks are too narrow and there are boulders everywhere for bullets to ricochet off. But the truth is, I don't know what actually happened when she was shot that day because I had already gone home.'

'Just take me through the day, would you? What do you remember?'

'We hunted the *jabali* that morning. But we did not fire any shots.'

Boyle found this hard to believe. 'No shots at all?'

'No. We didn't find any boar. Simple as that. It is not unusual to come back empty-handed. So, then we all had lunch in the lodge at the top of Pedralta.'

'The lodge?'

'It's the tiny house at the top of the mountain. You know the place,' said Lundgren, smiling.

'My house?' Boyle had never heard it referred to as a lodge before.

'Exactly, your house. It was a hunting lodge then. Well, as I said, we had lunch there and then I left. After I left, I presume they all had their siesta. That is what they told the police.'

'Why did you leave so early?'

Gunnar put down his fork. 'Wine is always served with the food on a hunt and the hunters can drink a lot. That was why I only hunted with them in the morning. Sure, I had a drink or two with lunch because I had no intention of using a gun afterwards. Some of them can get through a bottle each. And even though they have a siesta after and sleep for a couple of hours, that doesn't mean they are totally sober when they wake. So, I always went home. I was not about to hunt on a mountain crawling with inebriated hunters. What made it worse for Eduardo was that he had given Felipe a high-powered rifle exactly like his own. Felipe had just been a worker on the estate, so he could never have afforded it otherwise.'

'The Tikka?' said Boyle, remembering the make from his last conversation with Gunnar.

'Yes. It's a Finnish rifle. I used it and introduced it to the group. Before I knew it, everyone had one, Quimet and Sal as well. So, I suppose, I started a craze. That day only Felipe and Quimet were using their Tikkas. But the ballistics showed clearly that the bullet that killed Teresa had come from Felipe's rifle. Ballistics do not lie.'

'Did they find out which direction the shot had come from?'

'The bullet came from the area they had hunted all that afternoon.'

'Where was that?'

'Just off the track that leads over to Santa Nuria. You must know it.'

Boyle nodded. He had walked it many times. The route was a popular hiking track that ran straight through the hills that separated Pedralta and Roca Alba from the village of Santa Nuria. It was the same track where Cisco had fallen to his death.

'They were never certain of the exact spot because the police never found any shell casings, but the bullet definitely came from Felipe's rifle. The rifling marks on the bullet matched his gun.'

Gunnar got up and began to clear the plates. Boyle rose to help. Gunnar told him to relax and, after putting the dishes neatly in the sink, turned on the espresso maker.

'So, what happened after lunch?' Boyle asked.

'Not much. Tina had prepared lunch.'

'Tina? You mean Teresa?'

'No, Tina. She often cooked lunch for us.'

'Eduardo knew Tina then?'

'Yes, of course they knew each other. They were both from Santa Nuria. I think her father did some manual work for the Clavagueras and the mother, and sometimes Tina, both worked in their kitchen. Tina was young, about eighteen, I think. She was still living at home, in a farmhouse just down the track from the Clavagueras' *masia*. They grew up within a few hundred metres of each other.' Gunnar brought two cups of espresso over and set them down.

'Did she eat lunch with you?'

'Well, normally the cook would not eat with us; when her mother cooked, she did not. Here in Spain, especially in those days, the rich people did not mix with the help, but Tina was so pretty that no one minded her joining us. And she was well-known, even then, for her marksmanship, so she sometimes accompanied us on hunts as well.'

Boyle wondered if Tina was in on the shooting. Was Eduardo planning to run off with her after his wife had been killed? An eighteen-year-old? He would have to find out when the couple were married.

'Did she hunt on that day?'

'This was thirty years ago.' Gunnar laughed, showing his tanned face was covered in fine wrinkles. 'But, from what I remember, no.'

'Where did she go after lunch?'

'Home, I think.'

'She drove, did she?'

'No, she did not have a car. Salvador had dropped her off at the lodge that morning. I think I offered her a lift back but she said that she preferred to walk home. Thirty years ago, very few young people had their own cars. And a girl like Tina, from a poor family, had to rely on others to give her lifts. She must have walked on the path over the hills back to Santa Nuria. It is the shortest way.'

Boyle thought about asking Gunnar if Tina had her rifle with her but then decided against it. If Tina did shoot Teresa, she would have used Felipe's rifle. Perhaps she didn't go home straightaway.

Boyle's interview with Gunnar had left him as baffled as before, but it did give him an idea, and he wasted no time in checking it out. There were no snoops trailing him when he left Gunnar's house so he drove over to Casa Cielo at Pedralta and left his car in the driveway. It was quiet but for the occasional gust of wind whipping through the umbrella pines. It was coming from the north, building up to a *tramuntana*. He went down the potholed path where Cisco fell, stepping over crevices, then followed the track as it wound its way through the hills that would lead back to the Santa Nuria urbanisation and beyond that, to the farms in the valley and finally the village of Santa Nuria d'Aro. It was the same route Tina Clavaguera would have taken thirty years before after cooking lunch for the hunters in the lodge, walking home to her parents' farmhouse. Ten minutes into the walk, Boyle was not surprised to arrive at a spot which was high above Casa Cielo. Most of the house was hidden behind umbrella pines, but one part of the house was crystal clear. The roof and turret were laid out for all to see. Especially visible was the sunken terrace in the roof, where there was a perfect angle overlooking the exact spot where Teresa Clavaguera had been sitting when she was shot.

29

Boyle asked to see Deirdre and she agreed to meet him at a house in Santa Nuria that she was presently showing to some clients. She gave Boyle directions to the house.

The enormous, newly restored Catalan *masia* was situated near Solius and overlooked the sea from one side and the Pyrenees from the other. The umbrella trees to the right of the house were sighing in the breeze. Boyle parked in the wide gravel forecourt and watched Deirdre as she saw the young clients off in their sports car. She waved Boyle over to a side gate in the stone wall that surrounded the house. At the back were two apple trees bulging with fruit being whipped around by the battering wind. She took off her dangerously high heels – he was surprised at how petite she was without them – and she handed him one of her large supermarket bags. Together they began to pick the fruit off the ground. They laughed as they picked, several times nearly losing their balance as they were buffeted by the wind. When the bags were full, they carried them to their cars. One went into Deirdre's boot, one into Boyle's.

After a few minutes' discussion on the gravel drive about the proposed urbanisation on Pedralta, which Boyle decided would have to wait until he finished with the investigation into Teresa Clavaguera's death, he changed the subject and asked, 'Tell me, Deirdre, how much do you know about Eduardo's first wife?'

'I never knew her. I met Salvador a couple of years after she died.' She gave him a quizzical look. 'What's this all about?'

Boyle told her what he knew about the doubts over Felipe's guilt. 'I heard Tina was there the day Teresa was shot. Making lunch.'

'That would be Tina, alright. But to be honest, I don't know a lot about what happened then. No one talks about it.' She began to laugh. 'I'd love to see Tina banged up in prison, just for what she's done to me.'

After wiping her stockinged feet, she put on her shoes and took him to a protected terrace at the side of the house where they sat on comfortable garden chairs, the hills of the Ardenya rising up before them.

'I know you've been through a lot, Deirdre, but I just want you to tell me the truth, alright?'

Deirdre smiled. 'Of course.'

'Do you think Tina was interested in Eduardo then?'

'She always had a thing for Eduardo,' she said. Boyle looked at her sceptically. 'I am telling you the truth,' she said, as she laughed. 'Tina was always talking about how she'd been in love with Eduardo since she was twelve. She was brought up in the farmhouse right next door to him.'

'Not exactly the same social circles, no matter how close their houses were.'

'True, but she loved to tell this story,' said Deirdre, her anger with Tina seeming to fuel her excitement. Boyle would have to take what she said with a pinch of salt. 'Tina was twelve at the time. She said she was walking into Santa Nuria from her house when she saw the most handsome *chico* she had ever seen walking towards her. It was Eduardo, of course, on his way to his house. He must have been in his late teens then. She said that when he passed her, he looked her straight in the eyes and smiled. Her heart was all aflutter,' Deirdre said with sarcasm. 'She said that at that moment, she knew she would marry him one day.'

'She must have been devastated when he married his first wife.'

'It was strange. After Teresa died, Tina didn't hang around but went off to Barcelona to train as a chef. I didn't meet her till she came back. Then she was already going out with Eduardo. She said she came back because she missed the Costa Brava. But after they married, she told me secretly that she came back for Eduardo. She knew he was still unattached and she had never given up on her desire to marry him.'

'How did they meet up again?'

'Oh, that's another big romantic story she loved to tell. She became assistant chef at La Terrassa on Sant Pol beach. Eduardo came in one night with his friends and loved the food so much he asked to meet the chef. Imagine his surprise when Tina emerged from the kitchen with the chef.'

Or was it a surprise? thought Boyle. He wondered if there was a possibility that together, Tina and Eduardo had planned to kill Teresa. Boyle remembered Carmen telling him that Eduardo didn't marry again for five years. Was he waiting for Tina to return? Was that what they had planned? Tina would run off to Barcelona after they had shot Teresa, she would bide her time there until Felipe was tried and sent to prison, then she would return and they could marry?

Boyle woke suddenly. It was still dark. The winds had

died down and it was quiet. The digital clock on his bedside table read six forty-five. Pulling the duvet over his shoulders, he curled up and watched the curtains lighten with the cold, blue dawn. He heard the crackle of gunfire in the woods below and then remembered it was Thursday – a hunting day. The hunters began early in the day when the wild boar were on the move in search of food and water. That is most likely what woke him, but something was wrong; he felt uneasy. He heard dogs barking nearby and then it happened. One loud crack of gunfire hit the bedroom window. Instinctively, he rolled down under the bed. For the next few minutes, as the warm daylight crept into the room, he stayed low, fearing more gunfire. He listened to intermittent pops of rifles across the valley but there were no more shots nearby. As he lay there, he wondered how accidental that shot had been. It was one of two things: either there was an amateur hunter loose on the hillside or someone had taken a deliberate shot at his house.

When enough time had passed, Boyle crawled out from under the bed and immediately saw the burn damage to the pale curtains. He got up, pulled them aside and found a perfect bullet hole in the window. The glass had not shattered, suggesting the gunman was close. How close, he was unable to tell, but however unintentional the shot was, he knew it would not have been easy to get that angle on the house because it was perched high on the hillside and there was a steep drop to the woods beneath. It would have been awkward, unless the gunman had climbed to the top of one of the massive umbrella trees, as they often did in the middle of the night, to shoot wild boar. Is that what had happened? It was quiet now down in the woods. Boyle stood by the window and waited while the sun rose brilliantly over the sea, lighting up the landscape, leaving a ghost of the moon hovering over the Pyrenees. Remaining inside, he took his binoculars and scanned the trees. There was no one.

Boyle searched for the bullet and found it in his bedroom wall. This unnerved him. If the shot had come from the woods, even from the top of a tree, the angle would have been acute, piercing the ceiling. This indicated that the shooter was on the same level as the house. Carefully, he dug the bullet out with a screwdriver and rolled it over in his palm. It was impossible to tell what calibre the tiny lump of metal had been. Staring at the wide terrace outside his bedroom, he felt a chill, realising that the shot must have been fired just on the other side of the French doors. He opened the doors and stepped onto the terrace. There, lying on the tiles, was a handgun. What idiot leaves his gun behind? He moved closer to it. It was a Walther P99 pistol, just like those many of the police in Spain used, and like the one he used as well. He went back inside, grabbed a pen off the night table, slipped the pen in the finger grip and raised the gun to get a closer look. The gun was very familiar indeed. It had a small metal plate, fastened to the end of the butt, engraved with the initials AB. The bastard had used Boyle's own gun.

Boyle searched the area for the spent cartridge but found nothing. He slid back into the house and looked in his nightstand drawer. Inside was his empty clip-on holster. How did the shooter gain entrance to the house? It was useless checking all the metal shutters because he rarely closed them. He knew that if someone wanted to break into your house, there was no way of stopping them. If the *ladrones* were unable to pick your lock, they had an oxyacetylene saw that would cut through your metal shutters like butter. Down in the towns, crowded with nosy neighbours, there was more of a deterrent but up here, on top of a mountain, or in one of the wealthy urbanisations with some houses left unoccupied for weeks on end, there was little protection. You would need a private security company with a couple of man-eating German Shepherds to watch your house twenty-four hours a day.

Boyle had been robbed three years before. They had taken an old camera and some of Ana's costume jewellery, nothing of any great monetary value. One thing Boyle had in his favour was that he had nothing to steal. There was a bulky television, a smart phone purchased five years ago and an old laptop – nothing worth going up a mountain to take and the *ladrones* knew that. But it was obviously not robbers who had broken into his house this time. Someone was trying to scare him. He guessed the person was in some way related to Eduardo; one of his body guards, a member of his family or one of his friends, or perhaps even Eduardo himself. Eduardo must know by now that Boyle wasn't about to drop either investigation. If Felipe was innocent, that would implicate all the other hunters who were on the mountain the day Teresa Clavaguera died, including Eduardo Clavaguera, Quimet Navarro, Faustino Duran and Salvador Clavaguera.

He needed to get out of the house. After showering and dressing, he packed a small suitcase then drove down to Sant Martí, keeping an eye out for anyone on his tail. At the police station, Rosa swore with anger when Boyle told her what had happened. She handed the bullet over to forensics and immediately sent police up to his house to collect any other evidence. While he waited, they checked his gun for fingerprints but they found none but his own. Once back in his possession, he tucked the gun into his holster, which was fastened to his belt. He had put on the pale baggy jacket he always wore when he was armed. It hid the gun well. He didn't have to ask if he could stay with Rosa and Montse for a few days. Rosa insisted on it.

30

Boyle and Rosa went to see Montse in her office. 'There is something very suspicious about this property deal of Quimet Navarro's,' said Montse, as she ushered them into the room. She took a sheaf of papers from a pile on the desk and spread them out in front of them. 'It appears that Quimet has been paying off people in the planning department over the past four years.'

'How do you know that?' asked Boyle.

'They are being paid more than just a salary. There are infusions of cash into their bank accounts. Look,' she said as she tapped four different bank statements, one after the other.

Boyle read each one. Jose Font, Maria Fonells, Pau Castello and Rafael Moya had each received a payment of twenty-five thousand euros in May 2009. All from Quimet Navarro. There was no attempt to hide the fact that the money was coming from a local property developer. Why didn't he just pay the officials in cash? It showed not only how corrupt but also how arrogant the town council had become under Salvador Clavaguera's rule. It was common knowledge that the councils were funded through the payments for planning agreements, but the money was going directly into the officials' personal bank accounts.

'They were paid once a year over four years,' said Montse, handing Boyle more statements, which he perused. From May 2005 to May 2009, every member of the planning council received a total of one hundred thousand Euros.

Not an extravagant sum, but better than a poke in the eye, thought Boyle, *and more than enough to make the officials amenable to reclassifying the acreage on the mountain from rural to residential land.*

'What I don't understand is why he would buy now when the property market is on its knees?' said Rosa as she took the statements from Boyle.

'Prices are low. His good friend Salvador Clavaguera is there to change the zoning restrictions – we don't know how long he'll remain in office. Salvador told me that he has already sold plots for his development Marvista. The rich will always buy,' said Boyle.

'But the development is huge. Quimet won't build, unless he is crazy,' said Rosa. 'All the *inmobiliaria*s in Sant Martí are closing down.'

'The price of property will eventually go up. He just has to play the waiting game,' said Boyle. 'I heard that the Navarro family once owned the land on Pedralta but lost it to the Clavagueras.'

'Yes. It was after the Civil War. I don't remember the story but Papa would know,' said Montse.

Boyle made a mental note to talk to Narcis about it, see if he could fill him in on the details. It was telling that some of the land that had been taken from the Navarro family was now back in their hands. This was not a coincidence, Boyle would bet on it. Also, it was interesting that Quimet Navarro should be such good friends with Salvador Clavaguera. Had the requisition of his family's property been the grand plan of Quimet Navarro? It would be a disaster for the mountain and Boyle if the building plans should go ahead for Marvista.

Narcis was waiting for Boyle in the foyer of his house. He handed him a green envelope. The content of the card was more of the same: CONGRATULATIONS, WE HOPE YOU ENJOY YOUR DAUGHTER'S WEDDING. Narcis told Boyle that the card must have arrived that morning, but that neither he nor Esther had been out. Boyle tucked the card inside his jacket pocket and took the tape for the security camera from the high shelf in the foyer.

Boyle took the tape to *Mossos* and watched it in a special suite with Rosa. It took them no time to find the spot. The card had been delivered that morning at 8.14. They clearly saw the person shove the card under the door. Rosa exclaimed, 'Madre mía.' It did surprise Boyle that the deliverer had worn no disguise, not even a hoody to hide her face. She must have thought Narcis and Esther too out of touch to consider a security camera. In the recording, she showed no interest in what was around her. She just slid the card under the door and left. When it came to covert activity, she was an incredibly stupid girl.

Boyle waited outside the building where she lived. With any luck he wouldn't have to wait too long. When Isabella rounded the corner, she was staring at the ground, lost in her own world, lugging her school bag. She had come straight back from school, which was a relief. She started when she saw Boyle.

'*Oncle*,' she said as she gave him a peck on the cheek. 'Why are you here?'

'I want to talk to you.'

Rosa and Boyle had agreed that he should interview Isabella first, to ask about the cards. At a back table in Café El Cisne, Boyle ordered a hot chocolate for his niece and an espresso for himself. He then took out the green envelope and slid it across to her. Isabella looked at it and froze.

'Go on. Take the card out and read it,' he said.

'No,' she said, pushing it back towards him.

'You don't have to read it, do you? You know exactly what's written inside.'

She turned her head and watched the people in the rambla, refusing to look at him.

'Why on Earth would you do such a thing?'

She turned back to him, her pretty face distorted with anger. 'I hate all the dishonesty with Montse and Rosa. This is the twenty-first century. Same-sex marriages should be accepted by now.'

'Sending those cards was cruel.'

'Since no one was going to tell them, I thought my grandparents needed to know. Now they can get used to it.'

'Why didn't you tell them yourself?'

'Because my mother would have killed me.'

'It has created the most tremendous rift in your family. Your grandparents refuse to speak to your Aunt Montse and Rosa.'

'I didn't know.' She was surprised, clearly having no idea about the impact of her messages.

'And why did you send them more than one card?'

'No one was discussing it. Mama had said nothing, so I thought the cards were not getting through.'

'Your mother doesn't know about them.'

She took a deep breath. 'It was never my intention to upset them. Honest,' she said. Her lip was beginning to quiver.

'Not your intention? What did you expect?'

'I'm sorry, *Oncle*, I really am. I thought they would be shocked and then in a few months it would all be forgotten. But the most important thing was that my grandparents should know. I mean, what happens when Montse has a baby?'

Now it was Boyle's turn to be surprised. 'What? Is she pregnant?'

She leaned in and whispered. 'Not yet, but *Tía* Montse and Rosa want a child. Don't say anything about it. I'm not supposed to know. I overheard my mother discussing it with *Tía* Montse. My grandparents need time to get used to it – it's only fair – before the children come along.'

'Children?' Boyle was beginning to feel weak. If she knew about it, why hadn't Carmen told him? Was it another one of her secrets, like her internet boyfriend, Jordi?

'They'll want more than one, of course,' she said, getting back her confidence, pouting at Boyle like he was an idiot.

'But they'll adopt, surely?'

'No, no. *Tía* Montse told my mother that she definitely wants to give birth to them. And she's already in her late thirties, so she has to get moving.'

Speechless, Boyle stirred his espresso, which was already cold. He suddenly felt deeply sorry for his dead wife and her childlessness, which had never been explained. The doctors had told them there was nothing wrong with either of them. So, they had hoped it would happen, month after month, year after year. Boyle had minded less than Ana. He had liked having her all to himself but he hated to see her suffer. Ana and Boyle could have adopted but they chose not to because they were too busy waiting for what increasingly, as she aged, would have been considered 'a miracle'.

Reaching out, Boyle took Isabella's hand. 'Despite your good intentions, I think it was deeply unkind to inform your grandparents the way you did.' That much was clear to him. He would put the camera back and think about what to say to Narcis. At least the cards would stop now.

'I am sorry. Please don't tell anyone. And don't say it was me who told you about the children, please.' She grabbed hold of his arm and tugged at his sleeve like a child.

'That is impossible, Isabella. We must go and see Rosa at *Mossos*. She has more questions to ask you.'

As soon as Isabella entered the doors of the police station, she became a different person. "Meek" was the best way to describe her. In the interview room, Boyle sat next to Isabella across the table from Detective Inspector Rosa Pujol. Isabella's eyes were downcast.

'Isabella?'

The girl looked at the woman who would be her aunt soon. 'You have nothing to worry about,' said Rosa. 'Just answer every question truthfully.' Isabella nodded.

Rosa pressed down the button on the recorder. 'We found another one of the congratulations cards, filled out by you, in this bag.' Rosa set the small blue backpack on the table. Isabella blanched but studied it, a curious look on her face, as if seeing it for the first time. 'Have you seen this bag before?'

'No.' Her eyes flicked to the left. She was lying.

'Do you know where I found it?'

'No. Where was it, *Tía* Rosa?' She was sweetness and light.

'On the track to your Uncle Adrian's house. Were you there?'

'Where?'

'With Gabriel Osorio at Roca Alba, vandalising houses, the day Cisco Perez died.'

'I don't know what you are talking about. I don't know how those cards got into that bag.'

Rosa took two spray cans of red paint out of the bag. 'What if I tell you we found fingerprints on these cans—'

'They're not mine.'

'—the same fingerprints that were found on the inside of the cards – which I am sure we can verify are yours by taking your prints. Would you like me to take them now? Or will you be honest with me?'

Isabella paused, unsure what to do.

'Did Gabriel Osorio ring you?'

'Who?'

'Don't lie to me, Isabella. I don't know how you know him, but I know you do. Is he your boyfriend?'

'Alright. I know him. But I wasn't there that day. He was there alone.' Boyle wondered if they were in regular contact. Did Gabriel Osorio ring Isabella and warn her that Boyle had been questioning him? When Boyle had first confronted Isabella, she seemed genuinely surprised, which would suggest they weren't. He signalled for Rosa to stop the tape. He got up and whispered to Rosa. She nodded and began to record again.

'You say he was there alone.'

'Yes. But I don't know for certain if he was alone or not,' said Isabella.

'You haven't discussed this with him? He hasn't rung you?' Rosa asked.

'No.'

'Where did you meet him?'

'I can't remember. In Sant Martí maybe, down on the front.'

Rosa held up a photograph of Gabriel Osorio. 'Is this your boyfriend?'

'He's not my boyfriend. I'm not allowed to have a boyfriend.' Isabella's lips were quivering.

'Then why would he have your bag?' Rosa was gentle.

'I don't know, maybe he stole it. I did nothing, *Tía*.' Isabella began to cry. 'I'm sorry about the cards. I really am. I didn't mean to hurt anyone.' Rosa pressed the button to stop recording, reached across the table and took Isabella's hand. The interview was over. Boyle felt frustrated. He was certain that his niece was lying about something, that she was probably protecting Gabriel Osorio for some reason. What better reason than they were involved somehow? Isabella had pleaded with Rosa and Boyle not to say anything to her mother. They agreed they would keep it to themselves for now. They knew that for the moment, there was nowhere to go with this latest bit of information. They may be able to get her prints off the cans of spray paint but they had no actual proof that Isabella was in Roca Alba spraying graffiti the day Cisco died.

Boyle walked Isabella back to the family flat. When she unlocked the door to go in, Boyle held it open and said, 'Don't think the problem has gone away, Isabella.'

'What problem?'

'The lie you are hiding in here.' He pointed to her

head. 'I know you are lying about something. The truth will eventually come out.'

Her expression turned mean. 'Well, the police believe me and *Tía* Rosa is on my side, unlike you,' she said, as she slammed the door in his face.

31

Ever since Boyle had seen Carmen with Jordi, he had stayed away from Restaurant El Dorado. He had spoken to Carmen a few days ago, but as much as he tried to keep his distance, it was dawning on him how much he missed her company. Just before opening time, he walked into the restaurant. The first person he saw was his father-in-law, Narcis, standing next to the bar and entertaining the waiters with one of his stories. Narcis, who had retired from the restaurant business a few years before, was a witty raconteur. The waiters laughed as Narcis told his tale, but Boyle wasn't listening; he was scanning the room for Carmen. She was nowhere in sight. Was she with Jordi?

Narcis's face lit up when he saw Boyle and he moved towards him, putting his arm around his shoulder and hugging him in that continental way that still made Boyle, after all the time he had spent on the Costa Brava, uncomfortable.

'How are you?' Boyle tried to hide his disappointment in not seeing Carmen but appreciated the warmth of his father-in-law.

'Not too bad. Sit down. I'll get you a beer.' Narcis held up his hand to one of the waiters and motioned to the chill cabinet. They both watched the waiter pour the beer then leave.

Boyle changed the subject to the engagement cards, telling Narcis that whoever delivered them was wearing a hoody and that he was unable to make out whether they were male or female. He had decided that it would break Esther's and Narcis's hearts if they knew that all along, their granddaughter had been sending the cards; not to mention the fact that he had promised Isabella he would say nothing to her grandfather.

'What will we do now?' asked Narcis.

'I'll put the receiver back tomorrow. Possibly we will be able to identify the culprit next time,' said Boyle, knowing there wouldn't be a next time. 'But whoever is doing it isn't asking for money. It will probably stop soon, after the ceremony.'

Narcis nodded his head and closed his eyes. The ceremony was something he clearly didn't want to think about. Boyle wondered that if the idea of the wedding caused Narcis and Esther so much distress, then what would happen when Montse presented them with a child, which Isabella seemed certain was going to happen in the not-so-distant future? Even Boyle was confounded by that possibility.

Narcis failed to mention Carmen so Boyle finally asked where she was.

Narcis scowled with nonchalance. 'She's on a date.' Although parents were not supposed to have favourites, Boyle knew in his bones that Carmen was her father's.

'With Jordi?' Boyle asked, ever the masochist.

'Yes. We met him on Sunday. He seems alright. From Barcelona. Carmen has had such a tough time since Pau left. I hope it works out for her.'

Boyle smiled, trying his best to look happy for the couple. Then, in an attempt to forget about Carmen, his mind alighted on the death of Teresa Clavaguera. He had been meaning to ask Narcis if he had known her personally.

'Do you remember anything about the killing of Teresa Clavaguera?' Boyle asked.

'That was so long ago,' said Narcis.

'Do you know the Durans?'

'I knew the family back then but I rarely see

Faustino here in town. He and Teresa used to holiday here with their parents. They were from Barcelona – in the textile business. It wasn't like now, where a few families turn up during the summer; then, dozens of outsiders would arrive.' Narcis leaned close to Boyle and lowered his voice. 'There were lots of parties. It was the late seventies. Franco was finally dead and people were in the mood to have a good time. Everyone was having affairs – all ages. And this is no exaggeration. It was one big orgy up there during the summer,' he said, his face grave, as it always became when he spoke about sex. 'And Teresa was a very popular girl. It was unusual for a Spanish girl from a good family to be so friendly in those days, when girls were still chaperoned. In fact, she had once been Salvador's girlfriend.'

'That must have created some tension in the Clavaguera household,' said Boyle.

Narcis laughed. 'Well, all the young men were in love with her, and she… how can I put it politely?…'

It was Boyle's turn to laugh. 'Don't hold back on my account.'

'She offered herself freely. Then one day, Eduardo announced that he wanted to marry her. Everyone was shocked. His father disapproved of her, as you can imagine.'

'Not the mother?'

'Eduardo's mother died when he was young. He

was brought up by his father and grandparents. The father was very strict. He was never going to agree to the match. You might ask how the father knew that Teresa was such a friendly girl.' Narcis leaned close and whispered – not that there was anyone there to overhear. Boyle smiled at him with affection. 'The father had known about Teresa's reputation, rumour had it, because for a while he had bedded her as well.' Narcis held his palms up to ward off dissent. 'But don't quote me on that. It was just a rumour. But then the father died and the first thing Eduardo did was marry Teresa. Behind his back, everyone said he was a fool.'

Boyle thought that Eduardo sounded like a romantic, a stubborn romantic. He wondered if Eduardo was devoted to Tina in the same way. 'Did you ever meet Teresa?' Boyle asked.

'Once. Briefly. Down on the front in the Bar Carolet. She was already well known for her exploits. And when I was introduced to her, I was struck by how plain she was. "Handsome" was the best way to describe her. My first response was to feel sorry for her, this used woman. But then when I spoke to her… I don't remember the conversation, but I remember how confident she was and, most importantly, how she made me feel – like I was the only man on earth who mattered. Teresa was enchanting.'

Teresa had many admirers. Jealousy must have

been rife on the mountain. Was Felipe Perez in love with her also? Did he shoot her on purpose? Did the right man go to prison but get off with a lighter sentence for accidental death when he should have been charged with premeditated murder and locked up for life? Boyle thought about Quimet Navarro. Was he another boyfriend of Teresa's? Quimet must have held a grudge against the Clavagueras for filching his family's land after the war. Did he pay them back by having an affair with Eduardo's wife? Wife number one, that is. And thirty years later, was it still payback time, considering his affair with wife number two, Tina? A tangled web, alright.

'Do you know anything about the land that the Clavagueras supposedly took from the Navarro family after the war?'

Narcis held up his hand. 'Not "supposedly". It was true. The Navarro family was one of the wealthiest in the area before the *Guerra Civil*, but they fought against General Franco and lost nearly everything. Like so many rich families, they went to France to escape the danger of the war. When they came back, they found that their land was no longer theirs, that it now belonged to the Clavagueras. Eduardo Clavaguera's grandfather, Luis, had been a captain in the Nationalist army. When the war ended, Franco, as a thank you, gave him most of the Navarros' land. In the sixties, the Clavagueras built the Santa Nuria golf course and urbanisation. That's how they made their fortune – buying more property and developing it. You know the huge *masia* where Eduardo lives now?'

Boyle nodded.

'That was where the Navarros used to live before the war.'

'Imagine having to go through the hardship of war and then being booted out of your house afterwards,' said Boyle. He felt some newfound sympathy for Quimet Navarro begin to chip away at his dislike for the man.

'It can't have been easy for them,' said Narcis. 'Also, in exchange for the new money just after the war, Quimet's family lost much of their monetary wealth.' Narcis glanced at the door to the restaurant, waiting for the first customers to arrive, his anxious manner reminding Boyle of Carmen. He then peered at Boyle. 'You look hungry.'

Narcis moved to the bar with a walk that showed all of his eighty years. Boyle felt an unexpected surge of affection for him combined with a fear that he might lose him. Narcis had been a child during the *Guerra Civil*. The effects of the war, namely hunger and political repression, continued long after. Narcis's family was well-off, so there was always food on the table, at least. Esther's family had lived in the Vall d'Aro for over two hundred years. Her father had been a doctor who died just before she was born, fighting with the Republicans in Barcelona. The family was thrown into poverty and her mother had struggled to take care of her four children. Esther had told Boyle how she remembered following her mother, who had a shotgun tucked under her arm, over the hills of Les Gavarres in search of rabbit and birds, well into the 1950s. She became an expert shot and kept the family fed. There were long walks down to Sant Pol beach, where the family fished from the rocks. They also gathered edible delights that grew all over the valley and hills; wild mushrooms, pine nuts, tiny strawberries and weedy asparagus.

Boyle had once asked Narcis why the Spanish he encountered seemed reluctant to discuss Franco and the Civil War. Boyle suggested that they refused to open up to him because he was a foreigner. Narcis said that it had nothing to do with Boyle's nationality, but that during the dictatorship it was more important to forget than to remember. In order to survive the regime, they all kept silent and adopted a manner of obedience. Most of the people were poor so focused on their families and finding food. They avoided discussing politics and, as a result, the Spanish became a country of amnesiacs. Narcis had ended the conversation by saying, 'But slowly, we are waking up and remembering.' *No doubt all of this remembering is fuelling the Catalans' desire for an independent Catalonia,* thought Boyle.

Boyle's father-in-law took a plate of olives, sliced chorizo and bread off the bar and placed it on the table. Boyle thanked him and bit away at one of the tiny green olives.

'The Clavagueras weren't all bad though,' said Narcis, sitting back down. 'Eduardo's grandfather began the first irrigation system in the valley. They were now able to grow fruits and vegetables on a mass scale. It was a major change. The Clavagueras have contributed a great deal to the modernisation of this valley. No one can take that away from them. But despite that, I think that the Navarros have always held a grudge. They feel that the Clavagueras owe them something.' Narcis pushed the plate of food closer to Boyle. 'Have another and then I will take your order.'

'I think that Eduardo realises that he owes Quimet and is now trying to help him. When he sold him that land along the bypass, I heard Quimet paid next to nothing for it,' said Boyle.

'He paid absolutely nothing for it, is what I heard,' said Narcis.

The winds began to blow early that evening. The *tramuntana* blew all night, keeping Boyle awake in Montse's spare room. When he got out of bed it was quiet in the house but he could still hear the strong wind whining through the beams. The clock on the nightstand read 9am. There was a knock on his door and it opened. Montse peeked into the room.

'We have found the telephone number and address of a Doctor Bosch, who performed the autopsy on Teresa Clavaguera,' she said, breezing in and handing Boyle a piece of paper. 'I rang him but haven't told him anything. I just asked if it's alright for you to contact him. He sounds like a lovely man,' she said, then left.

Boyle was doubtful the autopsy report still existed, thinking that it most likely disappeared with the case report. He picked up his mobile from the bedside table and immediately tapped in the number. It was answered on the fifth ring by a man with a quavering voice. Boyle introduced himself and asked if he could have access to an autopsy report that the doctor did for Teresa Clavaguera in 1978.

'Of course. I have it here. We kept everything,' said Doctor Bosch.

That information was encouraging. They agreed to meet in an hour. Boyle showered, dressed and clipped on his gun. The doctor lived in Romanya, a tiny village perched on top of the Les Gavarres range of hills that bordered the north side of the Vall d'Aro. Several old stone buildings comprised the hamlet. There was a tiny tenth-century church, Iglesia de Sant Martí de Romanya, one restaurant and a municipal building, and the rest were residences. Although the sun was bright, when Boyle got out of the car he shivered in the icy north wind. The house was massive, in biscuit-coloured stone with an iron-studded door. Boyle rang the bell. A small, elderly man opened the door to Boyle and smiled.

'I am Doctor Bosch,' he said, proffering a hand.

'Thank you for seeing me, Doctor Bosch,' said Boyle, shaking the doctor's firm hand.

'My pleasure. Please come this way.' He was so happy to see Boyle that Boyle guessed the man had few visitors. They walked on a dusty path along the side of the house, exchanging pleasantries and talking about the fast-developing *tramuntana*. The doctor was short, bow-legged and walked with a pronounced limp. 'I had a knee replacement two months ago and it's changed my life. No more pain. It is amazing what modern medicine can do for an eighty-eight-year-old man.'

They approached what looked like a time-worn coach house with high wooden doors. 'We kept copies of all the reports for forty years. I should throw them away but I can't. I like to have them on hand when people enquire. I still get enquiries.' Doctor Bosch struggled with the key for the padlock to the door, but the padlock was broken. The doctor said it was old and that he must replace it but Boyle got a bad feeling. He helped the doctor to open the doors and switched on the light. But for a few tools and gardening implements that hung from the walls, most of the space was filled with about sixty file-sized cardboard boxes, stacked four high. 'My wife died last year,' said the doctor, moving aside for Boyle to enter.

'I'm very sorry,' said Boyle.

'I have her to thank for all of this.' He indicated the boxes. 'She was my secretary and a great organiser.' The doctor walked up to one of the boxes and squinted at the label. 'What year are you looking for?'

'She died in November 1978. Her name was Teresa Clavaguera.'

'I don't recall that one off hand. The oldest reports are at the back. I suggest we begin there.'

They searched amongst the boxes. Boyle found the correct box for 1978 and heaved it onto a table. When he opened the box, his stomach sank. It was partially empty. Boyle flipped through the files. October, November and December were missing.

The doctor rummaged through the files from January, looking confused. 'Where are they?'

'Have you had anyone enquire recently about the files?'

'No. Not for at least five years.'

'No files have gone missing before?'

'No, absolutely not. Why would they?'

Why would they? Because someone is trying to hide something. Clearly they had broken in and taken the forensic report, and that someone was several steps ahead of Boyle. Who was it?

'Tell me about the case,' said Doctor Bosch, offering Boyle a seat on a bench. 'Perhaps you can jog my memory.'

They both sat down. 'Her name was Teresa Clavaguera. She was accidentally shot by a hunter on Pedralta – in Roca Alba.'

'Ah, yes. That's beginning to sound familiar. Married to one of the Clavagueras? The property developers from Santa Nuria?'

'That's right.' Sometimes Boyle forgot that Clavaguera was a common name in the area.

'Very sad. She was so young. I can't quite picture the wound she had. Many times, I can visualise the wounds when I hear a name, even after forty years. Strange, isn't it?'

Boyle nodded even though he did not think it was strange at all. He was able to remember every horrific death scene he had witnessed; the images were safely tucked into his subconscious and every once in a while, he dreamt about them. 'She was shot in the chest,' Boyle said.

The doctor stared out of the window in deep concentration, his mind off somewhere in an operating theatre thirty years back. He looked at Boyle. 'No. I can't picture the wound, but I do remember something very clearly. She was pregnant when she was killed. Very tragic for the whole family.'

Why had no one mentioned this? thought Boyle. 'Are you absolutely sure about that?'

'Oh yes. Absolutely. She was already two and a half months along.'

'The reason I ask is because it wasn't mentioned anywhere in the newspaper reports of the trial.'

'I don't remember the trial, but I know the woman was pregnant. I have no doubt about that. And the husband... what was his name?'

'Eduardo,' said Boyle.

'That's it. Eduardo. He was totally devastated.'

As Boyle drove down the winding road from Romanya, he tried to tease out the implications of the latest disclosure. He was certain of one thing: that if Eduardo was unable to have children, he was not the father of Teresa's unborn child. So, was Salvador the father? Did Eduardo call in his brother to donate, as he had done with his present family? When did Eduardo find out he was infertile? Boyle wondered. Was it during his marriage to Teresa? If so, perhaps the discovery that she was pregnant would have been sufficient motivation for him to have murdered her. The next question he grappled with was this: if Teresa was having an affair, then who was it with? Salvador? Boyle's father-in-law had mentioned that Salvador had had an affair with Teresa before she hooked up with Eduardo. Did they carry on the affair after Teresa had married? Or was it someone else, perhaps one of the hunters there that day – Gunnar, Felipe or Quimet?

If Felipe was framed for the shooting, then, perhaps he was the one having the affair with her. Or perhaps Felipe was framed because out of the group of hunters, he was the lowest one on the social scale and so the easiest to frame.

Boyle headed back to Pedralta. He turned down the track to Roca Alba and drew up outside Can Bosc, the house of Faustino. There were scarves of smoke coming from the chimney. Faustino was outside, hefting a piece of luggage into the back of his SUV.

Boyle got out of his car and greeted him. Faustino said hello with a smile. Boyle had never seen the man smile before. 'Do you have a few minutes?' Boyle asked.

'Of course. Come in and have a coffee,' he said, ushering him into the house.

Boyle was surprised by Faustino's sudden friendliness. They entered the large L-shaped living space. It was rustic in style; animal skins on the tiled floor, heavy, rough-hewn furniture and old iron farm tools hanging on the walls. At one end was the dining area. The dining table and floor were full of packing boxes.

'You're moving?' asked Boyle.

'Yes, they're tearing down all these houses in a few weeks.' This sent a jolt of fear through Boyle. So soon?

'There are some people with serious money who are itching to buy plots here. I'm taking a few things now,' added Faustino. 'The movers are coming tomorrow and they will take the rest.'

Boyle dreaded the whole idea of the new urbanisation. 'I'm surprised you sold to Quimet.'

'He has been after me for years to sell. It's time to go. Yeah, I have some good memories of Roca Alba but… this is where my wife died and, of course, Teresa as well.'

'Where are you going?'

'Back to Barcelona. I have a house there that is more of a family home. My son and his wife are there.' He glanced around. 'So, you'll be alone up here most of the year now.'

Boyle had been alone on this mountain since Ana died but he wasn't about to argue that point with Faustino now; he needed his help.

Faustino showed him into the lounge where the fire was lit. 'Have a seat. I'll get the coffee. Or would you prefer something stronger?'

Boyle glanced at his watch. Eleven forty-five. Better not. 'A black coffee would be very nice. Thank you.'

Faustino disappeared into the kitchen. While Faustino was occupied getting the coffee, Boyle took in the place. A boar's head was mounted over a large brick and stone Catalan fireplace, with the characteristic thick wooden beam serving as a mantlepiece. Several hunting rifles, too old for Boyle to identify, were displayed on the wall. Faustino's hound was stretched out in front of the fire. He lifted his head slightly when Boyle sat down on the leather sofa, but that was it. Boyle listened to the wind rattling the shutters.

Faustino came back in with two black coffees and set them down, then took a seat opposite Boyle.

Boyle thanked Faustino for the coffee and Faustino said it was nothing.

What? Nothing? Blimey. Are you kidding? After all this time living on Pedralta and being ignored, it's a bloody miracle you're serving me coffee, thought Boyle. *Faustino must be one of those people who can only be friendly once they know they are leaving,* he decided.

'So why are you here?' asked Faustino.

'I would like to ask you a few questions concerning the shooting of your sister, if that's alright?'

'Who is paying you for this?'

Boyle paused, hoping that Faustino would not refuse once he heard that it was Cisco's mother who had hired him. 'I'm investigating it for Juanita Perez. She thinks her husband was framed for the shooting.'

'I figured that was the case.'

'Is it alright if I continue?'

'Okay,' he said, shrugging.

'I've just spoken to the doctor who did your sister's autopsy. He said that she was several weeks pregnant.'

'I knew that, yes.' He nodded his head. 'She would have been a good mother.'

'It wasn't mentioned anywhere in the newspapers.'

'It was a secret. No one knew but Teresa, Eduardo and me. You see, it took her longer than expected to become pregnant. My sister, never a patient girl, wanted to announce it to the world straight away, but Eduardo convinced her to wait until she was three months along. Unfortunately, that never happened. She was only seven weeks pregnant when she died. Eduardo and I decided to keep it out of the papers, and it was not brought up during the trial.'

'Why?'

'Eduardo was too upset,' said Faustino.

'And the police and judge went along with that?'

'Of course.' Faustino smiled, held his hand up and rubbed his fingers together. Money.

Boyle took a sip of his coffee. It was strong and bitter. He needed a moment to frame the next question. 'Did you know that Eduardo is infertile?

'Then?'

'Always has been.'

Faustino looked confused. 'What about his children? Who is the father?'

'Salvador was the sperm donor.'

Faustino put down his cup and sat back like he

had been slugged in the solar plexus. He stared into the distance, lost in thought, as though trying to add it all up. He then looked at Boyle. 'Are you sure?'

Boyle nodded.

'How can that be?' Faustino asked.

'I thought you might be able to enlighten me.'

'Who told you that Eduardo is infertile?'

'I am not at liberty to say.'

'Perhaps they are lying. Have you thought about that?' said Faustino, once again showing the belligerence Boyle had come to love.

Boyle hadn't thought of that. The question was, why would Deirdre invent a story like this? Why would anyone? 'I don't see why my informant would make this up.'

Faustino went quiet again. He put his elbow on the arm of his chair and rested his head on his hand, a look of bewilderment on his face.

'Do you mind if I ask you a few more questions?' said Boyle.

'Yes, it's fine. Go ahead.'

'Were you close to your sister?'

'Yes, I would say so. We confided in each other.'

'Is it possible she was having an affair?'

'If what you say is true, then she must have been. Though I cannot imagine with whom.'

Clearly Faustino lacked imagination, if what Narcis had told him was true about Teresa's reputation for bed-hopping. 'I heard that she had a relationship with Salvador Clavaguera before she got involved with Eduardo?' Boyle stated with care. 'Perhaps they carried on after she married Eduardo?'

Faustino looked at him askance. 'That imbecile? She wouldn't touch him with a barge pole,' he said, shaking his head. 'No, impossible.'

'Salvador is not a popular man,' said Boyle, trying to lighten things up. 'I'm amazed that he was elected mayor.'

'That's right. My sister would never have had an affair with him. I knew my sister.'

Boyle guessed that Faustino knew his sister about as well as Juanita Perez knew her husband – not well at all. He realised at this point that he was not going to get any more helpful answers from Faustino. Faustino was either right, and his sister was as pure as the driven snow, or he was in total denial about her promiscuity. Boyle had a hunch it was the latter.

32

NOT ALLOWED TO PASS THROUGH THE SECURITY gates at the Vespella Nou complex with his car, Boyle had parked at the beach and walked up into the exclusive neighbourhood built on a headland overlooking the sea. He kept his eye out for people following him. The wind thrashed the umbrella pines, scattering needles in the wide, empty streets. The well-kept mansions and luxury cars were hidden behind the high walls that surrounded each property. Boyle found it strange, considering that Franco had given Quimet's family land to the Clavagueras, that Quimet would then decide to live here, in a development that Franco had originally built for his cronies.

Montse had copied the bank statements of the planning officials in Sant Martí for Boyle, showing the dubious payments that Quimet Navarro had made to them over four years. Boyle had then rung Quimet Navarro.

'There is something shifty going on between you, Salvador Clavaguera and the planning commission,' he had said.

Quimet asked him what he was talking about.

'Jose Font, Maria Fonells, Pau Castello and Rafael Moya. Do you know them?' asked Boyle.

'No,' said Quimet.

'They all work for the planning commission and they each received one hundred thousand euros from you over a four-year period. Now that can't be right,' said Boyle.

'That's outrageous. You can't look into my private accounts!'

Boyle laughed. 'So, ring the police.' There was an even longer pause, just Navarro's audible breath rasping down the phone. How could Navarro defend himself? He was a crook. 'Take it from me, Señor Navarro – these days, nothing is secret. But if you don't want to talk to me, that's fine, you don't have to. I'll just put all the information I have into a jumbo-sized envelope and send it over to my dear friend at

Mossos, *Comissari* Marc Saldoni. I'm sure he will be interested.'

'If I talk to you?' asked Quimet.

'I will forget all about it.'

In Calle Sant Pol, Boyle saw the nameplate Las Brisas and approached the grey wrought-iron gate, behind which lay a pale ochre mansion with an emerald green lawn. He introduced himself on the entry phone and was let in by a uniformed maid, who directed him to a door just off the main foyer and showed him in. It was an office with comfortable seating. Quimet was standing by a window overlooking the sea. Huge waves whipped up by the *tramuntana* crashed against the rocks below. "Worried" was how Boyle would have described him.

'Please, take a seat,' Quimet said, indicating an armchair. Quimet sat on a sofa opposite.

Without wasting time on pleasantries, Boyle said, 'I'm here to discuss the shooting of Teresa Clavaguera, nothing else.'

Navarro's mouth tightened. 'I know nothing about that.'

Boyle glared at him. 'You were hunting that day. You must know something.'

'Well, it was a long time ago. I don't remember much.' He picked up a pack of cigarettes from the table and offered one to Boyle. He declined and waited for Quimet to light up. He wanted his full attention.

Boyle then said, 'Teresa Clavaguera was pregnant when she died. The child could not have been Eduardo's because he is infertile.' Navarro exhaled and nodded. 'Someone else must have been having an affair with Teresa. Do you know who?'

'It's not a secret that Teresa was having affairs. The last person was Felipe. The baby was Felipe's.'

Boyle expected this to be the case but was pleased to have confirmation. 'So, let's start at the beginning. How well did you know Felipe?'

'He and I had grown up together in Santa Nuria. At one time, we were best friends.'

'How did he start working for Eduardo?'

'I was managing a farm for Eduardo. One day, Felipe approached me for work. I was wary of introducing him to Eduardo. You see, Felipe was irresponsible. He'd miss work without a second thought if he wanted to go fishing or go to a fiesta. He never let work get in the way of having a good time. Consequently, he was always losing jobs.' Quimet took a drag, blew out a cloud of smoke and sank back into the sofa. 'He convinced me that he had changed his ways, said he would work hard if I got him the job. I asked Eduardo if I could hire Felipe to help me on the farm and he agreed. Felipe had grown up in Santa Nuria; in fact, he grew up on one of the Clavaguera farms, and Eduardo liked to hire local people. Felipe and Eduardo took to each other straight away. Felipe was charming and good-looking; people were drawn to him. But what really surprised me, though it shouldn't have, was how much Teresa was attracted to him. They flirted openly with each other. Of course, it was toned down when Eduardo was around, but it wasn't long before Felipe was working at their house, Casa Cielo, as a gardener and handy man. About two months later, Felipe was bragging that he was having an affair with her. I was furious. He put me in an impossible situation. I could have lost my job.'

'Tell me what you remember about the day she was shot.'

'Nothing much happened that morning. I remember that the boar had disappeared. We all drank wine but Felipe was the worst. Because I had introduced him to Eduardo, I felt responsible for the way he acted and by this point he was becoming a liability. On that day he must have poured a bottle of wine down his throat. I told him to take it easy but he paid no attention to me. But what was strange was that Eduardo was opening one bottle after another, encouraging Felipe to drink.'

Easier to frame a drunk man, Boyle thought. 'So, you had a siesta after lunch?'

'Yes. If I remember correctly, Gunnar, Faustino and Tina went home and the rest of us had a siesta for a couple of hours.'

'So, it was just you, Eduardo, Salvador and Felipe.'

'That's right.'

'What time was that?'

'It's usually three or half past.'

'You were using your Tikka rifle that day?'

'Yes. But I don't know what that has to do with anything.' Quimet reached over to an ornate crystal ashtray and cleaned the ash off his cigarette.

'Felipe was convinced that he was framed for the shooting of Teresa.'

'Well, don't look at me. I had nothing to do it.'

'The police are looking into the death of Felipe. They now believe that his wife didn't kill him but that he was executed,' Boyle said, stretching the truth somewhat. They had yet to convince the police that outsiders killed Felipe. They were still waiting for the results for the blood tests from the lab in Barcelona.

'Executed? Why?'

'Because the killers thought that Felipe had proof as to who really shot Teresa.'

Quimet stubbed out his cigarette and rose to his feet. Hands in pockets, he stared down at the sea.

'You know something you're not telling me,' said Boyle.

'I don't have to tell you anything.'

'You do if you don't want to go to prison.' Quimet glared at him. 'And by the way, if anything happens to me, all the papers automatically go to the authorities,' said Boyle.

'I'm not a gangster, for God's sake.'

'Then tell me what you know.'

Quimet sat down. He looked like a cornered animal and Boyle knew he was ready to talk.

'Where were we?'

'The siesta.'

'There are three bedrooms in the lodge, as you probably know, since it's your house.'

Boyle nodded. 'Go on.'

'Sal slept in one, Felipe in another and I took the last, which I had offered to Eduardo, but he insisted on sleeping on the sofa in the salon.' Quimet leaned forward, his manner intimate, and said, 'I fell fast asleep after lunch. But then I woke suddenly. I thought I had heard a shot, but I wasn't quite sure. You know how sometimes you wake and you're not always sure what woke you? This was about four o'clock. I know because I remember checking my watch. I got up and went into the salon and discovered that Eduardo wasn't there. I went back to bed and drifted off to sleep again.' Quimet took a drag of his cigarette and gazed down at the sea.

Boyle gave him a few moments then asked. 'What happened next?'

Quimet looked at him, as if trying to gather his thoughts. 'Something must have woken me again. I remember that I heard footsteps on the gravel path. I looked out the window and saw Eduardo walking back towards the house. I thought that he must have tried to shoot a rabbit. But it was strange because he was carrying a Tikka rifle under his arm and he wasn't using his that day. My first thought was that Eduardo was using my rifle – I was using my Tikka that day – and I don't like anyone touching my things, especially my guns. But I wasn't about to say anything to him; after all, he was my boss. So, I went back to bed. But this time I couldn't get back to sleep. I was worried about my gun. After a while, I got up and went into the salon. Eduardo was already asleep on the sofa. I went to the entrance where we kept our guns and smelt my rifle. I was relieved that it hadn't been used. And then I smelt the only other Tikka there, the one belonging to Felipe. There was the distinct smell of sulphur and I knew it had been fired.' Quimet paused and rubbed his hands together. 'And what you must understand is that none of us saw any wild boar that morning, not one single shot was fired. I came back through the salon and although Eduardo's eyes were closed, I don't know how, but I knew he was just pretending to be asleep. Later that afternoon, when we heard that Teresa had been shot, I thought that possibly Eduardo had done it.'

'Why didn't you tell the police?'

'Because we all thought Felipe *had* shot her. He was in the right area that afternoon and still inebriated from all the wine he had at lunch. And later, the ballistics confirmed that the bullet came from his rifle.'

'When did you know for certain that Eduardo had shot his wife?' asked Boyle.

'I still don't know if he did.'

'Come on. You have some hold over Eduardo. It isn't out of the goodness of his heart that he's allowed you to acquire so much of his land. And from what I hear, some of it *gratis*.'

Quimet appeared to be struggling with what to say next, as if he hoped that what he had revealed already was enough. It was not. He lit another cigarette. 'Just before Teresa was shot, she had told Felipe that she wanted to end the affair. That she was pregnant with Eduardo's child. Felipe, of course, told me about it. He was upset to see it end. But I was surprised that in all that time leading up to her death, Eduardo never mentioned the pregnancy to me. Usually men are happy when their wives become pregnant. It is a cause for celebration. It wasn't until about six years ago that it all made sense.'

'What happened?' Boyle asked, although he had an inkling of what he was about to hear.

'Deirdre Clavaguera found out that her husband Salvador was the father of Eduardo's children and told my wife Lola. She said that Eduardo was infertile and always had been. Then I figured that Eduardo must have killed his wife because he found out that she was expecting a child that didn't belong to him, but to Felipe. You see, that would have driven Eduardo wild because he really trusted Teresa. Actually, I'm not surprised he killed her. She was a tramp.'

Things were beginning to drop into place. 'Is that when you began blackmailing Eduardo?'

'How do you mean?'

'Don't mess me about. All the land you've taken.'

'Taken?' Quimet stood up and glared at Boyle. 'I haven't taken anything. I was taking possession of land that belonged to my family in the first place. Land that was stolen from us.'

Boyle waited for Quimet to calm down and sit. He had some sympathy for the man but he wasn't going to let it interfere with the investigation. *Everyone has lost something important to them and don't we all lose in the end?* Boyle focused on the final question. 'Do Salvador and Tina have any idea that Eduardo killed Teresa?'

'I don't think so. I certainly have never discussed it with either of them.' Boyle stood up to leave. 'You won't say anything about my business deals?' asked Quimet.

Your crooked business deals, thought Boyle. 'Only on one condition.'

'What's that?'

'That you don't go ahead with the urbanisation on Roca Alba.'

Quimet looked puzzled. 'That's not what we agreed.'

'Start tearing up Mount Pedralta and I promise you, all hell will break loose,' said Boyle.

33

Boyle sat in his office feeling cold. The temperature had dropped. The *tramuntana* was in full flow, whistling through the window. He went to the thermostat and turned it up to twenty-one degrees. He wanted to ring Eduardo Clavaguera but was uncertain he would be in a talking mood. Taking out his mobile phone, he began to send him an email.

> *Eduardo*
>
> *Today I spoke to the doctor who performed the autopsy on your first wife Teresa. He says that she was pregnant when she died. The child cannot*

have been yours because you are infertile. Good motivation for murder, don't you think?

Within five minutes, Eduardo rang. There was no greeting, just, 'I would be interested in seeing a copy of the autopsy report that states what you say.' Eduardo seemed so confident that the report would never appear that Boyle felt he must have had it stolen from the house of Doctor Bosch. He wondered if Eduardo had managed to get rid of the old police report for the shooting of Teresa as well. A nice backhander to a member of the *Guardia Civil* would have done the trick. 'You don't actually think you can form a case against me, do you? You need some proof.' Eduardo was baiting him. 'Anyway, haven't you done enough damage to my family?'

Was the damage to Eduardo's family worse than what Eduardo had done to the family of Teresa? Eduardo was a cold-blooded killer. Surely that was worse. 'I have a witness that says your wife was pregnant when she was shot.' Boyle said, holding back Quimet's eyewitness account of Eduardo's use of Felipe's gun that day. 'That would certainly get the investigation moving again.'

'Is that all you have? That my wife was pregnant?' Eduardo gave a fake laugh.

'No, there is more.'

'What?' he asked with scepticism.

'I want to ask you a few questions.'

'I suppose I could give you a few minutes of my time.'

Boyle was surprised by Eduardo's quick change of mind. He knew that Eduardo would want him nowhere near his house, so suggested, 'Do you know the Bar Aurora in Sant Martí?'

'Of course I know the Bar Aurora. I have lived here all my life,' he snapped.

'I'll meet you there in half an hour,' said Boyle, and then disconnected.

Exiting his office, Boyle was hit by a blast of the cold north wind. He zipped up his cagoule and with his head down, bracing himself against the torrent, he made his way along the pedestrianised rambla towards the bar. The fierce winds had cleared the streets of people. Workers from the cafés along the rambla were being blown about as they attempted to stack and chain the outside tables and chairs.

In Bar Aurora, Boyle had a *café solo* and read a copy of *La Vanguardia* while he waited for Eduardo to arrive. The café was empty but for the owner Diego, who was washing up the lunch dishes at the far end of the bar. A few minutes later, he saw Eduardo's security man Pedro park a navy-blue Porsche SUV just opposite the bar and get out. Boyle recognised the Porsche as the one that had followed him when he met Tina Clavaguera at the stables. Boyle's eye was still smarting from their encounter in Barcelona.

When Eduardo stepped out of the vehicle, he had a look of such dread that Boyle briefly felt sorry for him. That was, until the man entered the bar and uttered his first words.

'Señor Boyle, what trouble have you cooked up now?' he said. The dread was gone from his face and replaced with a phoney easygoing expression. How often Boyle had seen the guilty person throwing the blame on someone else, attempting to make the investigation the crime. Eduardo ordered a brandy from Diego who was practically bowing with deference to the head of the powerful Clavaguera clan. Eduardo turned to Boyle and asked, 'Will you join me?'

Boyle accepted the brandy. He glanced at the rambla and recognised Eduardo's other security man – the Galician – standing outside. He was leaning against the door of the vehicle keeping an eye on him, no doubt with an automatic weapon of some sort within easy reach. He gave Boyle a menacing grin.

Eduardo approached the table, closely followed by Diego, who set down two large snifters and a bottle of Torres 10. As Eduardo sat, Diego began to pour the brandy into a glass. When the snifter was a third full, Eduardo held his hand out for him to stop. The men quietly watched as the same amount was poured for Boyle.

Boyle waited until Diego was back to his

dishwashing before he asked in a lowered voice, 'Whose baby was your first wife expecting?'

'Mine, of course. But that is none of your business.' Eduardo cupped the snifter in his hand and swirled the brandy around. Boyle noticed that his eyes were unfocused. He clearly had had something to drink beforehand. His reckless manner was new to Boyle.

'Everyone in the Vall d'Aro seems to know that Salvador is the father of your children.' Eduardo took a drink, saying nothing. 'A simple DNA test will prove that Salvador is the father,' Boyle added.

Eduardo shrugged and said. 'So what? The question of my children's paternity is no one's business but mine.'

'Did you kill your first wife and frame Felipe for it?'

Eduardo smirked, 'If I did, I certainly wouldn't tell you.'

Boyle leaned towards Eduardo. 'Tell me, how did you do it? Did you take Felipe's gun during the siesta, leave the lodge and then shoot your wife at Casa Cielo? I have a witness to say that is exactly what happened.' There was a flicker of surprise in Eduardo's eyes. *Quimet has probably been blackmailing Eduardo for several years, so he must know the identity of the witness,* thought Boyle.

'Cisco befriended your family to find out the truth about what actually happened to your first wife.

Felipe had told his son that he had doubts about his conviction.'

Eduardo laughed.

'My guess is that Cisco didn't paint the portrait of Teresa as a memento for you, as you told me before. No, he painted it as a reminder that you killed your wife all those years ago and then framed Cisco's father for it.' Boyle knew there was no statute of limitations for murder in Spain. And rightly so. Why should anyone ever get away with murder?

Eduardo's demeanour changed, the way it does with those who have had just that one drink too many. He glowered. 'Don't you think you've done enough damage to my family?'

'I haven't even begun yet,' said Boyle.

'That's it,' said Eduardo, rising to his feet. 'Don't bother me again.' He picked up the snifter, gulped the rest of his brandy down, then whispered to Boyle, 'If you don't keep out of my business, the next time a gun is fired at you, it won't miss.' Eduardo looked out at his body guard, standing alert by his car. 'I warn you, Pedro is an excellent shot.'

Boyle had to hold back from slugging him. Eduardo left and strode to his car. Pedro opened the door to the SUV and he climbed in. The vehicle swung around quickly, squealing complaint before taking off to Santa Nuria.

Boyle looked out at the rambla. The precinct was

now deserted. He drank his brandy, watched the branches of the jacaranda trees lashing in the fierce wind and thought about the case. There were still many unanswered questions, but one in particular nagged him. He wondered how Felipe knew for certain that he had been framed and how much he had told Cisco. He picked up his mobile and rang Quimet Navarro. When Quimet picked up the phone, he sounded uneasy.

'Look, Señor Boyle. I've told you everything I know. I hope you aren't going to start threatening me again.'

'I need more information.'

He sighed. 'What is it?'

'You met Felipe at Bar Can Pijuan a couple of years ago. Alfonso told me. What did Felipe say to you?'

'What do you mean?'

'Why was he so convinced he was framed?'

'*Vale*. When Felipe first read the ballistics report, he, like everyone else, was convinced he had accidentally shot Teresa. But in prison he had time to think, and he said that one thing never made sense to him.'

'What was that?'

'At first we thought that Teresa was hit by a ricocheting bullet that had bounced off one of the boulders on Pedralta. That's what all the hunters thought. But in the ballistics report, there was no evidence that the bullet had hit anything before it entered Teresa's body. When I met Felipe at Can Pijuan he told me that it had never made sense to him.'

'Why?'

'Because although he was a beginner, he was an incredibly good shot.'

'But he had had too much to drink that day. You said so yourself.'

'If the bullet had hit nothing before it hit Teresa, then the shooter would have been aiming straight towards the terrace where she sat. And Felipe told me that even drunk he would never have fired directly towards Casa Cielo, or any house for that matter. He said that there was no way that he had shot her. He was convinced of that and told me he was determined to clear his name.'

So, all along Felipe had doubts about his guilt.

'I asked him who he thought had done it. He said he didn't know.'

'He didn't suspect that Eduardo had murdered her?'

'Eduardo would have been the last person he would suspect. I was worried because we had both used the same rifles that day and I was hoping that Felipe didn't think I was responsible. He never said. He was aggrieved because after the shooting, no one took anything he said seriously because he had drunk so much. He was confused after the arrest and browbeaten, he said. He asked me if I knew anything at all that could help him and I said, "To help you do what?" and he said, "To prove my innocence".'

'What did you tell him?'

'That I knew nothing. There was no way I wanted Felipe to know the truth.'

'Did Cisco ever talk to you?' Quimet was quiet and Boyle added, 'I'm not going to implicate you in any of this. Just tell me.'

'Cisco came to my office one day. I can't remember when. Two years ago, perhaps. He said that his father had gone to prison for something he hadn't done. He accused me of the shooting because I had the same kind of rifle and said that there must have been some kind of mix-up that day. But I knew that the only fingerprints that were found on the rifle that killed Teresa that day were Felipe's. I reminded him of that. Later, Cisco and Miguel vandalised my flats. Cisco was the ringleader.'

Boyle remembered Eduardo telling him that he had told Cisco about his father's crime; that up until that time, Cisco was unaware of his father spending any time in prison. 'Who told Cisco that his father had shot Teresa?'

'His father did.'

'Not Eduardo?'

'Why would Eduardo confide in Cisco? He was the murderer.'

'Will you testify to this?'

Quimet lowered his voice. 'You can threaten me all you want. I'll deny I ever spoke to you.'

'Do you think Miguel Clavaguera knows anything?'

'I doubt it. When he sprayed my properties, he was so high on drugs that he probably didn't know who they belonged to. He was just along for the ride. He followed Cisco like a puppy.'

Boyle left the café and made his way to Montse's house in the dark. The narrow streets were deserted. The wind had disappeared and everything was quiet. Boyle turned into Calle Sant Pere. The Porsche SUV was back, parked in front of Montse's. Pedro was in the driver's seat and the Galician was in the road, looking through the windows of the house. Boyle turned around and headed for his office. There he typed up the case report for the murder of Teresa Clavaguera on his laptop. The report consisted mostly of the testimony of Quimet Navarro, unnamed, and took two hours to complete. He printed out one copy of the report and put it in a manila folder. He rang Rosa at the *comisario*.

'There is enough here to open up an investigation into the murder of Teresa Clavaguera. I'd like you to take a look at it,' said Boyle.

'Murder, you say? Who killed her?'

'Eduardo, so the witness says.'

'*Dios mío.*'

'I'll scan you a copy.'

'Let me read it, then we will talk.'

Boyle sent the report to Rosa and then walked back to Montse's house. The *tramuntana* was building again and the icy wind cut through his bones. Luckily, the SUV had left. He didn't fancy camping out in his office all night; he wanted a hot shower, a hot drink and a hot fire.

The first thing Boyle did when he entered Montse's house was draw all the curtains. Montse and Rosa came home at eight o'clock with a take-away paella. Rather than eat in the chilly dining room, they sat in the living room in front of the wood-burning stove with plates on their laps and listened to the wind battering the shutters. Rosa told Boyle that she had read his report and showed it to judge Jordi Llfranc, and he said that they were going to look into it. They had already called Eduardo Clavaguera and he had agreed to come in for questioning the following morning at eleven. Rosa had requested that Boyle watch from the observation room.

The next day, at five to eleven, Boyle stood in the observation room next to the two-way mirror. Eduardo was in the interview room, seated opposite Detective Inspector Rosa Pujol. The family lawyer, Jaume Sanchez, entered the room and sat next to Eduardo. Rosa was checking the tape recorder.

Chief Superintendent Marc Saldoni entered the

observation room and stood near Boyle. They shook hands. Dressed in his smart *Mossos* uniform of navy blue with a red stripe down the trousers, he had large Catalan eyes and a moustache and wore a perpetual hangdog expression. Boyle hadn't spoken to him since Ana's funeral. They had been best friends until the day Marc's ex-wife Rosa had moved out of the marital home, straight into Montse's house. Marc had taken a lot of ribbing from the men on the force; it was bad enough that his wife had left him, but that it had been for another woman was beyond humiliation. He blamed the failure of his marriage on Montse. Boyle thought Marc would let Rosa return, that he still harboured deep feelings for her, but Boyle knew that Rosa was never going back to him.

'Is it alright for me to be here?' Boyle had to ask. Marc was Rosa's superior.

'Of course, *amigo*, I hear you've been very helpful,' he said, taking a seat near him.

'Has Rosa filled you in on the case?' asked Boyle.

Saldoni laughed. 'No. One of her detectives did. Rosa doesn't talk to me anymore,' he said, feigning the tone of a man with a broken heart. He laughed again, a hard, hearty laugh. 'I can't believe it,' he almost shouted.

'What can't you believe?' asked Boyle.

'That my sweet Rosa is to marry your fat sister-in-law.' Boyle looked perplexed. How did Marc know? 'The chief of police in Sitges rang me. I don't know why there's all this secrecy surrounding their relationship, the whole world knows about them,' said Marc.

Back in the interview room, Rosa pressed the recording machine to begin the interrogation. She faced Eduardo and cut to the chase. 'Did you kill your first wife and then blame it on Felipe Perez?'

Eduardo lowered his head, his hands in front of him as if he were praying. 'This has been weighing on my mind for many years now. Yes, I did kill my wife. My lovely Teresa. I purposely shot her with Felipe's rifle and put the blame on him.'

'*Dios mío*,' said Marc Saldoni from the observation room. 'What is this?'

Boyle was taken aback. Eduardo wasn't willing to confess to the murder last night, and now he was doing so. What changed Eduardo's mind to make him admit to this? What could possibly influence someone to confess to a murder they did years before when there was only Quimet Navarro's eyewitness account, which he wasn't about to share in court, and no forensic evidence?

Eduardo's lawyer was frantic. He began to whisper to his client. Eduardo shook his head and turned away from him.

'Why did you kill her?' asked Rosa.

'Because she was having an affair with one of my

labourers and she was pregnant with his child. I was overcome with rage when I found out.'

There was no official record of the pregnancy so Boyle was surprised when Eduardo also mentioned this. He would now be charged with two murders, that of Teresa and her unborn child. In Spain, it gave him a better defence for a crime of passion, but proving that it wasn't planned would be the real difficulty for him. Wouldn't the framing of another man for the shooting indicate that the killing had been planned? Had Eduardo thought about this murder days in advance, or was he so overcome with feelings of jealousy and rage on the day of the shooting that he grabbed Felipe's rifle, went to his own house and shot his wife?

'Can you tell us what you did that day?'

'Yes. On that particular day in question, at the hunting lodge on Pedralta, I took Felipe's rifle while he was sleeping. I walked from the lodge along the track to a point that overlooked the house where I lived at the time, Casa Cielo. I shared that house with my wife Teresa. I could see her reading on the terrace. She liked to do this most afternoons.' Eduardo stopped. The look on his face was one of shame. He rested his head in his hands. 'I don't know how I could have done such a thing.' Eduardo began to shake his head.

'What did you do, Señor Clavaguera?'

He looked up at Rosa. 'I took aim at Teresa – at her heart – and I fired.' Eduardo lowered his head again and began to sob. Rosa switched off the machine and handed Eduardo a tissue.

Boyle and Marc Saldoni watched from the observation room with surprise.

Saldoni turned to Boyle. 'Do you believe him?'

'Believe he did it or that he is repentant?'

'He did it alright,' said Saldoni, 'but is he really sorry for his sins?'

Boyle wasn't sure about any of it. Saldoni said that Eduardo would most likely be given bail at some point. He figured that without any previous criminal convictions, they would go easy on him, telling Boyle that Eduardo probably wouldn't even spend time in prison for his crime because the killing had happened thirty years before, and – most importantly – because it was a crime of passion; the men in the court would understand, anyway. It would take at least two years to bring Eduardo to trial but for now, until they sorted out bail, he would remain behind bars.

Boyle reckoned that Teresa's brother Faustino and Juanita Perez would be interested in knowing what was going on with Teresa's murder investigation. He rang them both. When Faustino heard that Eduardo had confessed to the murder of his sister, he said that he wasn't surprised after what Boyle had told him about Eduardo's infertility, that the man was the obvious killer. Teresa's pregnancy must have driven him to the edge. Faustino asked if Eduardo was being held in prison and said that he would like to visit him, that he had questions that needed answering. Boyle told him that as of yet, Eduardo hadn't been bailed. When Boyle rang Juanita and informed her, she said she was shocked, that she hadn't thought of Eduardo as an evil man before and that, in light of that, perhaps Eduardo *had* pushed her son off the roof that day as well.

With Eduardo's arrest, things went quiet and the threat against Boyle seemed to go away. The trial wouldn't happen for at least two years. He couldn't stay at Montse's house all that time, so he moved back home to Pedralta.

At the house, the first thing Boyle did was clear out Ana's wardrobe. It was a day he had dreaded for months but once he began, it was surprisingly easy. Carmen and Montse came to pick what clothes they wanted. He had given them all her jewellery, most of which had been handed down from her family. Carmen chose Ana's engagement ring – a small solitaire diamond on a gold ring, something he could barely afford at the time on his policeman's wage – and Montse took Ana's gold wedding band. The expected tears never came. After they left, Boyle bagged up the rest of her clothes and shoes into three large black bin liners and drove them down to the supermarket car park, where he put them into an enormous orange metal charity container marked *Ropas de Amigos.*

34

THE NEXT DAY, BOYLE WENT TO HIS OFFICE to catch up on work. Rosa rang him from the police station to say that Gabriel Osorio had been shot and was in Trueta hospital in a coma and under armed guard. 'Isabella is at the police station. She says she's ready to talk. I thought you might like to watch the interview.'

When he first arrived at the police station, he saw Carmen sitting in Rosa's office, crying. Boyle went straight up to her and she threw her arms around him and hugged him with tremendous force. 'What if the people who shot Gabriel try and hurt Isabella?' she whispered in his ear. He disengaged from her and told her that he would make sure that didn't happen, but that first they needed to find out exactly why Gabriel was shot.

When Boyle reached the observation room, he could see that the interview had just begun. Isabella was sitting opposite Detective Inspector Rosa Pujol, her face red from crying. Her long, tangled mane had been cut into a chin-length bob and the pink stripes had disappeared. The girl looked scared. Did she think that the people who shot Gabriel would come after her as well? Montse was sitting next to Isabella as her legal counsel.

'Why do you think that Gabriel Osorio was shot?' Rosa asked Isabella.

'Perhaps it was because of what we both heard that day.' Isabella stared down at the table, making no eye contact with Rosa or Montse.

'What day was that?'

'About three weeks ago. The tenth of September, the first day of the hunting season.'

'Where were you on the morning of September the tenth?' Rosa asked Isabella.

'I was up in Roca Alba on Pedralta with Gabriel.' At the mention of his name, she teared up.

'That's Gabriel Osorio?'

She nodded. 'Yes.'

'What were you doing?'

'I'm a vegan. So is Gabriel. We don't believe you should hurt innocent animals. We were painting anti-hunt graffiti over the houses there.' She ran her hand through her new haircut and pulled on the ends, as if to make them grow.

'Did you hear or see anything unusual there?'

'Yes. The boy who died, Cisco Perez. We heard him scream when he fell. It must have been him.' Isabella swallowed hard.

'What time was that?'

'Midday, I think.'

As Boyle watched from the observation room, he felt for the first time since he took on this case that they were approaching the truth.

'Then what happened?' asked Rosa.

Isabella now made eye contact with Rosa. 'A couple of minutes later, we saw a car racing up the track towards the road.'

'Can you describe the car?'

Isabella nodded. 'It was an economy car, silver. I can't remember what kind. I don't really know cars.'

'Do you remember who was in the car?'

'A man was driving, and then there was a woman beside him and a girl, sort of my age, in the back seat.'

'What did the man look like?'

'Like a man, I guess. Old. I don't remember him,' said Isabella.

'Who can you describe?'

'The girl. I've seen her in Sant Martí before.'

'What did she look like?'

'She had long, straight, light brown hair. Pretty. And I remember the woman in the front seat. She had dark hair, tied to one side.' *Tina Clavaguera,* thought Boyle. *She was wearing her hair that way the day Cisco died.* 'I've seen them around Sant Martí before but I don't know who they are.'

'Do you recognise any of these girls?' Rosa laid out six photos in front of her. Laura Clavaguera's photo was mixed in with those of girls of a similar likeness and age. Isabella immediately pointed to a photograph. 'There she is. It's her.'

Rosa spoke into the machine. 'Just for the record, Isabella has pointed to the photograph of Laura Clavaguera.'

Laura Clavaguera and her mother and father, thought Boyle. *Of course it was.*

'But what was so strange was that even though we had wrecked the place, they were all so out of it, they didn't seem to notice all the damage we'd done. The man just drove like a maniac,' said Isabella.

Como un murciélago del infierno, *like a bat out of hell,* thought Boyle.

The police decided to bring in Tina Clavaguera and her daughter Laura for questioning. The interviews were arranged for 3pm and 4pm. Rosa was going to go to Girona to see Eduardo in Girona prison and organise his transfer to Sant Martí for an interview later that day.

Things were moving quickly now. Boyle went home and early that afternoon he heard vehicles entering Roca Alba below. He looked down from the terrace. There was a *Mossos* SUV and a white forensics van travelling through the woods towards Casa Cielo. He rang Rosa on her mobile. She answered immediately.

'What are you doing down there?'

'Come down, *guapo*, and I'll tell you what's going on.'

35

When Boyle reached the track, he saw two uniformed forensic police scouring the rocks and brush where Cisco fell. Inspector Rosa Pujol stood by, watching them.

'What is going on?'

'I saw Eduardo Clavaguera in Girona prison. He confessed to killing Cisco.'

Why did he need to confess to the killing of Cisco as well? Was the guilt getting the better of him? 'Eduardo must be having a good clear-out, he's clearly in the mood for getting it all off his chest,' said Boyle, feeling that it was all a bit too facile, although he wasn't certain why.

'Don't scoff. Anyway, it makes sense. First, he kills his wife because she's pregnant with another man's child and many years later, he kills Cisco. We don't know why yet, but we will when Eduardo comes in for questioning today. Unless, of course, there are two murderers in the family. What are the chances of that?'

'Not an impossibility,' said Boyle.

'Yes. The odds?' Rosa asked as she made her way down the track.

'I haven't got those numbers at hand.' He felt uneasy and looked up at the police rooting through the bushes on the hillside. 'What are you looking for?' he asked.

'Eduardo says he threw Cisco's smart phone into the brush.' She looked at Boyle. Her eyes showed fatigue. 'Eduardo is now on his way to Sant Martí. Will you come to watch the interview?'

'Of course. I thought you looked for the phone the day Cisco fell.' Boyle had had a good look for it as well but found nothing.

'There is a possibility we missed it.' There was a snarky tone to Rosa's voice. She stared out over the valley. 'Perhaps you don't want to watch the interview, after all.'

Boyle smiled. 'I want to be there. Anyway, what did Eduardo say happened with Cisco?'

'He says he came here alone to Casa Cielo at eleven

forty-five to discuss Cisco's upcoming exhibition. That Cisco was on the roof painting at the time. He claims that the boy confronted him – said that his father Felipe had spent time in prison for the killing of Teresa Clavaguera, but that he had been framed. They argued and then Cisco tried to kick him. Eduardo pushed him back in self-defence and Cisco slipped and fell off the roof. Eduardo knew the boy was dead because of the angle of his neck. He then threw the smart phone over the cliff.'

'That's not what Eduardo told me at Felipe's funeral,' said Boyle.

'What are you talking about?'

'Eduardo claimed that months before, *he* had told Cisco that his father had been in prison. That it was the first time Cisco had even heard about it. And they had discussed it in great detail then.'

'He must have been lying to you. I think his confession to the police is most likely the truth.' She was on a roll and clearly irritated by this conflicting information.

'Did he mention the packet of cocaine?'

'No.' Rosa closed her eyes as if to shut Boyle out.

Boyle wondered why Rosa didn't ask about the cocaine, because whoever pushed Cisco over must have thrown the packet of cocaine down as well. It was found near his body.

'What about Isabella seeing Eduardo in the car

with Tina and Laura, is that a lie as well? And where was Miguel?'

'He had clearly left by the time his father arrived. Or, and I favour this one, *hombre*, he was never here in the first place,' said Rosa.

'Why would Luis Sureda and Isabella make all that up?'

'I don't know what Isabella's problem is, except that she is overindulged and a bit of a drama queen. But I do know that Luis Sureda is a well-known drug addict and liar. He doesn't need a reason to make things up. Eduardo was adamant. He went alone and he saw no one,' she said.

Rosa was quiet. They both watched the forensic team as they moved over the boulders and through the bushes.

'Did Eduardo say why he didn't report it to the police in the first place?'

'Why do you think? He was scared. He knew Cisco was dead,' Rosa snapped.

'Dare I ask about Cisco's sketchbook?'

'Eduardo has admitted to taking the sketchbook. We have picked it up from his house.'

There was a shout. 'Got it!' One of the police lifted a smart phone out of the bushes and held it up for Rosa to see. She beamed.

Why would Eduardo lie about going to Casa Cielo alone? To protect a family member – his son Miguel or daughter Laura, or even his wife, Tina? They all had reasons to fight with Cisco. Tina had told Boyle that she had never liked Cisco, that she thought he had been a bad influence on her children. Miguel was competitive with him. But most damning of all, Luis swore that he left Miguel at Casa Cielo that day.

Boyle joined Rosa in the first of the two squad cars and they drove in a convoy to the Clavaguera *masia*. Boyle waited in the car while Rosa and the constable arrested Tina and her daughter Laura. As Tina followed her daughter out of the *masia*, she shouted to her, 'Don't say anything. Don't let them bully you. You weren't there. Don't let them convince you that you were.' When she caught sight of Boyle, she glared and said, 'We have our lawyer coming from Girona. You'll never work in Catalonia again. *Gracias a Dios.*' Boyle thought Tina looked like a wild animal, bristling, trying to control her temper – a hyena came to mind, one that wasn't in a laughing mood.

The interview with Tina Clavaguera was scheduled to begin in twenty minutes. Boyle was with several of the police in the garage behind the Sant Martí police station. They were waiting for the van that was carrying Eduardo from Girona prison to arrive. Five minutes later, the navy blue *Mossos* van squealed into the drive followed by two motorcycle police outriders. The van doors slid open and Eduardo stepped down onto the oily garage floor. He was handcuffed and wearing a grey prison uniform and he looked surprisingly well. He had a policeman on either side of him, holding his arms. He appeared relaxed, almost ethereal. When he saw Boyle, he nodded in recognition and gave a small smile. Was there an expression of surrender on his face?

Boyle caught sight of him at a distance before anyone else. Faustino was crouched behind a police van, the glint from the sun on his pistol. Boyle ran for him but it was too late. Faustino rushed up to Eduardo and shot four times straight into his chest. Eduardo held his hands to his bloodied chest, gave Faustino a look of surprise and collapsed to the ground. There was the scraping sound of steel against leather as Eduardo's guards, the outriders and the waiting police drew their guns. Boyle hit the floor, spread-eagled to avoid the crossfire.

The police opened fire. Faustino was shot as he ran away. He grabbed his arm, ducked between the wall of the garage and an enormous metal refuse bin. His gun poked out from the side of the container, now trained on the police. Boyle rose to his feet and crept to the back door where about seven police were standing, stock still, their guns aimed at the container. Boyle was breathing hard and his palms were sweaty, and he chose not to draw his weapon.

The police guards sneaked back to Eduardo. One picked up his legs and two grabbed an arm each and, protected by a line of vehicles, they carried Eduardo's bloodied body towards the back door. As the men passed Boyle, he saw the ashen face and limp form and knew that Eduardo Clavaguera was gone. No one survives a hail of bullets like that – he would have died instantly.

Chief Inspector Marc Saldoni exited the police station, his weapon already drawn.

Boyle thought he was best able to prevent a blood bath if he had the chance to persuade Faustino to give himself up. With his arms raised, he turned to Marc. 'I'm going to talk to Faustino,' he said.

'Don't, Adrian,' cried Marc.

Boyle walked out into the forecourt, approaching the back of the garage where Faustino was hiding. He went straight up to him, his hands raised. Faustino was bleeding profusely from the arm. He pointed the gun to Boyle's chest, shaking, cringing in pain. Two of the police crept around the back but were unable to get a clear shot.

'Put the gun down, Faustino. We can talk about it and get you some help,' said Boyle.

'Talking won't help. But it doesn't matter what happens now, justice has been done,' said Faustino.

'Not exactly what I would call justice.'

'No, but then you are a foreigner – you don't understand us. It looks like Eduardo is dead. That is good enough for me. But I do have you to thank for finding out for me. You told me of your suspicions that Cisco and Teresa's deaths were connected in some way. That idea had never crossed my mind, but I immediately thought there could be something behind it. I went to see Juanita in prison and told her to ask you to investigate what happened to my sister. I paid. I did it through Juanita because I didn't want anyone to know that I was after them. But when you told me that Eduardo couldn't have children, I guessed he was the murderer. It was so obvious…'

The police appeared at the side, their guns aimed at Faustino, but Boyle was in the way.

'Give yourself up, Faustino. Please,' Boyle pleaded with him.

Marc Saldoni shouted for Faustino to drop his gun. Rather than obey, Faustino shoved Boyle aside and moved out from behind the wall. Boyle dropped down flat on the garage floor again. Faustino, his body totally exposed to the police, discharged the last bullets from his gun, aiming high – he had no intention of hurting anyone else. It was purely a suicidal move. The police fired several rounds and Faustino went down with a resounding moan. He was dead before he hit the ground. There would be no inquest into his death, or Eduardo's for that matter.

Both Faustino Duran and Eduardo Clavaguera were hurriedly buried, each having a small funeral, the kind that are afforded criminals, and then both of them were locked up in large family vaults to do their time.

That's it, case solved, thought Boyle, but he felt none of the satisfaction he normally did after the termination of a case. There were still many loose ends, unanswered questions, the main one being, why would Isabella say she had seen three people in a car speeding out of Roca Alba the day Cisco died, if she hadn't?

But as much as it bothered him, it wasn't up to Boyle to solve them, and he knew he would finally have to let it go. Overcome with exhaustion, he went home and slept for two solid days.

36

A MAGNIFICENT ORANGE GLOW SPREAD across the sky. Boyle watched the sunset from his kitchen window as he stirred the Bolognese sauce on the stove and drank a bottle of beer. A pasta dish was just what he craved. The temperature had dropped so he had lit a fire – the first of the season. The two cats had taken up residence near the hearth and were fast asleep.

The water for the pasta had reached a rolling boil. He cut open the spaghetti and was just ready to tip the pasta into the pan when there was a knock on the front door. It was curious because from the window he had a clear view of the track that led to his house and he had seen no one drive up. Whoever was at the front door had come on foot. That was strange because he was the only one living on the mountain now. The thought crossed his mind that Pedro had been sent over to do some damage. But Eduardo was dead – he didn't have to worry about the Clavagueras' security guards harming him, did he? Boyle turned off the hob, wiped his hands and went into the spare bedroom. Peering through the curtains, he saw Laura Clavaguera at the front door. Dressed in a quilted jacket and jeans, she was holding her left arm. Boyle opened the front door. The forearm was bloodied.

'What happened?' asked Boyle.

'Someone tried to kill me.' She was pale and shaking.

'Who?'

She appeared distressed. 'I can't say.'

'I'll ring an ambulance,' said Boyle.

'No, please don't. The bullet went straight through my jacket and just grazed my skin. If you let me clean it here, then I can go to the hospital later.'

'Come in,' said Boyle.

Boyle led Laura into the bathroom. 'Where's your car?'

'I walked here,' said Laura.

Boyle pulled a metal first aid box out from under

the sink. 'Sit here,' Boyle said, putting the toilet seat down.

Laura sat. 'You are all prepared,' she said, looking into the box and forcing a smile.

'I learned first aid when I was with the police.' She took off her jacket and Boyle folded it carefully and placed it over the side of the bath. The left forearm of her shirt was soaked through with blood. Boyle undid the cuff and, with Laura's permission, cut the sleeve around the top of the arm, pulling it over Laura's hand and throwing it into the bath. He examined the wound. Although initially it had produced a lot of blood, it was slight. 'You're lucky. It is just a graze, as you said.'

'It's stopped bleeding,' Laura said with relief.

'Stand up and I'll clean it over the sink.' Laura obeyed. Boyle scrubbed his hands and then began to clean and dress the wound. 'Tell me, who did this?'

'It was from a distance.' Laura winced as Boyle dabbed the wound with cotton wool soaked in alcohol. 'I want to tell you but...'

What is going on? thought Boyle. He was unable to make sense of it. Was someone trying to kill Laura? Were Eduardo's security men still around, working for Tina now? Did they have anything to do with this? Boyle laid a patch of gauze over the injury and fastened it down with adhesive tape. 'Who is trying to hurt you, Laura?'

Laura was shaking. 'My mother. My mother tried to kill me.'

Boyle was horrified but kept his cool. 'Why?'

'I told her that I was going to the police.'

'Why, what do you want to tell them?'

'She killed Cisco and Teresa, not my father. My father was so good, so gentle. He would never hurt anyone!' Laura broke down and sobbed.

'Will you come to the station and tell the police?' Boyle asked.

Laura nodded her head. He took out his mobile and rang Rosa, telling her what Laura had just said.

'This isn't happening,' said Rosa.

'It is.' Boyle looked at Laura. 'Does your mother know where you are?'

'I don't know if she followed me here,' said Laura.

'I am bringing Laura down to you,' said Boyle.

'We'll drive up there to meet you, just in case Tina turns up.'

Boyle closed his mobile then dashed into his bedroom, grabbed his holstered gun off the nightstand and clipped it onto his belt. He then led Laura outside. They crept down the stairs to the drive and got into his Rover. It was dark now. His property was well lit but beyond the entrance to the drive there was the pitch black of a moonless night. He pressed the remote control and waited for the gate to open. It was slow, stuttering and starting; he had meant to get it fixed. They were sitting ducks for anyone lurking beyond. He rolled down his window to listen. Ahead, he heard footsteps on the gravel, walking down the track at a determined pace. It reminded Boyle of Quimet's story, how he had heard Eduardo's footsteps on the same track the day Teresa was shot. Then Tina came into view, holding a twelve-bore shotgun. Laura cried out with terror.

'No, Mama, please!'

Cold, expressionless, Tina lifted the gun and took aim. Boyle pushed Laura down and shielded her. When Tina fired, the windscreen exploded and bits of glass flew everywhere, striking Boyle and Laura. Boyle lifted up, drew his gun and fired a shot at Tina, just missing her. She backed off, disappearing into the dark. Boyle checked on Laura.

'Are you hit?'

'No, I'm okay,' she said, shaking glass out of her hair. She looked pale and shell-shocked. He gave her his house keys and told her to run inside and stay there.

Boyle got out of the car and moved down the track. He guessed Tina must be going towards her car but as he neared the end of the track, he stopped. There was no car and no Tina. She was hiding somewhere. On the mountain side of the track, it was sheer cliff, impossible to climb. On the other side, there was more of a gradual rocky incline downwards, overgrown with shrubs and cork trees, with a number of paths leading to Roca Alba below. Boyle listened for any movement. There were no crunching sounds on the gravel and no crackling of dried leaves, just dead silence. Then Boyle heard the thrumming of tires on asphalt and in the distance saw several cars with gently flashing blue lights speeding up the main road. There were no sirens but he knew it was the police.

Just up ahead of Boyle, he saw sudden movement in the shrubs and heard the sound of someone slipping down the slope towards Roca Alba. He ran to the path just in time to see Tina sliding down, out of control. Boyle rang Rosa on her mobile and told her where Tina was headed. He then followed her, moving as fast as was possible in the dark and downhill. Boyle got close enough to hear Tina's laboured breathing; she swore each time she fell. When she reached the properties below, she darted off.

Blue lights were flashing through the woods as several *Mossos* squad cars sped into Roca Alba, weaving their way through the trees. The cars lit up the woodland, allowing Boyle to catch sight of Tina running for her life. He figured she was going towards Casa Cielo. To what, hide? As Boyle tried to catch up with her, his lungs burned from the effort. He heard the police scrambling out of their cars to give chase.

When he came upon Tina, she had stopped. She was bent over with her shotgun across her knees, trying to catch her breath. Boyle approached her with care.

'Stand back, Adrian,' Rosa shouted. The police were surrounding Tina, their guns drawn. She dropped her shotgun and raised her hands in surrender. Whatever crimes Tina had committed, in her eyes, her guilt wasn't sufficient to warrant suicide by cop, like Faustino's chosen punishment. However restricted it would be, Tina wanted life. Boyle felt a stab of disappointment. If only it had been the other way around and Faustino had been the one who chose to live.

Tina was immediately arrested for the attempted murder of her daughter and Boyle. Boyle and Laura went to the police station with Rosa to make their statements. Laura was vitriolic about her mother and repeated what she had told Boyle at his house. After the statements, and in light of the girl's animosity towards her mother, Boyle suggested to Rosa that now would be a good time to interview Laura about Cisco's death. His niece Isabella had seen Eduardo driving Laura and her mother away from the scene after Cisco fell. Eduardo had admitted to killing Cisco but Laura said it was her mother who was responsible for the murder. He felt it was important to get the full story from the girl's point of view. They asked Laura and she readily agreed.

In the interview room, Laura Clavaguera sat slouched at the table, her arms folded across her body.

She was staring ahead at nothing, her eyes red from crying. The family solicitor, Juame Sanchez, was next to her. On the other side of the table sat Detective Inspector Rosa Pujol and her colleague, a young female detective named Nuria Vall, who said nothing throughout the interview. On the table beside the recording machine was a man-sized box of tissues.

Boyle sat in the observation room, eating a *bocadillo jamón* and drinking a steaming *café americano* that one of the new recruits had brought in for him. He had missed dinner and was famished. He was watching Laura. Her relaxed manner suggested that the anger towards her mother was fast disappearing and he wondered if she would open up. She sat up and started to twirl a gold band on her index finger, avoiding any eye contact with Rosa.

'When you can, Laura, tell us what happened,' said Rosa. Her voice was soft, accepting.

'Cisco was on the roof, painting, when we got to Casa Cielo.'

'Who was with you?'

'I drove up with my father. My mother had been hunting and met us there.'

'What time was this, Laura?' asked Rosa, angling her head as if to get the girl's attention.

Laura rested her head in her hands. 'I don't know. Perhaps eleven thirty, eleven thirty-five.'

'Was anyone else there at the house?'

'Just Cisco. Luis and Miguel had already left.'

'Tell us what happened next.'

'Cisco was painting the tower. I told my mother and father to stay downstairs. I went up. You see, I wanted to tell him something important that I didn't want them to hear.' She then hesitated, clearly uneasy about discussing whatever it was in front of the police.

'What was it, Laura?' asked Rosa.

Laura faced Rosa and shook her head.

'I know this has been an incredibly difficult time for you.'

'Yes,' Laura whispered.

'Tell us what is bothering you.'

Laura looked at Rosa. 'I was pregnant and had an abortion.'

'I am so sorry.'

Laura tightened her mouth to ward off tears. 'Cisco wanted me to have the baby and knew nothing about the abortion. I was going to lie, tell him that I had miscarried. But he was so involved with his painting that I couldn't get his attention. So, I blurted out that I had had an abortion.'

Her solicitor put his hand over hers and whispered something in her ear. 'I want to tell them everything,' she said and pulled her hand away. Then she faced Rosa. 'I don't want my father to take the blame for this.' Boyle found it poignant that Laura was now referring to Eduardo as her father.

'When you can, Laura, continue,' said Rosa.

'When I told Cisco about the abortion, he was so shocked. He jumped down from the roof onto the terrace and moved towards me. He looked at me with such hatred, it was frightening,' she said. Her words were beginning to tumble out. 'He screamed at me. Said I was a murderer. I thought he was going to kill me. Then he pointed to the painting he was working on, and he asked me, "Do you know who this is?" "No," I said, "I have no idea." He told me it was my father's first wife Teresa.'

Already her evidence is sounding more real than her father's evidence ever did, thought Boyle.

'Did you know about Teresa?' asked Rosa.

'Sure, I had heard about her, but I didn't know what she looked like. There aren't any photos of her in my parents' house. I sometimes forget that my father was even married before my mother.'

'What happened next?' asked Rosa.

'Cisco screamed at me, said that he was the son of Felipe Puig. I asked who he was. But Cisco was crazy now. He screamed in my face. "Felipe Puig went to prison for shooting Teresa Clavaguera."' Laura paused, looked at Rosa and shrugged. 'I didn't know much about the death of Teresa. I knew she had been shot in a hunting accident. That was all. My father never spoke of it. Cisco got closer to me, pinning me against the wall. He looked so mad. I'd never been so scared of him. His father never shot Teresa, he said. Someone had framed him. He said it had ruined his father's life and was the cause of his stroke.'

Laura took a sip of water, then went on. 'He pressed me harder against the wall and so I pushed him away. Then he said that he had only befriended my brother and me to get near my father and his friends, to discover who had really killed Teresa. To clear his father's name because his father was too ill to find out for himself.' Laura dropped her head, devastated. 'He lied to me. I felt like everything we went through meant nothing to him.'

'Did he find out who had murdered Teresa?'

'Yes.' There was a long, uncomfortable pause for her. 'He said that my mother did.' Laura laid her head in her hands.

Boyle thought about the ongoing affair between Quimet Navarro and Tina Clavaguera. Was Tina doing this to keep Quimet quiet?

'How did he know your mother had killed her?'

'He didn't tell me.'

'How did Cisco fall, Laura?' Rosa asked.

Laura paused and fidgeted with her ring, her face tense and pale.

Boyle watched her through the glass. Rosa was being diplomatic. Laura had already said that her mother had killed Cisco, but the "how did it happen?" question in a murder investigation, however delicately put, seemed to be the most difficult to answer. And it was especially so for someone like Laura, who, Boyle thought, was close to both Cisco and her mother.

Laura sat up straight then closed her eyes, took a deep breath and began slowly. 'He said he never wanted to see me again. Then he got back onto the roof and began to paint, just like that. I stood there watching him in disbelief. I had trusted him and all he had told me was lies. He wasn't who he said he was. He had been spying on my family all these months. I was so shocked, I couldn't move. He continued to paint, ignoring me. Then he stopped. He looked vicious. "Are you still there?" he said. "You're a murderer. Just like your mother!" I couldn't believe he was the same Cisco I had known all this time. I didn't know what to say. Then I suppose he didn't think I was moving fast enough, so he walked across the roof, stuck his foot out and kicked me in the shoulder. I fell backwards onto the terrace. I saw my mother and father standing at the door. My mother was so angry, I'm sure she wasn't thinking. She ran in front of me, caught his foot in her hands and pushed him hard. He wasn't expecting it and lost his balance. It happened so quickly. He grabbed on to the roof tiles but they were too slippery. He pleaded with my mother to help him, but she turned away. He looked at me with surprise and stretched out his arm to me. I ran towards him but I was too far. I couldn't catch him and he fell.' Laura covered her face with her hands and cried. She then looked up at Rosa. 'He screamed. It was so awful. I wish it hadn't happened,' she said. She began to sob. Stony-faced, Detective Nuria Vall pulled a couple of tissues from the box and handed them to Laura. Laura took them and held them to her eyes.

Rosa asked Laura if she would like to stop the interview and finish at another time. The girl shook her head. Rosa waited for Laura to gather herself and asked, 'What did you do next?'

Calmly, she said, 'My father and I ran down to the patio at the back of the house and looked down at the track. We could see him there. His body was at such a weird angle. My father said he was dead.'

'But you didn't ring the police. Why?'

'We were frightened. We knew nothing could be done for him and we knew that my mother was responsible. My father told me to tell no one. He worshipped my mother, she was his life; he couldn't face her going to prison.' Boyle realised that this was the truth. Eduardo was willing to do anything for Tina, even take the blame for her crimes. He was clearly enthralled with her. She was the power behind the Clavaguera throne.

'What about the packet of cocaine that was found near Cisco? Where did it come from?' Laura looked defeated. 'Was the packet Cisco's cocaine?' asked Rosa.

'No. Cisco had given up long ago. It was my

cocaine. I was going to use it. But after the accident, I threw it into the bushes. Not to make Cisco look like a user, but for me to give up.' Boyle thought about Cisco's mother. Juanita never believed the cocaine was Cisco's. She did indeed know her son well.

Laura lowered her head and let out a long sigh of relief.

Tina Clavaguera was so distressed about her husband's death that she refused to be interviewed and her solicitor, Señor Sanchez, demanded that they give her bail and let her go home immediately. His request was denied and she spent two nights in a prison cell before she agreed to be interviewed.

It gave the forensic team time to gather evidence. They scoured Pedralta, Boyle's drive and Roca Alba, combing the areas for evidence, but most of their efforts were focused on the Clavaguera estate, in the grounds where Laura had been shot.

Rosa and Boyle discussed how the interview would go – first, the attempted murder of her daughter Laura and Boyle, then the killing of Cisco, and finally her alleged involvement with the shooting of Teresa Clavaguera.

Tina seemed relaxed when she finally agreed to talk with the police. She sat at the interview table and yawned. She was wearing a fresh change of clothing, her hair was pulled back and she wore no makeup.

Boyle watched her from the observation room. Her solicitor, Señor Sanchez, sat beside her. He appeared to be saying something to reassure her. She patted his arm in friendship and gave him a sad smile.

Rosa pressed the record button to begin the interview. Her assistant Nuria was there with the box of tissues, but Boyle sensed there would be no need for them like there was with Laura. Tina didn't seem like a crier.

Rosa stared at Tina with a puzzled look. Then she shook her head. 'Señora Clavaguera, I have yet to interview someone like you.'

'What are you talking about?' snapped Tina.

'Two days ago, you tried to shoot your own daughter! I'm not a mother myself, so enlighten me – what possesses a woman to do that?'

'You would make a terrible mother. You are too hard.'

'Answer the question.'

'I don't like your tone!'

'Tough.'

'Don't you dare speak to my client that way,' said Sanchez.

Rosa switched off the recorder. 'Señora Clavaguera, we can take a break if you like, send you back to your cell until you feel like talking.' Tina glared at her. 'Of course,' continued Rosa, 'I would advise against it. We have a lot to deal with.' She flipped through the sheaf of papers in front of her. 'The attempted murder of your own daughter and Señor Boyle, and the murder of Cisco Perez. So, answer the first question please.'

'I was angry at the time. I had no intention of killing my daughter, or Señor Boyle for that matter. I aimed high on the car window.'

'Why were you angry?'

'I felt my daughter was responsible for the death of my husband. I warned her not to get involved with Cisco. If she hadn't got involved with him, then none of this would have happened.'

Boyle watched from the observation room. Cisco was also good friends with Eduardo and Miguel Clavaguera, so her answer rang false.

'But shooting at her is a bit extreme, isn't it?'

Tina hung her head. 'My husband's killing by that mad man Faustino has left me... grief stricken.'

Funny, she didn't look grief stricken to Boyle. There was no grief anywhere in sight, just arrogance.

'But Señora Clavaguera, your daughter says you also shot her in the arm at your *masia* before she went to hide at Señor Boyle's house. She says she was afraid for her life.'

Tina shook her head. 'That just isn't true. She shot herself.' Tina raised her palms up, like a supplicant. 'Look, I love my daughter dearly but she is a drug addict. And she makes up the most incredible stories.

She has told so many lies that she doesn't know what truth is anymore.'

Rosa rifled through the papers in front of her, picked one out and handed it to Sanchez. 'Our ballistics report says that it would be impossible for your daughter to have grazed herself on her forearm with the rifle. From that angle, without a doubt, physically impossible.' Rosa gave Tina a controlled smile.

Her lawyer handed Tina the ballistics report and pointed to a diagram. Tina looked at it briefly and threw it back to Rosa, clearly underwhelmed.

'Can you explain how you daughter was shot, Señora Clavaguera?'

'It's not for me to explain.'

Rosa leaned towards Tina. 'Oh, I think it is.'

Tina took an impatient breath. 'I don't know how she was shot at my house. I know nothing about that. I admit, I fired at my daughter and Señor Boyle in his car. I did that because I miss my husband.' There was a long pause. Tina looked thoughtful, as if reaching into the past. 'My family was fine before Cisco came along. When Cisco entered our lives, everything changed.'

'What did he do?'

'He was the one who introduced Laura and Miguel to drugs.'

'They hadn't tried drugs before that?'

'No. Never. We had a perfect family before he ruined it.'

'Is that why you killed him?'

Tina sat up straight and stared at Rosa with incredulity. 'What?!'

'Your daughter tells me that you pushed Cisco Perez to his death.'

'How dare she!' Tina turned to Señor Sanchez as if to convince him. 'I wasn't even there that day.'

'We have a witness who has identified you leaving the scene at the time.' Tina appeared to take in that piece of information with seriousness. She leaned back again, pensive.

Boyle had his forehead on the observation window, fascinated by Tina. As she sat there, saying nothing, he thought that she must be remembering the two anti-hunt protesters at the scene that day.

'Alright, I was there,' Tina finally admitted.

'Why did you lie?'

'I was trying to protect my daughter.'

Rosa laughed. 'You attempt to shoot your daughter twice and then you expect me to believe that you lied about the circumstances surrounding Cisco's death in order to *protect* her?'

'My Eduardo never pushed Cisco off the roof, it was my daughter. She's wicked. I have tried to cover for her all her life, but this is too much. You have to accept that sometimes they turn out like that. She was the one who pushed Cisco off the roof. Not my darling Eduardo, who spent his life covering up for her.' Tina pointed to Rosa. 'Now that is the truth. I saw it.' She paused and gazed at her hands, which were folded on the table, her eyes glassy.

Boyle studied Tina. She was faking her emotions. She was a narcissist, a psychopath, a thoroughly nasty piece of work.

'I was horrified,' she went on. 'But she was high on cocaine. She became a monster when she took drugs.'

Boyle had seen Laura under the influence of drugs and although she was unpleasant, he would never describe her as a monster.

'We would now like to ask you some questions about the shooting of Teresa Clavaguera.'

Tina looked stunned and then leaned her head to the side, quizzical.

'Your husband's first wife,' said Rosa.

Tina glowered at Rosa and then whispered something to her lawyer.

'Why weren't we told about this beforehand?' asked Señor Sanchez.

'Your daughter just informed us,' said Rosa.

There was a long pause before Tina spoke. She turned and glared at the mirror behind which Boyle was observing, a look of pure evil on her face. It was a look that he hadn't seen often in his career with the police, but he had seen it enough to recognise it. It was as if the temperature in the room had dropped several degrees. Tina went on to deny that she had shot Teresa Clavaguera.

The interview with Tina had gone as Boyle had expected it would. He knew she would blame her daughter for the killing of Cisco. She said that if her husband had been alive, he would have testified to this as well. Boyle believed that. Eduardo would have supported his wife over his children. Boyle had no doubt that Eduardo had lied when he told him that his first wife Teresa had meant more to him than Tina. Tina was everything to him, Boyle realised. Eduardo would have hidden her crimes to protect her from punishment. That is what he had been doing since he had allowed her to kill his first wife and then cover up for her. The question was, had they planned this or had Tina shot Teresa and Eduardo just covered it up for her after it had happened? But, whichever way it transpired, Tina must have convinced Eduardo that it was better for him to take the blame for what she had done.

Tina claimed in her interview that she wasn't even there when Teresa was murdered, that she had gone home after preparing lunch for the men. In the meantime, she was held in custody for the attempted murder of her daughter and Boyle, but Rosa told Boyle that they would need more evidence to pin the murders of Teresa Clavaguera and Cisco Perez on Tina.

37

That afternoon, Boyle drove to Vespella Nou. He pressed the buzzer at Las Brisas, was let in by the maid and shown straight to Quimet's office. Quimet was at the window, observing the sparkling sea. He motioned for Boyle to take a seat.

'You know that Tina Clavaguera has been arrested for the attempted murder of her daughter?' said Boyle.

'Yes, I think by now everyone in the Vall d'Aro knows that,' said Quimet as he took a seat opposite Boyle.

'Cisco told Laura that Tina Clavaguera was

responsible for the murder of Eduardo's first wife, Teresa.'

'Well, I don't know anything about that,' said Quimet, his eyes averted.

Boyle stood and looked down at Quimet. 'When you told me that you saw Eduardo Clavaguera walking down the track with a rifle, you were lying. Weren't you?'

'No.'

'It was Tina Clavaguera who was walking down the track with the rifle, wasn't it?'

'I told you what I know and I have nothing to add.'

'That afternoon, she came and took Felipe's rifle, shot Teresa, her love rival, and then brought the rifle back to lay the blame on Felipe. And then you and Eduardo covered for her. Eduardo never left the lodge that afternoon. He slept. And as for giving Felipe lots of wine, I'm guessing that never happened either. It was Tina, the perfect hostess, who was pouring the wine for Felipe while she made lunch for all of you.'

'I don't know what you are talking about.'

'What? Are you protecting your lover? Are you so in love with her that you will let her get away with murder?'

Quimet stood up, went to the picture window and stared at the sea, saying nothing. Finally, he turned to Boyle. 'I would like you to leave my house.'

Boyle approached Quimet from behind and

wrapped his arm around his neck in a choke hold. 'Tell me I'm right. It was Tina. Just say it.' Boyle squeezed the man's neck tighter. Quimet brought his hands up and dug into Boyle's arm but failed to loosen his hold. His eyes bulged; he was struggling to breathe.

'No,' he said with a rasp. Boyle held his arm firmly around his neck. 'Alright, she did it. It was Tina.'

Boyle let go. Quimet sank into a chair, laid his hand on his neck. It took him a few minutes to catch his breath. Boyle stood over him and waited. When Boyle saw that Quimet had recovered, he sat down and continued with the interview. 'So, now tell me what really happened.'

'You are right, it was Tina who shot Teresa. I didn't see her come to the lodge and take the rifle but I heard her on her return. Like I said before, it woke me. I watched Tina moving towards the lodge; the rifle, which I soon realised was Felipe's, was under her arm. She appeared calm. At the time, of course, I didn't know what she had done. But when we were told that Teresa had been shot dead and they arrested Felipe for the crime, I knew immediately that Tina was responsible.'

'How could you get involved with someone like that?'

'Knowing what she had done didn't make me love her any less.'

Boyle sat back in his chair. He was unable to

fathom that kind of love. Quimet must have seen the confusion on his face and answered Boyle's unasked question.

'You see, I was always in love with Tina. Tina and I grew up together in Santa Nuria. Her farmhouse was near ours. Our families socialised together, hunted together, worked our farms together, planting and harvesting. Both our farms were rented from the Clavagueras.' Quimet's face turned sour and he leaned forward. 'Do you think my family liked that? Renting a property that had been ours in the first place? How would you like that? They stole everything my family owned. Well, I had always wanted to be with Tina. We went through the village school together and then high school in Sant Martí. We had our first kiss together. Our families assumed we would marry one day, and what can I say? From early on I was in love with her. But when we were teenagers, it became clear to me that she wasn't interested in me at all; she wanted Eduardo Clavaguera. Not me, a worker on the Clavaguera estate.' He paused and smiled. 'But later, I had something on her. I knew that she had killed Teresa and that Eduardo had helped her cover the crime. So, I took Tina. I couldn't marry her but I could still have her. She had no choice in the matter and neither did Eduardo – if they wanted to stay out of prison, that is,' continued Quimet with a smirk. He then smiled and gave a gentle laugh. 'I even think that Tina's son Miguel is my child, not

Salvador's. I have no proof but the family resemblance is clearly there. He looks uncannily like my son Josep. I am the same blood group as Salvador. I know there has never been a DNA test, just blood groups. But that feels like divine justice to me. You take my family home and property, and later, I have your wife every Sunday or whenever I please. And there's a child into the bargain. It's win, win.'

'I wonder why Tina and Eduardo didn't have you killed.'

Quimet laughed. 'Because I did your little trick.'

'What little trick is that?'

'Remember you told me that you had written down everything I did, and that if I harmed you in any way, then all that information would go to the police? Well, I had Eduardo and Tina's story written down, every sordid detail hidden away in a safe deposit box, and they knew that.'

'And Eduardo accepted all this because he loved Tina so much?'

'Yes. But I love Tina more. Always will.'

'Even though she is a murdering psychopath?

'It is unconditional.'

Well, good luck with that mate, thought Boyle. He felt sick to his stomach hearing about this old, warped love, these dirty attachments. He'd need a long, hot shower to remove the filth.

Boyle looked at Quimet. The man got up and lit

a cigarette, his hand clearly shaking. 'What are you going to do now?' Quimet said it not with his usual sarcasm but quietly. The dog had rolled over and exposed his underside.

'I want you to tell the police what you have just told me,' said Boyle.

Quimet slowly shook his head.

'Tina Clavaguera, no matter how much you may love her, is a danger to everyone she comes in contact with. She shot and killed an innocent woman thirty years ago and recently pushed a young, talented artist to his death. Are you really telling me that you want to protect her? She just tried to kill her own daughter. Who knows? She may come after you, your wife or even Miguel, the son you say you share with her. You can love her all you want, but please just help us to remove her from society.'

Quimet pulled himself away from the sea view and came and sat down in the chair opposite Boyle. There was a look on his face Boyle had never seen before. He had seen it many times on those he had interviewed over the years and it always gave him a thrill. It was the look of surrender. Quimet would talk.

'I won't be prosecuted for withholding evidence?'

'I'll make sure of that,' said Boyle, at this point saying anything that would get Quimet into the interview room at the *Mossos d'Esquadra*.

Twenty minutes later, Boyle walked into the police station in Sant Martí with Quimet Navarro, who, after his interview, agreed to give testimony in court. Later, Tina Clavaguera was charged with the murders of Teresa Clavaguera and Cisco Perez. There would be no bail.

On the drive to Girona, Boyle felt like he was embarking on a holiday, a *tramuntana* having left glorious, clear skies in its wake. It was Saturday and the women's section of Girona Prison was crowded – with men mostly, there to see their wives, girlfriends or sisters. After a two-hour wait, Boyle finally came face to face with Juanita through a smudged glass window. They talked about the murder of Felipe. She was waiting for the results of the blood analysis that would prove that they were both gassed by intruders and that she was not responsible for her husband's death. He told her that he hoped it would not take too long. She said that prison was preferable to an empty house. Finally, he said, he was able to tell her who killed her son.

'Not Tina?!'

'She has been questioned by the police and charged with killing Teresa Clavaguera. She is saying that although she pushed Cisco, it was an accident. She never intended for him to fall off the roof. But it is more difficult for her to explain how she killed

Teresa Clavaguera, since Quimet Navarro will testify that he saw her with Felipe's rifle on the day of the hunt all those years ago.'

'The Clavagueras. What a fine, upstanding family they are, huh?' she said. Boyle smiled at her. 'And my Felipe?'

'It looks like Eduardo's body guards killed your husband.'

Boyle then asked her how the friendship between Cisco and Miguel Clavaguera began.

'Cisco and Miguel met by chance in Girona at Gavarres Graffiti Park nearly four years ago,' she said. 'After knowing each other for two years, they became friends. I realise now that it was just after Felipe had his stroke and that Cisco became friends with Miguel in order to get close to the Clavagueras. Cisco wanted to help his father find out who killed Teresa. I understand it all now.'

Early one morning in late October, Boyle heard the distinct sounds of demolition coming from Roca Alba. When he looked down from his terrace, he saw dust rising up from the woods. His heart sank. Quimet had promised not to touch the urbanisation. Boyle rang him and left a message to call. He then took the shortcut down to the urbanisation. Faustino's and the seven other houses in the development appeared to be untouched. The sounds were coming from Casa

Cielo. When he came upon it, he saw the bulldozer crashing through the house. The painted walls were crumbling. There was dust and dirt everywhere.

Later, Quimet returned his call. 'What do you want?' he asked.

'There is a bulldozer in Roca Alba. What is going on?'

'We're tearing down Casa Cielo. Nothing else. Laura and Miguel requested it. I'm doing it for them. The other houses will be rented out during the summer months. You have nothing to worry about.'

The bulldozer worked for two days to demolish the house. After that, there were three days of drilling as they broke up the foundations. When the workmen left, Boyle went down to have another look. The pool had been filled in and nothing remained of Casa Cielo but dirt and rock. Leftover boulders and rocks were piled up to mark the perimeter of the terraced land and the dirt inside had been neatly raked in a swirling pattern, reminding Boyle of a peaceful Japanese garden.

Epilogue

Boyle drove with Montse and Rosa to Sitges on their wedding day. He had wanted to drive them himself in the old Rover and had had it cleaned specially. But they declined the offer, both thanking him, and then Rosa had added, 'It's our wedding day, Adrian.' So, they had all ended up in Montse's newer, smarter Volvo. The three of them arrived at the Sitges nineteenth-century Catalan gothic town hall with half an hour to spare before the ceremony and waited in the car park for Carmen to turn up with her children and Jordi. There was another small wedding party, next in line, waiting on the steps.

'How are you, Adrian?' Montse asked with a knowing look. He knew she understood how difficult today would be for him, with Jordi there, but he brushed it off as nothing. It was Montse and Rosa's wedding day; he wasn't going to let anything get in the way of that.

'How do we look?' asked Rosa. She put her arm around Montse and they posed.

'You both look beautiful,' he said.

Montse and Rosa were dressed in smart trouser suits and their lapels bore tiny wild orchids that they had picked in the Ardenya hills situated behind Sant Martí. Taking out his mobile, he snapped several photos. They kissed on the lips in one of them. Boyle noticed the other wedding party frowning at the women and felt a twinge of fear for them. If there were frowns for them in Sitges, a place known for the acceptance of lesbians and gays, then what was in store for them in conservative Sant Martí once the residents became aware of their marriage?

Montse looked at her watch. 'She's late, as usual,' she said under her breath. Rosa told her to stop worrying.

Ten minutes later, a burgundy Prius pulled into the square and parked next to Montse's car. Isabella and Antonio got out. Boyle noticed that his nephew was looking sullen. Antonio hugged Rosa and Montse, then gave Boyle a hug and stood by his side, where he remained for most of the day.

'*Tío, ¿que tal?*' said Antonio.

'*Bien, et tu?*'

'*Fatal.*'

'Why?' he asked in a confidential voice, although he needn't have. He knew very well why Antonio's spirits were low and he found it interesting that Antonio was speaking to him in Spanish, not the Catalan that he normally spoke, using *tío* rather than *oncle*.

'Just because,' said Antonio as he hooked his arm through Boyle's.

They all watched Jordi open the car door for Carmen and she slid her elegant legs round and lifted herself from the seat with ease. She was wearing a pink silk dress with a matching coat that Boyle had never seen before. It was as if Carmen and Jordi were getting married, they were the couple on show today.

After her arrest for vandalism, Isabella had had a personality change. Gabriel was out of hospital and healing well and had already met Carmen and Antonio. Isabella now treated her mother with respect, bordering on the sycophantic, and tried her best to behave impeccably around her new aunt, Inspector Rosa Pujol. She beamed at her mother and Jordi.

'Doesn't Mama look happy?' she said, turning to her Aunt Montse.

Carmen and Jordi walked towards them, wearing

the secret smiles of those in love. They walked from the car in perfect time with each other, as if part of the same animal. Boyle felt a stab of jealousy, unable to manage a smile. What was there to smile about? How could she not know how he felt? But he realised that how he felt was the furthest thing from Carmen's mind. Montse laid a hand on his back and gave him a smile of reassurance.

After the couple greeted Montse and Rosa, Carmen turned to Boyle. 'Adrian,' she said. 'I'd like you to meet Jordi.' Boyle held out his hand, which Jordi gave a firm shake, looking Boyle straight in the eye, making an effort with him even though Boyle was not a family member – and, even worse, an *extranjero*.

'Hello, very nice to meet you, Adrian. Carmen has told me so much about you,' Jordi said in perfect English. It was going to be a long day.

Montse and Rosa were married by a woman who carried out the service in Catalan. They then drove to a restaurant on the front that was set in an old fishing warehouse. Montse, Rosa, Boyle and the children drove down together. The restaurant had high ceilings and a sky light which gave it a romantic atmosphere. They were shown to a table set for seven with a crisp linen tablecloth, and a centrepiece of red roses and crystal that sparkled in the sunlight.

Boyle scanned the room. Carmen and Jordi had yet to arrive.

'Can I take your jacket?' asked Antonio.

'No, thank you,' said Boyle, feeling the cold. The winter was not far off.

'Where is Mama – and Jordi?' asked Antonio once they all sat down.

'You don't expect your mother to be here before us, do you, Antonio?' said Montse with a touch of playfulness, although Boyle knew her well enough to detect the undercurrent of annoyance.

'This is a special day for Mama,' said Isabella in defence of her mother, and then she realised what she had said and added with a smile, 'I know it's a special day for you, Tía Montse and Tía Rosa.'

'Your mother has always been like this, Isabella. I remember when we were children, hungry, waiting at the dinner table for her so we could begin to eat. But she had to make her entrance,' said Montse, taking the napkin off the table and placing it on her lap.

They nibbled on olives and slices of chorizo, Boyle lifting his head regularly to glance at the front door. He was reminded of a time when he was a boy, waiting, staring at the front door in the cold foyer of the children's home for his mother to come and rescue him and take him on a special Sunday outing. Unable to put up with the memory one second more, he switched seats with Isabella so he faced the back of the restaurant.

'I didn't want to talk shop, but here we go,' Montse said to Boyle. 'Last week I gave Lola Navarro the photos of her darling husband Quimet cavorting with Tina Clavaguera.'

'Don't tell me,' said Boyle. 'She's just filed for divorce.'

'With Tina Clavaguera set to spend the rest of her life in prison, I don't know if that will be necessary. But the very good news is that Juanita is going to be released. The tests came back showing that she had traces of nitrous oxide in her blood, and there were also traces in the body of Felipe. We are presenting the evidence to the judge on Monday and she'll be released then.'

Boyle was aware that many robbers in the Costa Brava used sleeping gas to knock out the occupants of a house so they could steal without disruption. But this was normally done in the more upmarket homes, not in a poor neighbourhood like Juanita's. This time it was clearly done to kill Felipe and place the blame on Juanita.

'Do they have any idea who did it?'

'They have some DNA from some skin found under Felipe's nails. It doesn't belong to Juanita, Felipe or the nurse who regularly comes in to help. They put it through the database and came up with ex-army Pedro Gonzales, former body guard of Eduardo Clavaguera.'

'He scratched him.'

'No doubt. They have an arrest warrant out for Pedro and another body guard, Manel Bosc, who the next-door neighbour, Mrs Deulofeu, described to the police. Both men quit their jobs after Eduardo was killed and they have since disappeared. There is speculation that they are now working in Eastern Europe.'

The waiter came up and asked if they should begin serving lunch. Montse looked at the front door and gave a theatrical sigh. Carmen and Jordi had disappeared like Eduardo's body guards. Montse told them to hold off for a few more minutes.

'They're probably walking along the front,' Antonio whispered to Boyle. His grimace told Boyle that although they may not be on the same team when it came to graffiti, they were definitely on the same side when it came to the interloper Jordi.

Montse overheard. 'I gathered that,' she said, taking a drink. 'But the least she can do is not keep us waiting on our wedding day.'

Rosa put her arm around Montse. '*Tranquillo, mamasita.*'

Carmen entered with Jordi thirty minutes later. Boyle saw Antonio's mood drop; he became sullen again.

'I'm sorry we're late,' said Carmen. 'I had to give Jordi a tour of the marina. You know he hasn't been to Sitges before?'

'How nice,' said Montse. 'Perhaps there's a tour bus to take you all over.' Clearly fighting an impulse to shout at her sister, Montse turned to Rosa and asked, 'Do you know if they have bus tours of Sitges?'

Carmen and Jordi stood still, appearing to feel unwelcome.

'I'm not sure, *cariño*,' Rosa said, trying to normalise the situation while Montse fumed. 'Sit down, please,' Rosa said to the couple. 'Antonio? Why don't you pour your mother and Jordi some cava?' Antonio was sulking and hesitated a moment too long. Rosa looked over at Isabella. '*Reina*? We're dying of thirst here, pour us some bubbly.' Isabella was up on her feet, lifting the bottle out of the ice bucket and filling the glasses, miss goody two shoes. Boyle had to smile.

Antonio held out his empty glass when she came by. 'You've had yours already. You're not allowed more than one,' she said.

'A bit more. Please!'

'No,' she said, passing him.

'It's alright, Isabella. He can have a tiny bit more. It is a special day after all,' said Carmen, beaming at her sister and Rosa in an attempt to make amends.

Boyle was glad that he was placed at the opposite end of the table from Carmen and Jordi and found comfort from sitting next to Antonio, who pulled discreet faces all during lunch at the couple's expense. Carmen smiled throughout lunch, a smile stretching from ear to ear. She was quick to laugh at anything said to disguise the smile that Boyle knew was there for only one reason – she was in love with Jordi. And Jordi was just as bad, compulsively touching Carmen – her hand, her arm, her back – and every time he touched her hair, he came dangerously close to her décolletage. Boyle felt Antonio tense with foul humour beside him.

After the main course, Boyle said a few words about Montse and Rosa and led a toast for them in their new life together. During the dessert, crema Catalana, Montse stood, lifted her glass and began another toast, welcoming Jordi into the family. Everyone raised their glasses and said, '*Salud*'. This more than made up for her outburst at the beginning of lunch.

'*Merci*,' said Jordi, who apart from the original English greeting with Boyle, spoke only Catalan throughout. 'I am touched by your generosity of spirit.'

'*Gracias, Tía y Tía*,' shouted Antonio, who, as if in protest against Jordi, hadn't uttered one word of Catalan the whole day. His mother's new boyfriend was a stickler for Catalan and, like many Catalans, preferred English to Spanish.

The only time Carmen looked at Boyle was when they all toasted Montse and Rosa and the couple kissed on the mouth. Carmen turned to Boyle and opened her mouth in an expression of mock horror.

After Ana had died, he had wondered what would

happen to his relationship with her family. There was no blood connection between him and the Ferrans, so would they continue to be his family or would it come to a point where the relationship with them would end? And once Carmen had hooked up with Jordi, where did that leave Boyle? Would he feel happy about having dinner at the family restaurant three or four nights a week? Would he still be invited to family dinners? Or would Jordi take his place? Perhaps the only reason he wanted to be with Carmen was because he wanted to remain connected to the Ferran family. If Carmen married Jordi, then he would take Boyle's place as father figure to Antonio and Isabella. Montse and Rosa were now married and, from what he had heard from Isabella, were looking forward to having children. He would no longer be needed. All this overthinking was ridiculous. *Pull yourself together,* he warned himself.

There was no wedding cake; neither Montse nor Rosa had wanted one. The seasonal marzipan sweets, *panellets*, served during All Saints' and All Souls' Day in Catalonia, were laid out on the table with coffee. Antonio gobbled down three of them and then asked to be excused from the table.

'I want to see the boats,' he said. When his mother said no, he blurted out, 'You looked at the bay. We had to wait for you!'

His mother said nothing, fighting back her fury.

Boyle got up. 'I'll take him out, if that's alright?'

'I don't mind,' said Montse.

'¡*Vete!*' snapped his mother with a wave of her hand.

As soon as they were outside the restaurant, Antonio's face creased up and tears ran down his face. Boyle hadn't seen him cry since he was a young boy. He placed his hands on his shoulders.

'I hate him! I hate him!'

'Who?' asked Boyle, just to make sure.

'Mama's boyfriend.' He said it with such disdain, Boyle wanted to laugh.

'Although Jordi seems like a decent man who we shouldn't dislike,' said Boyle.

'I'll never like him. Isabella loves him because she has met his daughter and likes her. She's awful too. And when he touches Mama, I want to punch him!'

Boyle quietly agreed with the last one. 'Come for a drink, Antonio.' He put his arm around his nephew and they walked along the seafront, both pleased to share this aversion to Jordi. However, Boyle was now certain that Carmen was the most unpleasant of the two. They watched the seagulls circling the arriving fishing boats. There was a café just opposite the marina and they went inside.

Antonio soon tried his luck. 'Can I have a beer?'

'No, Antonio, you have had enough alcohol today. It's a lemonade for you.'

Acknowledgements

I wish to acknowledge the invaluable assistance of the following people: Tom Bromley and the Faber Academy, Steve Savage and Caroline Gallup, Xavier Sureda for his help with Catalan law and the police, former British policemen Roland Hawkins and Trevor Waters, Rene Harriman for his information on all things graffiti and lastly the hunters Leif Nordstrom and Luis Puig. Thank you all for your help.